EMILY'S I

CW00982932

DEDICATION:

To my brother-in-law Neil Elkins, who passed away December 2007

CREDITS

I would like to thank all those who helped and advised me with this project. My special thanks to Petersfield Writer's Circle, who listened for hours as I read excerpts from this book, and then pointed out the errors and repetitions. In particular I am grateful to the late Charles Goatley, who read the whole of the first draft and was helpful and encouraging in his comments. I must give special thanks to Michael Glannister, who proof read the manuscript, and Jo Smith who typeset the final draft. I am also most grateful to Kate Williams, Judith Young and George Harvey-Nevin, who with Erin and Toby, came up with the book's front cover.

Emily's Hour is a sequel to my first novel, *The Nemesis File*. I liked my central characters, Steve and Kirsten, and wanted to see how they had fared over the years. Once again I have used places that I know and are important to me. Chichester Harbour, that great south-coast sailing centre, figures again. The imaginary Branham Lake and its surroundings are based on a real setting. If some people believe they recognise the sailing club featured, they may not be mistaken. However this is fiction, and no character bears any relation to a person in the real world. The nearby Branham Little Lake is based on a beautiful secret place that I know, but if you go there you will not find abandoned cottages, or the nine hundred acre forest. These are in my imagination, but also I hope in yours when you read this story.

AUTHOR

Jim Morley has sailed and raced small boats all his life. He spent forty years in farming and forestry, combining this with a career in freelance writing.

He has published three novels, reflecting his interest in boats and also rural matters. He lives near Petersfield in Hampshire and sails a small family cruising yacht on Chichester Harbour.

EMILY'S HOUR

James Morley

Emily's Hour
First published 2008

Published by Benhams Books, 1 Fir Cottage, Greatham, Liss, Hampshire GU33 6BB

Typeset by John Owen Smith

ISBN 978-0-9548880-3-9

Printed and bound by CPI Antony Rowe, Eastbourne

CHAPTER 1

'I understand that your wife is foreign,' said Dolly Pembelty.

'She's got dual nationality,' Steve replied. 'That makes two of you,' he grinned back.

Dolly failed to take offence. 'Stephen, I am Commonwealth – your wife is foreign. Where was her nation when my Gerry and I were fighting and dying for freedom?' Her Australian accent was breaking through the veneer of Home Counties.

'Hold on, Dolly. You can't have been dying, and I don't think the Danes had any choice, they had a German army breathing down their necks.' That was true, but the less said the better with Kirsten's family skeletons still well concealed.

'I see from the roll that your wife has a vote in our British elections. May I ask how she will exercise it?'

'I don't know, she's never said. Lib Dem I would guess, or Green Party I wouldn't be surprised – you'd better ask her yourself.' Steve glanced at the open front door.

Dolly ignored the hint. 'Then I suppose I would be wasting my time calling for her membership subscription to my Conservative branch.'

'As I said – ask her yourself.'

'I might if she was ever in a fit state of dress.'

'So, this is what we've been coming to,' Steve sighed.

'Yes. Group Captain Pembelty, my Gerry, has been most offended by your wife's public nudity.'

'If that's what's upsetting him he'd better complain to her himself. Kirsten's not here at the moment by the way – she's fetching the kids from school.'

Steve was not certain if he wanted to swear or burst out laughing. He wondered what the stout Dolly would look like unclothed. He really didn't want to quarrel with her. Dolly Pembelty was a kindly soul who worked tirelessly for their home village of South Marshall on the Sussex-Hampshire border. Her husband, Gerry Pembelty, retired Group Captain and Battle of Britain veteran, was a charming if muddled old gentleman who commuted between the village pub and his allotment. Although he seldom mentioned the war, Gerry could bore for England with his gardening hints.

Dolly departed. Steve watched her walk down the drive, her rear view giving the impression of a disgruntled teddy bear. She had almost reached the curve by the rhododendrons when Kirsten's Renault Megane came into view. The car slowed to a halt; Dolly ignored it and walked stiffly out of sight. Oh dear, Steve thought and not for the first time.

Kirsten parked the car by the front door and Steve limped forward to greet his children as they jumped out and ran to him. Life as a one-time Olympic sportsman had left Steve with a painful arthritic legacy and he winced as thirteen-year-old Emily bounded into him. John-Kaj aged eight followed struggling with his oversize backpack.

'Em, can't you give Johnny a hand – he's busting a gut with that load?' Kirsten called.

Emily had so much of her mother about her – the same mobile face and dark hair and already a talent for sport. John-Kaj, on the contrary, was showing an academic ability beyond his years. He couldn't have inherited that from his father; Steve had to agree. Maybe he drew on his Danish side and the long line of scientists and shrewd business-men. John-Kaj, or Johnny, had been so named in memory of Kirsten's tragic Uncle Kaj, while his elder sister had earned her name inspired by Pink Floyd's "see Emily play". Thank God, neither of his children had the tainted blood of their great-grandmother's notorious lover. Steve hoped that they would never know the full truth of the Elgaad family's disgrace. Steve still had dreams: visitations of that dramatic month that had brought Kirsten and him together and so very nearly concluded in their violent death.[†]

'Right, tell all?' Steve addressed Emily. 'Did you get in the team?'

The girl's face clouded for a few seconds. 'I don't know. Mrs Zeigler was going to tell us but she never came into school.'

Emily was a pupil at the comprehensive while John-Kaj attended the primary at the edge of the village.

'That's unusual,' he remarked. 'Is she ill?'

'I dunno, Mr Cotton rang her several times and got no answer. Then I rang her on my mobile and she didn't pick up then either.'

'Then you'll have to wait patiently for tomorrow.'

Kirsten emerged from the sitting room and threw her coat across a chair.

'What did Dolly Pembelty want?' she asked. 'And why wouldn't she say hello when I passed her on the drive?'

'It's what I've tried to explain a hundred times.' Steve stared at his

---

[†] See *The Nemesis File* by James Morley

wife with mock severity. 'This is not Denmark. In Southern England nudity is top of the socially unacceptable activities list. I think your mowing the lawn in the buff has mortally offended poor old Gerry.'

Kirsten smiled. 'If Group Captain Pembelty is so offended, why does he sit for an hour on the hill watching me through his binoculars?'

Both Steve and Emily laughed. 'I wouldn't begin to speculate,' he said.

At seven a.m., the Chief Ranger of Branham Country Park steered his Land Rover around the perimeter of the lake. At least it had stopped raining and the scene had the makings of a perfect spring day. Branham Lake was eighty acres of water held in place by an earth dam that had stood the test of eight hundred years. The ranger was responsible for the expanse of sand hills and heathland that bordered the lake, plus the beach and swimming area on the north shore. Across the water he could see the masts and jetties of the sailing club. No pompous moneyed yacht club this one, thank God. The members were a dedicated bunch from all social backgrounds, practicing their sport fifty-two weeks of the year, even breaking the ice in January. Well, they were welcome to it; swimming around a capsized dinghy at any time of the year was not his idea of fun and in sub-zero water temperatures the idea was a definite no-no.

The behaviour of the wildfowl by the jetties was wrong. He could hear the calls of the ducks, not the contented quacking of a normal day but sounds of distress and alarm. The swans had moved away from the reed beds and were grouped in the centre of the lake, as had the Canada geese. He could see the source of the trouble now, an oily stain drifting around the jetty area from a metallic object – the roof of a sunken car.

The police constable waded into the water and attached the strop on the cable to the tow bar of the Mercedes. He crossed the two metres to the wooden jetty, hauled himself out and pulled off his wellingtons now filled with the murky liquid of the lake.

'That water is shit cold,' he muttered.

'Never mind,' replied his sergeant pointing to his civilian companion; his features held an undisguised smirk. 'The Commodore says you can use her club showers.'

'We've opened the kitchen and there's hot coffee when you've done.' Liz Preston ignored the policeman's chauvinism; his patronising pronunciation of the title Commodore was too blatant and deliberate.

Liz was angry and worried. She was proud of her record as Branham Sailing Club's first female commodore. She was in the second year of a successful term in the post, and she did not need vandals pushing stolen cars down her slipways.

'All right, Mr Grogan – haul away on the foretop main sheet.' The sergeant waved to the civilian in the tractor cab and turned back to Liz. 'Is that correct nautical, Ms Commodore?'

'Not really – mainsheets belong in dinghies, like the ones here. We really must take you out in one, Sergeant.'

He ignored her. He was staring at the glistening shape of the Mercedes as it emerged from the lake. 'Bloody hell!'

'There's a stiff in there,' said another PC, as they saw the limp body fall across the front seats.

The driver's door swung open, and a torrent of water flooded onto the concrete apron above the slipway. 'I know that car,' said the sergeant. 'That's Arnold Evans' motor. Is that him in there?'

'Yeah, that's Arnold,' said the second PC. 'Poor bugger – how did he come to end up here?'

'One of your fellow Masons, I believe,' Liz remarked. Bad taste, she knew, but she couldn't resist the chance to kick the officious copper when he was down. It covered her horror and disgust. A drowned body was a nightmare for any sailor, even if the man in this case was no loss.

'Yes, Ms Commodore, I understand that you lot didn't like Arnold.'

'It wasn't personal and certainly not enough for any of our members to stick him in the lake.'

The policeman gave her a sharp look and grunted.

CHAPTER 2

Steve replaced the telephone and walked back into the kitchen. The others caught the look on his face and stared at him.

'We can't go to Branham on Saturday,' he said as he resumed his seat at the supper table.

'Oh why?' Emily asked, disappointment mirrored on her face.

'That was Liz Preston on the phone. Believe it or not the club's a crime scene. A man's been murdered in his car and by coincidence I knew him.'

'Who was it?' Kirsten asked.

'Arnold Evans; he keeps a boat in the old Birdham marina. Peter Terring's done some work on his engine.'

'I know you've mentioned that Evans before,' said Kirsten. 'What was he doing at Branham?'

'I don't know, but Liz Preston says the man owns the whole of the south foreshore including the sailing club site. They found him dead in his car this morning – car submerged in the lake between jetties seven and eight. You know where the disability boats launch. Apart from the body, there's oil smothering the water. Brian from the disabled sailing is not pleased, as you might imagine.'

'And the police really think it's murder?' said Kirsten.

'That's what Liz is so wound up about. The police are as thick as two planks. They're trying to accuse the sailing club because the entrance gate was locked and only members know the key code.'

'That's silly,' said Emily. 'I know it. It's 41476 – and I'm only a family Cadet member.'

'Trust you – meddlesome little girl,' Steve laughed.

'I'm not a little girl – I'm nearly fourteen,' replied Emily.

'But it's true,' said Kirsten. 'Anyone could know that key number: the club house cleaners and there were people working on the car park.'

Branham was famous as a proving ground for young competitive sailors. Steve coached there once a month, and Kirsten took both children most Saturdays to sail their Cadet dinghy. The whole family was steeped in boats, but Emily had found a taste for the competitive side in both sailing and track running. This year she had won her county's award for outstanding female athlete under sixteen. The subsequent television interview and local publicity had gone dangerously to the girl's head. Her parents were ambivalent about this. Both former Olympic sailing medallists, they knew the pitfalls and disappointments that lay in wait for even the most talented.

'It appears that Evans wanted to repossess the sailing club and then run it as a commercial concern. The man's mega rich, he doesn't need to do that, so there must have been some spite involved. Liz said that's what the police have fixed on, and they've been giving her and Harry Preston the third degree.'

'Why Harry?' Kirsten looked startled.

'The police wanted to know if Harry had it in for Evans, because Evans might be going to muck up the wildlife around the lake. It seems that Harry was seen arguing with Evans. These coppers appear to be an uncultured lot – they were prejudiced against Harry from the start.'

'Wow,' said Emily 'It's like Midsomer Murders on the telly. But it won't be old Harry…'she paused. 'More likely Beale the Bosun – he's a shit.'

'God, what are you kids growing up like,' Steve replied. 'When I was your age it was Mister Preston and Mister Beale, or whoever it was in charge then. And Bob Beale was quite right to blast you. You were joy riding in a safety boat without permission and you're unqualified and too young.' He beckoned Kirsten to follow him and left the room.

'Who told her the S word? Don't let me ever hear either of them use the F one.'

'Oh yes,' said his wife. 'And was your speech so pure in your footballing days? It certainly wasn't in your sailing, or so I have been told.'

'You always have the last word. But I'm still full of doubts about that school. Why can't we go private? God knows we're not short of money.'

Kirsten deflected the question. 'Are the police sure that man was murdered?'

'Yes, they're floundering around trying to implicate Branham. But Liz has had words with a reporter from the local *Herald*. It seems the forensic people say Evans was beaten over the head with a metal bar some place else, then driven to Branham and submerged in the water.'

'Doesn't that let Branham off the hook?'

'No, because of the key code on the gate they say it must be a Branham member. They're setting out to question all four hundred and sixty of them.'

10

'While the real murderer runs away to Spain, your English Keystone cops waste our money chasing shadows.' Her Danish accent was accentuated in contempt.

'A lot of use your Danish police were when Lindgrune was around Copenhagen.'

'I wish you had not said that name – I thought we said never!' Kirsten strode back into the kitchen.

'Sorry, love,' he replied to the door firmly closed in his face.

Linda Zeigler was worried she'd overslept. Her girls' night out at the Green Dragon had extended to closing time, and following that, they'd returned to her apartment in Havant for coffee. She had finally rid herself of the last of her friends at one-thirty. She had woken at seven, feeling mildly queasy and staggered into the kitchen for a roll and a cup of black coffee. Linda was head of geography at the local comprehensive, a post she combined with athletics coach. She was a good teacher; she was well aware of that and she knew her students respected her. She was grateful that most of them were docile, with some genuinely wanting to learn and pass their GCSEs and A levels. Twenty years ago Linda had been an international gymnast, and today she coached the school's athletic team. She was fortunate that this earned her respect from the girls in her care. She knew, without conceit, that she still had a supple and fit body and a residual glamour from her earlier days. She also knew how to deal with the overt attentions of some of the male staff, and equally, the doe eyed ogling and whispered comments of teenage boys. Yes, Linda was confident, and she knew she was good at what she did.

Cautiously she backed her little Fiesta into the main road. Be quick, and she would have time to take her readings at Mounts Farm and then make it to school in time for assembly. It was still raining and dismal: typical England in May time, blowing hot and cold with winter not quite letting go. The windscreen wiper had a half perished rubber giving less than perfect vision as the driving rain enveloped her car. She nearly missed the turning for the farm, and would have done had she not seen a car parked under the beech tree. A familiar car, she thought, but she couldn't identify it in this wet maelstrom.

Linda parked next to the grain-drying barn. Mounts Farm had given up livestock farming and was now arable. Her official Met station was in a caged area in the middle of the old open cow yard. She fumbled with her keys to select the one for the heavy padlock and unbolted the gate. Inside was the white box with its louvered sides.

She pulled the clipboard from under her coat. Her recording sheets were in a plastic cover in a vain attempt to protect them from the same rainfall she was recording. By holding the board under the lid of the instrument box she could just about read the temperature range and keep the wet out. She checked the rainfall, recorded the time and shut the box. That was it, she was happy now; just a short run down the A27 and she'd be into school with ten minutes to spare. Three more days to the weekend, she thought. She hoped the weather would improve before her sea fishing trip on Sunday.

She could hardly believe it; the bloody car wouldn't start. She turned the key again and again until finally the battery gave out and with it the last hope of reaching work on time. Linda was smouldering with anger as she walked around the car and threw open the bonnet.

'Hello, Linda – trouble?'

She turned round. 'Oh, hi, I thought that was your car.'

'What's happened?'

'Battery's dead.'

'In that case you're not going anywhere. Like a lift?'

Linda agreed with little enthusiasm. She had never liked this man, but she needed to reach school and in this situation she had no choice.

CHAPTER 3

Inspector Storey of West Sussex Police had mixed feelings. He had just entered his last year with the police force. He had almost reached the magic thirty years of service. Full pension and the little farmhouse in Burgundy beckoned. Storey's wife had suffered enough of his unsociable hours, the kids had long since fled the nest – there was nothing to keep him here anymore. He'd earned his retirement ten times over. His companion and driver WPC Samantha McGregor, turned left at the roundabout and headed for their destination, the Comprehensive School.

'Sir, can we pull over for a minute?' McGregor asked. 'I'd really like a smoke before we get to that place.'

'All right – stop in the layby.' He pointed. 'No willpower you younger ones. I gave up years ago – never felt better.'

McGregor parked the police BMW and fumbled in her bag.

'Not in the motor – outside please.'

Sam obliged. She stood on the edge of the lay-by drawing on the lighted cigarette. 'My lifeline,' she gasped. 'Sir, have we any background on this enquiry?'

'It's suspicious but very little detail. Missing teacher – not come into school for two days. No trace at her home; no one's seen her. Probably had enough of the little sods and done a runner.'

'Is that what the school think?'

'No, it seems. The lady: she's a Mrs Zeigler; single, divorced and very well liked by everyone except Mr Zeigler. Sporty one, got an Olympic bronze medal twenty years ago.'

'She was an athlete?'

'No, just a little girly gymnast.'

'Oh yes, not like a big macho male gorilla one…Sir?'

'Quit the feminist crap, McGregor and get in the car.'

Steve had spent the afternoon in the office. Not his favourite place on a hot sunny day but duty called. Easterbroke Europe had expanded since the time the company had passed into his wife's control. Kirsten, as sole survivor of the Elgaad family, had inherited the fortune that her Uncle Kaj had salted away for her. Danish law banned her from inheriting the pharmaceutical company that bore the family name, so it was an easy choice for Kirsten to invest her money

13

in the marine company her new husband managed. Steve knew that Kirsten was uneasy with an inheritance that sprang from her unstable grandmother's infatuation with Nazi Germany. But were it not for grandmother Gerda, Kirsten would never have been born. Gerda's intervention had saved Kirsten's German Jewish father's life in the darkest hours of World War Two and that alone ameliorated her conduct in Steve's eyes.

Easterbroke's Chichester premises had grown beyond the sail loft and chandlery. A new building housed a marine diesel and outboard motor franchise along with a maintenance workshop. This was the province of Peter Terring, a brilliant engineer who seemed able to diagnose an engine fault by hypnosis or some extrasensory quirk. Steve was pleased with Peter Terring's appointment but could not in honesty say that he liked the man. Terring was a forty-five-year-old confirmed bachelor. Not a gay one; just a surly middle-aged man obsessed with engines and with little joy in life outside work. It was rumoured that the man was deeply religious. Apparently, he enjoyed the occasional fishing trip but that apart there seemed to be something detached and unreal about him. Steve had heard that Peter had a brother with a garage business somewhere up country and it was there that he had first learned his trade. He was not sure he wanted to face the man on this lovely spring day.

When Peter came into the office he seemed uncharacteristically cheerful. 'A few fine days like this and we can get things moving,' Peter put a folded newspaper on the chair before seating his oily overalls upon it. He didn't manage a smile but his usual lugubrious tone was absent.

'It'll certainly encourage the punters to get their boats afloat,' Steve replied. 'We're putting ours back in tomorrow.'

'Good, I'll check your diesel today.'

Peter must be having a change of mood. Steve had been prepared to chivvy the man all week before Peter agreed even to a simple job such as fitting a water impeller. Customers before management was all very well, but Kirsten wanted a forty-eight hour trip with both of the kids in the school break. She would take it out on him if the ship failed to be ready to go. More than likely, Peter Terring did not care himself for a confrontation with Kirsten. The man, though definitely a misogynist and a transparent child-hater, was visibly nervous of forceful women. He avoided them wherever possible, dealing with husbands only. Kirsten, smoulderingly sexual and charismatic, probably scared the life out of him.

At last Steve was able to leave the office and stroll round to the boat park. There propped up on wooden shoring stood his pride and joy, *Traveller*: all forty-five foot of classic wooden sailing cruiser. *Traveller* was not a racing machine, and in that respect she was different from any other boat that Steve had owned. The yacht had been built in the middle nineteen-thirties by the Hillyard company in nearby Littlehampton. Unusually, she was rigged as a schooner, with mainmast taller than the foremast and with a central steering position.

Apparently the original owner had the yacht constructed around a vast coal stove providing heating for round-the-year cruising. That artefact had long since gone, leaving a cavernous saloon and galley area and a forepeak filled with sails. Behind the centre cockpit was a cosy little aft-cabin with space for both children. Nothing about *Traveller* could be described as elegant, but she had real sturdiness and security. It had served her well through seventy years and almost every condition the oceans of the world could throw at her. Today, she stood ready to be craned into the water and motor once more the two miles to her mooring at Itchenor.

Steve was about to climb the ladder and board the ship when his mobile phone rang. 'Steve, it's Liz from Branham.'

Inspector Storey had to admit the atmosphere in the school was nostalgic. The corridors, filled with the smells of cooking and floor polish echoed the shouts and chatter of the children. He and McGregor had divided their forces. Storey quizzed the Head Teacher and the staff who worked with Linda Zeigler, while he detailed McGregor to chat informally with her pupils, or students as the head had insisted he call them. Storey had handled dozens of missing person enquiries before; usually a cheating spouse, or some silly teenage runaway found a few days later penniless and half starved. Other investigations were different, he was still haunted by the murder of that little boy and never ceased from wondering if some sharper policing might have saved him. This present case was a puzzle. There seemed no reason why a popular teacher should cut and run and never leave a message.

'You say you saw Mrs Zeigler on Wednesday evening.' Storey eyed the young teacher. She was a pretty girl: dark skinned Caribbean, although her accent was polite Sussex.

'We went out for a meal at the Dragon and then back to her place for coffee. I left at half midnight but I wasn't the last.'

'Was this a mixed gathering – male and female?'

'No, it was a girls' night out – just the five of us.'

'All right, Miss, give me the names of the others and you can go.'

The girl spelt out the names while Storey wrote on his note pad. McGregor appeared in the school corridor and beckoned to him. 'I've had a call,' she said. 'Her car's been found at West Ashling,' she glanced at her notes. 'At Mounts Farm, it seems she did rainfall readings there.'

'Plenty of that these last few weeks.'

'Sir, we've been withdrawn – it's CID's call now. You see the car was abandoned and the engine had been disabled.'

'What, deliberately?'

'So CID say.'

'Right, suspicious disappearance – that lets us off the hook. You ever thought of applying for CID?'

'Wouldn't mind; you ever been there, sir?'

Storey laughed. 'They don't like me – they think I upstaged them over that girl at Dell Quay five years ago. CID were set on her being a suicide – nice clean solution.'[†]

'You said it was murder?'

'That's so, but it was that magistrate from Hampshire who twigged. I agreed with him, and CID have never forgiven.' Storey lapsed into his own world. To be honest that case had convinced him to remain in Uniform.

It was only as they reached the city outskirts that the radio call came through. A woman's body had been found in the town reservoir. They were required to divert in support of a suspected crime scene.

Liz and Harry Preston lived on the outskirts of the village of Tilford near Farnham. Judging by Liz's tone this was an emergency that wouldn't wait. Steve and Kirsten had left the two children at the Midhurst house of Steve's eldest daughter Sarah, and they finally reached the Preston house at half past five.

Steve parked on the gravel by the front door as Liz came to greet them. Steve could only describe her as unravelled. Her hair was ragged, her clothes untidy and Steve could see she had been crying. So different from the feisty businesswoman they had come to know.

Kirsten ran to Liz and flung her arms around her. 'What's happened?'

[†] See *Magdalena's Redemption* by James Morley

'Those stupid bloody police – they've arrested Harry.'

Steve could make no sense of this. Harry Preston was a talented artist. Unusually, he was a financially successful one. His wildlife and landscape pictures sold in four figures and he had two glossy coffee table books of his work. Apart from this, Harry was a meek personality, very much under the thumb of his wife.

Kirsten gently steered Liz into the house and sat her on a chair in the kitchen. Without asking, she rummaged for a set of cups and pressed the switch on the kettle. 'We are all going to have a cup of tea,' she said, 'and then we will discuss what we will do.'

It was one of those moments with Kirsten: the time of crisis when she took control and Steve loved her for it.

'Now, tell us what happened from the beginning.'

'The police found out that Harry had words with Evans the day before the car went in the lake. They are so stupid,' Liz put her face in her hands while Kirsten put a supportive arm around her.

'How do they know that?' Steve asked.

'They were seen arguing.'

'What does your solicitor say?'

'I don't know – she was going to call me but she hasn't...' Liz looked distraught. Kirsten glared at Steve and put a finger to her lips. He took the hint: it was for Kirsten to handle this.

'I had that bloody little reporter round here – nosy shit,' Liz muttered.

'Which paper – not the tabloids?' Steve couldn't help intervening.

'No, the local paper.'

'What, the Farnham one?'

'Oh no, I think it's the Mid Southern Times, the man said.'

Steve was baffled. 'That's a South Coast rag, what's the connection with Branham?'

Liz began to sob again. Kirsten caught Steve by the arm and her sharp nails bit through the thin shirt. 'Out of here,' she said. 'If you can't be tactful, you stay out of it. I'll talk to Liz.'

'No, Kirsten!' Liz was sitting up straight again wiping away the tears with a rather soiled handkerchief. 'I want your advice – both of you.'

'Sorry, if I was a bit abrupt,' Steve reached to a high shelf and handed Liz a box of tissues. 'Are you saying this incident, or whatever, took place in Sussex?'

'That's right, Harry was painting wildfowl at Pagham. When he packed up his gear and came back to the car, Evans was standing there. Evans grabbed one of Harry's sketches and stamped it into the mud. Then they had a right royal slanging match but that was all. Harry's not capable of killing a mouse, let alone a man.'

'How did Evans come to be there?'

'Unlucky chance. Harry went into the Seal pub in Selsey for a bite to eat, and there was Evans. Harry left at once, but he thinks Evans must have followed him looking for a confrontation.'

'What do the police say?'

'Practically nothing. The last thing I've been told is that they are applying to magistrates for more time to question him.'

'Where is Harry now?'

'He's in custody with the police in Bognor.'

'Liz?' Kirsten asked. 'How do the police know all this?'

'It all happened in the car park in front of several people.'

Steve's thoughts were in turmoil; there had to be something wrong here. 'Look,' he said. 'I'm not a policeman but this is crazy. Evans was dumped in Branham in his own car, someone must have driven it there from wherever he was killed and then driven away in something else. If Harry left his car at Pagham, at least forty miles away, how could he have done it?'

Liz wiped her eyes. 'They took his car away yesterday and some horrible woman sifted through his clothes and took some with her.'

'That's it,' Steve felt almost jubilant. 'What idiots; if he arrived home in his own car it can't be him.'

'It's no good,' said Liz. 'Yesterday our solicitor said the police were checking all the taxi firms in this area to see if he phoned one to take him back to his car. Then they said that he must have followed Evans to his place and killed him there.'

'I thought Evans lived in Haslemere,' said Steve. 'It's nearer than Pagham, but you've the same problem with the car.'

'They say Harry left the car in the lake and then walked home.' Liz was shaking and the tears flowed again. 'They refused to believe me when I told them he never left the house and I've no witness to back me up.'

'Steve,' Kirsten looked him in the eye. 'I think we should go and see Norman Fox.'

CHAPTER 4

Storey ducked under the police tape and walked the last few yards to the edge of the reservoir. Scene-of-crime-officers were already scouring the surrounds and the water's edge. He stopped with surprise as he recognised the police forensic officer, who was standing beside a covered object.

'Hello, Lucy, I heard you were moving onto this patch. How's your Dad?'

Lucy Watts was the daughter of Tom O'Malley the magistrate who had challenged the police evidence in The Girl By The Shore case. She and her doctor husband had recently moved to a medical practice in the area, and Lucy had been signed up as a police forensic surgeon. She was a pretty, blonde girl in her early thirties who had earned a reputation for sharp observation in the same case. More than that: she had been there at the end when the psychopath had died. An odd business: the Hampshire police never fully identified that mystery man.

'Hi, Inspector – Dad's fine; which is more than this poor woman is.' Lucy lifted the edge of the plastic cover.

Storey was not squeamish by nature, he'd seen enough dead bodies in his career, but there was something about this sodden corpse that affected him more than usual. Her face seemed so relaxed even though her skull was bruised and smeared with blood. This was Linda Zeigler. Someone would have to formally identify her but the face fitted the photograph exactly.

'She's the missing person we've been trying to trace,' he muttered. 'God, I must be going soft – what a waste.'

Lucy looked up at him and grimaced. Despite her professionalism she had a green tinge to her face. 'She's the school teacher?'

'Yes.'

'She was an Olympic gymnast, so I'm told. Superintendent Fox has a grandchild at her school.'

'It is foul play then.' Storey didn't have much doubt about that but it was for Lucy to rule on fact.

'You can't get much fouler than staving in someone's head. You've definitely got a murder investigation.'

'Any idea when it happened?'

'We can't say until we've done a PM in the lab, but the body's passed the rigor stage so it could be a couple of days.' Lucy stood up. 'You will get the bastard who did this.'

'It'll be CID's call but I'd say they'll nail whoever it was. She was popular at the school, but we don't know much about her private life: ex-husband; boyfriends, ex-boyfriends, other associates. There'll be answers somewhere.'

'Carol says come over and have dinner with us tonight – make it informal.'

'Thanks, Norman – we'd be delighted.' Steve put the phone down and looked at Kirsten. 'He's agreed to talk but he's being very cagey. Says they've just found another body in water on his patch. They're going to question Harry about that one too.'

'Oh, for God's sake…' Kirsten exploded. 'What did Carol say?'

Chief Superintendent Norman Fox was a local police supremo. Fifteen years ago Norman's wife Carol had been office manager at Easterbroke Sails. Norman had been a humble Detective Sergeant then, but his contribution to unmasking Kenneth Lindgrune had done much to launch his long-term career.

'Carol was in the background. From all the whispering I gather it was her that persuaded him to see us. But he was a bit sticky – says it's not his province: "…but the matter is in the hands of experienced officers who will pursue all avenues in their enquiries".' Steve mimicked the official police speak.

'I'll pursue his backside down as many avenues as it takes,' said Kirsten. 'He's not going to treat us like that, not after everything that happened those years ago.'

'Let's see when we meet face-to-face.'

'You reckon that's him then?' said Sam McGregor.

Inspector Storey studied the scene through the one-way window. 'He doesn't look like any sort of killer to me. He's the artist isn't he?'

'Yes, I paint a bit myself but he's a master,' Sam replied.

Harry Preston sat on one side of a table with a suit-wearing woman whom Storey supposed to be the suspect's solicitor; facing them was Detective Inspector Le Bois. Guarding the door was a young DC whom Storey couldn't put a name to. This must be one of the Surrey officers who also had an interest in the investigation. Storey didn't much care for Le Bois. That officer had cut his teeth as a young constable during the late 1970s in the rough area of a London Borough. He had never quite abandoned a robust and dubious type of policing that had no place in rural Sussex. The DI was a Channel Islander, born in St Peter Port. In Storey's experience Channel Islanders were sometimes bloody-minded and Le Bois was a bad-tempered workaholic, inclined to tunnel vision.

'He's the only suspect so far, but it's not conclusive.'

Storey spun round to face the speaker, Chief Superintendent Fox. 'Sir, you made me jump.'

'What's your interest in this?' Fox asked.

'Nothing to do with me officially, sir, but I'm interested as I was detailed to trace the missing teacher. I can't believe that bloke did both killings – what motive?'

'Phil Le Bois is doing his best to conjure one out of thin air, but there's nothing that we can trace about Preston that would make him a violent killer, and some friends have been bending my ear with character references for the man.'

Both turned their gaze to the scene in the interview room. 'Look, Mr Preston,' Le Bois' words were carried through a speaker in the corner. 'This is doing you no good. Tell me the truth, admit you did the killings and your confession will stand you in good stead with the jury. But keep playing silly buggers with me in here won't help you one little bit. You did it, I'll prove you did it, and when you go to court it'll be life, and in your case that'll mean life. You'll have fifty years to paint a portrait of every con in Lewes nick.'

'Inspector,' the solicitor spoke. 'You are going outside the rules. You are not permitted to use intimidation to force a confession.'

Fox muttered. 'Phil would use thumb screws, the rack and red hot irons given the choice.'

Storey couldn't disagree but he thought it wiser to say nothing. He returned to the unfolding drama.

Le Bois had pulled an object from under the table: it was long, bar like and sealed in polythene. 'The murder weapon – found in the bushes at Pagham not ten yards from where you were seen with Mr Evans. Blood on it's his, and surprise, surprise, it's the tiller of a boat and you're into boats, Mr Preston.' Le Bois had half stood and was leaning across the table. Harry Preston shied away before looking back at the object that Le Bois was waving in his face.

'That may be a tiller but it's from a really big yacht. It's nothing to do with me. I don't sail boats anywhere here and at Branham we're all small dinghies.' Harry sounded composed. 'I'll take a lie detector test if that will help.'

'We are not Americans so you can forget that.'

'Inspector, you are running out of time,' said the solicitor. 'You either charge my client or you release him.'

Le Bois glared at her then turned to the window and mouthed – "bitch". He stood up looking down on his suspect. 'Henry Preston, I am charging you with the murder of Arnold William Evans. You do not have to say anything, but it may seriously harm your defence if you fail to reveal something you later rely on in court.'

Nadine Rotherton was at the wheel of her open-top sports car, driving northbound up the A3. The police had given her permission to collect her things from the Haslemere house. She should have been grief-smitten, but the tears wouldn't flow. Arnold Evans was dead, murdered apparently by a total stranger. Nadine had been nervous when the police started to ask questions – luckily she had an alibi. She had been in the television studio presenting Travel with Children – her weekly live holiday program. An alibi witnessed by five million people was as cast iron as one could get. So Nadine, Arnold's common law wife, lover, or tame bimbo was out of the frame. She should feel nervous and vulnerable, but as the police had already caught the man who did it she would get on with life. Life without Arnold would depend, of course, on whether the bastard had remembered her in his will. She could cheerfully murder that ex-wife if the silly cow had scooped the pool. No, Arnold wouldn't do that to her, would he?

Why had that man killed him? The police wouldn't talk to her – as Evans' lover she had no legal rights, but the newspaper man had told her it was all about Branham Lake and Arnold's plans for the place. It still didn't make sense. Arnold had enemies a plenty – Nadine could list seven or eight who might have reason to take out a contract. So why should those people with their silly little boats want him done in? Anyway, couldn't those sailing people have bought Arnold off – some of them must be loaded, including the artist who topped him. Property was a very minor part of the Evans empire; peanuts compared to Maxstats.com, his Internet company.

It was raining again, and the top was down – sod it. Nadine pushed the accelerator flat to the floor, racing for the Farnham exit, cutting across the traffic in the inside lane. She stuck a finger high in the slipstream in response to the angry horn blasts. Now off the dual carriageway she was able to pull over and restore the hood. The rain was worse, pounding down on the replaced roof. The road sign told her she was on the A325 heading north – only ten miles from

Branham. Suddenly she had a memory of childhood in Thursley a few miles from the lake. She had this vivid flashback to the twins and herself riding bikes along the King's Ridge, gazing down on the wide expanse of water and the little yachts. She made a decision: she owed some respect for Arnold; she would make a detour via Branham for old time's sake, and then put up for the night at the Lakeview Hotel.

The Lakeview greeted her as if she was minor royalty. Nadine did not mind that one bit, although she doubted if all those men in the bar took much notice of her present career. They remembered the "Bikini Girl" of fifteen years ago. She'd enjoyed that role but would like to put it behind her. She'd been the weather girl presenter who had dressed for the weather: Woolly hat and jumpers in January and the stringiest bikini in the July heat wave. Even now, rising forty, she was proud of her figure.

She sat down with her drink and soon had a small queue lining up to have her autograph; then a couple of lads posed with her for a photograph. Bored with this, she had decided to go for a walk; after all it was still over an hour to dinner. She fished her waterproof from the boot of the car and started along the road past the sailing club. The gate was locked, but she could just see the water and the slipways. Again, she wished she could summon up some real grief, although from what she'd learned this was not the place where Arnold had been bashed on the head. That had been somewhere by the sea.

She was surprised to find she was enjoying this. The rain had stopped and the air smelt good; that sweet aroma of pines and heather somehow brought her closer to her childhood and the days before she was hardened and spiteful. She crossed the main road, and once again began to climb the ridge. The twilight was merging into darkness and, although she was alone she sensed that someone else was on the path, man or woman she couldn't tell. Well, they were all entitled to this place although she would rather have it to herself and her memories. She was hungry now and once more the rain was falling, blowing lightly but wetting her face and hair. Nadine turned and walked back down the track. Just short of the road she paused, turned, looked back up the hill and yawned. A man was walking towards her and, incredibly, she knew him.

'Hi,' she called. 'Surprise, surprise, I was just thinking about you...'

She never saw the other figure behind the bush and barely felt the blow that crushed her skull. Two figures emerged and looked down at the lifeless body. Lifting her doll-like, they wrapped Nadine in a plastic cover and carried her a few yards to the Land Rover discreetly parked in the trees.

CHAPTER 5

The Fox family lived in Bosham close by Chichester Harbour. A house near the water, a garden and a sailing cruiser on a mooring were all they had ever dreamed of, especially now that retirement on good pensions beckoned.

Steve and Kirsten were their close friends, and it was a friendship forged through troubled times. Carol had been office manager at Easterbroke Sails during those traumatic days when Steve's first wife Miriam had died. Carol had proved herself then in a male dominated industry, and two years later had watched events unfold that summer when their worlds seemed to fall apart.

It was the evening following their visit to Liz Preston. Steve and Kirsten were on time for dinner at the Fox house. Though the Fox family were among their closest friends, both felt nervous. The murder charge for Harry Preston had been a profound shock. Both knew that, regardless of evidence, the police were wrong; Harry would not, and probably physically could not, have killed a heavy-weight bruiser like Arnold Evans. Steve knew that this attempt to influence a senior police officer was risky, unethical and possibly illegal, but Liz was distraught and Kirsten insistent. Steve climbed painfully out of the car and stared across the waterside. It was cold and low tide revealed a wide expanse of bleak, rain-swept mud.

Carol and Norman had greeted them happily with hugs and ushered them into a warm sitting room.

'I think we'll discuss your business now – get it over and then have dinner.' Norman's opening words were not encouraging.

Steve, urged on by Kirsten, went through his case slowly point by point. Carol poured drinks while Norman listened; face inscrutable. In the background a television, sound turned low, lit up a darkened corner.

'All right,' said Norman. 'I hear what you say and I will take this seriously, but I must emphasise I can't intervene directly. This is in the hands of the investigating team and the Crown Prosecution Service...'

'This is an innocent man,' Kirsten was beginning to be angry.

'Listen,' Norman replied. 'I can't intervene but I can use my influence – OK?'

Steve's attention was drawn to the television. 'That's the Lakeview Hotel,' he muttered. 'Hey, Norman, turn up the sound!'

A reporter was speaking to camera. 'The dead woman, TV presenter Nadine Rotherton, was known to be a close friend of Arnold Evans found dead in this lake four days ago. The police will not comment on the cause of death...'

'Yes,' Norman allowed himself a smile. 'Our suspect would be rather unique if he was responsible for that.'

'Can you check on the cause?' Steve asked.

'Not tonight, but we will liaise with Surrey as a matter of routine. But frankly it's probably self-harm – who would want to kill a silly little celeb girl like that one?'

Steve and Kirsten looked at each other – both were unhappy although not surprised at Norman's attitude.

'Come on,' Norman grinned at them. 'Cheer up. This can only help your friend's cause.'

Carol put her head round the door. 'Come and have dinner.'

It was only when they were leaving that Norman made the suggestion. 'If you're dead set on some private sleuthing, why not give Frank Matheson a call?'

'That's a great idea,' Kirsten agreed.

Steve was less sure. 'Hasn't he retired?'

'Yes, officially. When all's said he's over seventy, but he did some legwork in the Girl on the Beach affair. His son runs his agency, but Frank's still fit and well and maybe a bit bored.'

'I might give him a call,' said Steve. 'But that's assuming you're still set on making idiots of yourselves over Harry.'

'Great dinner, Carol,' said Kirsten, 'but we'd better go and collect the children.' She smiled at him mischievously. 'You see, we left them in the care of the wife of your chief suspect.'

Liz had insisted they leave the children with her. This meant a twenty-five mile diversion in the wrong direction, but they accepted that, knowing both youngsters were happy at the Preston house. Liz and Harry had only one surviving child, an adult son who lived overseas. They tended to be kindly, if over indulgent with the Simpson children. Leaving them with Liz for a few hours might help ease her worries.

The Preston house was a blaze of light from every window. As Steve parked on the gravel sweep he noticed a police panda car

26

nearby. The front door was open wide.

'Something's wrong,' said Kirsten.

Steve stopped the car and Kirsten leapt out. Steve watched as she sprinted across the gravel to the open door as Emily ran into her arms. Steve reached them just as John-Kaj emerged from the house.

'Hello, where's Liz?'

Emily was crying, but John-Kaj simply looked bemused. 'It's the police,' said Emily. 'They've taken Liz away.'

'What!' Kirsten shouted. 'And they left you on your own?'

'No,' said Emily. 'There's a lady copper in there. Supposed to be looking after us.'

'When did this happen?' Steve snapped.

'About an hour ago. They said the copper would look after us until some other people came, but they're not here yet.'

'Let's go back indoors and see what we can do,' said Steve. 'Do you have any idea what the police want?'

'I heard them say something about a dead woman in the river.'

'What river?'

'The Wey – down by the bridge.'

Another voice spoke. 'Do you have the care order?' A young woman police constable stood outlined in the light from the front door.

Kirsten sprang at her. 'What the hell are you doing here?'

'I beg your pardon,' the policewoman looked startled. 'You're not from social services?'

'These are our children,' Steve also was not pleased and he showed it.

'Your children?' The woman looked puzzled. 'I was told they were Mrs Preston's children. Someone's coming to take them into care.'

'The hell they are. What's happened to Mrs Preston?'

'I can't discuss that – she's being held in custody for questioning on a serious matter.'

'We'll see about that,' said Steve. 'In the meantime I'm taking the children home.'

'I'm sorry, but you can't do that. As I say they're being taken into care.'

'Emily, John, get in our car. Now!' Kirsten yelled.

The WPC looked even more baffled. 'Are you related to these two? I mean, do you have legal guardianship?'

'You stupid little...' Kirsten, red-faced, leant forward into the

27

alarmed woman's face. 'They are my children – Mrs Preston was our sitter. So I am taking my own children to their own home.' Kirsten walked to the car and climbed into the driving seat.

Steve felt it was time to be diplomatic. 'It's true what she says – they are our kids.' He slipped one of his business cards into the policewoman's hand and walked to the car.

Kirsten drove to the entrance and pulled over for a Vauxhall with a woman driver and passenger. 'Christ,' said Kirsten. 'Did you see those two lemon-faced cows. Bloody social services written all over them – come to steal my kids – I'd bloody pulp them if they'd tried.'

'Then it's a good thing we left now.'

'What do we do, Steve?'

'We call Matheson.'

The telephone was ringing. Steve rolled over in bed and looked at the clock. It said six-thirty a.m. – who on earth?

'Yes,' he yawned into the handset.

'Steve – Norman here. Sorry to trouble you this early, but something's come up.'

Steve heaved himself into a sitting position and glanced at Kirsten still apparently asleep and oblivious. 'Go ahead.'

'We need to clarify something urgently. Social Services say you snatched two children that the police have sought a care order for.'

'Say that again!'

'It's what I said; Social Services say you've removed the two young children of a suspect in custody. The police asked for them to be taken into care and a court order has now been issued. The position is that if you want to keep them at your house, you'll have apply to a magistrate's court in the area concerned.'

Steve needed to keep his head. He told Norman the facts. He was not pleased, in fact he was forcing himself to exercise self-control in a way he had not required in years. He was relieved to see that Kirsten was still in her own dream world.

'Oh my God,' Norman laughed. Steve did not find the situation amusing and said so none too politely.

'All, right, leave it to me.' Norman still seemed amused. 'Social services…no, I'd better not say too much. It's like that French writer – Carol keeps quoting him – Kafka, that's the guy.'

Steve could hear some muttering in the background.

'That was Carol; says Kafka wasn't French.'

'Norman, please, this is a bloody nightmare – what do we do?'

'I would suggest you come into our station and make a statement. Does the Surrey's woman suspect have any children?'

'Only one: he's grown up and working in Spain, but they lost another little girl aged ten. Frankly they've suffered enough without this nonsense. By the way, you're talking about Harry Preston's wife, and I repeat, there is no way either of them are connected with any of these murders. If there is a connection it's about time you went out and found it before Frank Matheson makes you all look bloody stupid.' Steve slammed the phone down.

Kirsten was awake rubbing her eyes. Steve could see light filtering through the curtains and hear the driving rain spattering on the window. He told her and then lay back and let the torrent of her rage wash over him.

The morning television news seemed, in Steve's opinion, to have lost the plot completely. Iraq; Afghanistan; the Middle East; the Health Service, had all been consigned to the second or third items.

It was likewise with the tabloid press.

TV Girl Celeb Nadine In Horror Murder.

Arnie's Girl Dies In Copycat Killing.

The brasher tabloids were having an enjoyable morning outdoing each other in gore. *Lovely Nadine...a source revealed the body to have been decapitated.*

Then... *her head was crushed under the wheels of a heavy vehicle...*

These reports, mostly imaginative and contradictory were echoed in the more tasteful broadsheets. Steve and Kirsten ignored it all: they only had eyes for one paragraph ... *the police are reported to be holding a woman suspect and it is understood that she is the wife of the man already charged for the murder of Internet tycoon, Arnold Evans.*

'I've rung Frank,' Steve called to Kirsten. 'Do you want to have a word?'

He held out the phone to her as she ran down the stairs.

She seized the handset from him. 'Frank, it all lies, they never did it. Will you help us – please?'

'All right, young Kirsten,' the voice on the phone was mellow and well remembered. 'Calm down for half a minute. Right, that's better. I can call round this morning, eleven o'clock – how's that?'

CHAPTER 6

'I've done some checking; your friend Preston was up before the magistrates earlier this morning.' Frank Matheson sat at the kitchen table sipping the coffee Kirsten had brewed for him.

'What will happen?' Kirsten asked.

'It's only a formality, but his solicitor will ask for bail. My source with Sussex police says they're opposing that, partly to safeguard the suspect from harm.'

'What harm?' Steve asked.

'Silly rumour – there are people saying that he's a psycho, and that he killed the schoolteacher. The trouble is that Phil Le Bois is beginning to believe that too.'

'Who's he?'

'Local DI – got as high up the ladder as he'll ever get. Wants glory, and isn't too fussy how he finds it.'

'You mean a bent copper?'

Matheson looked shocked. 'Absolutely not – Le Bois's just a bit short of brain cells. Anyway, Sussex are expecting a demonstration outside the court; they're diverting officers to guard the place. Good news for every real villain for miles.'

Frank Matheson, one time Chief Superintendent, seemed to have aged little in the fifteen years that Steve and Kirsten had known him. Although in his mid-seventies, he looked fit and appeared mentally as sharp as ever. Forced to resign from the police under a cloud, Matheson had scored his greatest triumph as a free-lance private investigator. His personal quest to bring down the man who had destroyed his career had coincided with Steve and Kirsten's troubles. All three of them had witnessed Lindgrune's spectacular demise on the Itchenor shoreline: an event that had formed an unbreakable bond.

'Right, you two,' Matheson opened a notebook and placed it on the kitchen table. 'Tell all, just like you did that time at Xjiangs restaurant. Johnny's opening a branch in your Petersfield by the way.'

Between them, Steve and Kirsten told him the whole story. Apart from the occasional grunt Matheson said nothing but wrote copious notes in untidy shorthand. 'Is that it?' he asked as they finished their statement.

'Yes,' said Steve. 'Can you suggest anything that'll help?'

'Oh yes, I've picked up on several very interesting coincidences.

Let me start enquiries for a couple of days and I'll come back to you.'

'Can you do anything for Harry and Liz?'

'I certainly hope so, but as I say, give me a day or so. First port of call is a visit to Miss Marple.' Matheson chuckled as he saw their baffled expressions.

'By that I mean have a little chat with Professor Greta von Essens of Portsmouth University. Stop laughing – Pompey does have a university for real these days. Tempus fugit as we say down there – I don't think.' He looked at the kitchen clock. 'It's news time. Let's go and turn the telly on.'

The local woman newsreader's face filled the big plasma screen. 'Violent scenes erupted outside the court in Chichester…'

The picture changed to a police van driving past a jeering crowd holding placards. *Murdering bastard – Justice for Linda*. A large woman broke from the crowd pursued by two police officers. She reached the van and thumped angrily on its sides with her fists. The police seized her arms and dragged her away.

'Well what-do-you know,' Matheson exclaimed. 'Sid Everett and Andy Ikes,' he pointed at the screen. 'You remember Sid, from the *Banner*.'

'Of course,' said Steve. 'He gave us that tip-off.'

'That's right. He's the hack and Andy's the camera. Look at them milking that mob. I bet it's Andy that's orchestrated the whole show.'

Steve turned up the sound as a television reporter addressed the camera. 'These were the scenes outside the court as suspect Henry Preston was charged with the murder of Arnold Evans.' He paused and flapped a hand angrily at a scruffily dressed woman who had forced her way in front of the camera.

'Justice for Linda – hang the bastard…' Strong arms dragged her away.

'Sorry about that,' said the reporter. 'But this illustrates how feelings are running high in this town, following the murder of popular local teacher, Linda Zeigler…'

'God, almighty,' said Matheson. 'Right, I'll ring Greta now and then I'm on my way. This matter won't wait.'

Steve and Kirsten stood by the front door and waved Matheson on his way.

'It's embarrassing,' said Steve. 'But he's refusing to take a fee, not a penny towards travel or anything.'

'I know,' she replied. 'But he says he owes us for what happened in 1990. He lost his little girl remember.'

'Of course, but we owe him so much more. Everything we have in a way.'

Steve changed the subject. 'How was Emily this morning?'

'She's OK, but she's upset – they were all fond of Linda Zeigler, and of course they're frightened – expecting a mad murderer round every corner.'

Steve felt ashamed that he'd hardly spoken to his children at breakfast. His thoughts were elsewhere: with Harry and Liz, presumably locked in dank cells and facing false charges. Worse than that, in spite of Matheson's assurances Steve was not convinced. Police forces were not above offloading the blame on an innocent party in hope of an easy resolution and a quiet life. False convictions had been in the news lately. This inspector with the funny French name could bask in the reflected glory; or at least he could until the real killer struck again. He followed Kirsten indoors out of the rain that persisted relentlessly.

'Want me to make some lunch?' he called. 'Then I'll have to go to work. I've only just remembered we're launching *Traveller*. It's high-water at 1600.'

'I want us all to go on her in the school break,' Kirsten replied. 'But not if Harry and Liz are still in trouble.'

'Put your trust in Frank.'

Steve made soup and found some rolls and baguettes, products of the local organic shop in the village. They sat in the kitchen. Steve watched his wife across the table and smiled. She returned with her own rueful grin that he knew so well. What a supremely fortunate man he was to have found this wonderful woman, still as beautiful in his eyes as the evening he had first met her in Elgaad's house and next day encountered her naked on the windsurfer. For him she'd given up so much of her heritage, taken his name and his country's nationality. In spite of Dolly Pembelty's comments, he still loved to see Kirsten nude and natural: slightly fuller in the figure than fifteen years ago but in his eyes even more feminine. Hypocritical of him, as his prudish English upbringing had prevented him from ever joining her and the kids with their naked frolics in the pool.

He was even more grateful to his elder daughter Sarah, now married to her James and with a child of her own. A bizarre outcome, as little Christine, his first grandchild was the same age as her Aunt Emily. Sarah and Kirsten had accepted each other from their first meeting without jealousy or rancour on either side. How unusual was that? Steve knew he was a lucky man: maybe too lucky for his own good. Could some avenging force be restoring the balance with all this trouble?

'Car coming in,' Kirsten called watching through the window. 'It's the bloody police again. Another car as well, but I can't see who.'

Steve joined her. The two police officers, one female, were conferring with a third civilian girl who had just left the other car and was unfolding an umbrella. She was blonde and not unattractive he noticed. Crouching against the rain and wind the trio headed towards the front door. The male officer reached up and rang the bell.

The police displayed their warrants; the blonde girl had an identity square pinned on her clothing near her prominent left breast. Steve looked away; Kirsten had a nasty habit of almost reading his mind in these encounters.

'I'm from Southern social services,' the girl said. 'We've come to collect the children.'

'Oh hell!' Steve was really angry now. 'Whose children?'

'Mrs Elizabeth Preston has been released on police bail,' said the male copper. 'You are Mr Stephen Simpson?'

'Yes, but look here...'

'You were supposed to attend your local police station to give an explanation as to why you took them,' said the female police officer. 'Where are they now?'

'The children, as you call them, are our own kids and they're both at school.'

'You took them to Farnham?' The social services girl looked puzzled. She glanced at a note pad; already she was looking a lot less attractive and her furled umbrella was dripping on the carpet. Steve sensed that Kirsten was about to have one of her volcanic tantrums. He squeezed her arm until she blenched, then he gave her his best "keep your mouth" shut glare.

'Yes,' the woman continued not waiting for an answer, 'Jeremy and Rachel Preston, so county archives state. But our computer system has crashed and the birth dates and all current details seem to be missing.' The blonde looked up from her notes. 'I assume they are both at private school. We've checked local school rolls, and we can find no record of their attendance. You understand that that alone is not good.'

'You'd have been better informed if you'd checked dates of death.'

Steve scrutinised all three slowly and deliberately. He knew he could be an intimidating figure at moments such as this. 'Jeremy Preston is a thirty-six-year-old property developer based in Spain. I can give you his phone number and email. Rachel Preston, poor little kid, died from leukaemia eleven years ago. Didn't Mrs Preston tell you any of this?'

'She denied any knowledge of her children. She seemed rude and indifferent. This is one of the things that is influencing the current decision to remove them to permanent foster care.'

Steve was hard-put not to laugh at the vision of the debonair and lecherous Jeremy in foster care. The fact that Liz was released on police bail was a huge relief. While Kirsten fumed silently he ushered all three into the house. In his study he dug out the file with the children's birth certificates and showed them photographs and school reports. The police were inclined to see the funny side. The social services girl remained unconvinced. 'I will have to cross check your statement,' she said. 'But I must warn you we may be returning with a court order.'

'So, that's why we pay maximum rate council tax,' Steve grunted as the cars left.

Kirsten glowered. 'If we have any more of this bollocks, I say we go public – ring the media and the TV people. Anyway, another hour and I'm off to fetch the kids.'

'And I'm five hours late for work.'

Now she laughed. 'Who sacks you? We own the joint.'

CHAPTER 7

Dr Greta von Essens lived in Bishops Waltham, a tranquil little town in the midst of the Hampshire countryside. Her cottage on the outskirts was set in rural surroundings with a large garden. Greta was English born, a fact that became apparent the moment she spoke. Greta epitomised the ageing female academic nurtured by a top girls' school, then by five years at Cambridge followed by a postgraduate appointment.

Greta's father had fled his native Hanover in 1938. His aristocratic parentage had not saved him from the stigma of falling in love and marrying a beautiful Dutch Jewish girl. Rejected by his family, and under threat from the Nazi regime, Greta's parents had taken the only sensible course. British cousins had helped them obtain entry visas and the pair had settled in Southern England. Greta, their third child, and only girl, was born in 1946. Her parents had no thoughts of returning home to Germany. Both her uncles, father's brothers, were dead, killed on the Russian front, as were his three sisters by allied bombing. Her mother's entire family had vanished in the Holocaust.

Greta had made her personal pilgrimage to Auschwitz. Every spare moment during the next two years she spent researching the atrocities of Nazi Germany. She visited sites, spoke to those witnesses who were prepared to talk, including a few convicted or suspected of committing horrific crimes. Greta was surprised how many of these were prepared to talk frankly. Though a few were contrite and tearful, as many more seemed to be proud of actions that they believed to be right and patriotic. Many of them registered indignation at the way public opinion regarded their crimes.

Greta had concluded her research and then taken a sabbatical from her university to write a thesis on criminal psychology. It contained pages of new radical thinking that provoked hostility from conservative opinion in both the police and medical professions.

One policeman who did not scoff was Frank Matheson. He read the thesis and contacted Greta the next day. Her analysis of a stalled investigation led Matheson to arrest the Portsmouth serial rapist. Not so many people scoffed after that. Greta's services as a criminal profiler had earned her the title: Female Sherlock. She had not forgotten her career debt to Matheson. She had applied for the new post at Portsmouth, and with Matheson's support, had gained it over competition from two distinguished younger applicants.

Matheson parked in the lane outside Greta's house and opened the little wooden garden gate. It had stopped raining and sunlight was warming the green countryside. Greta's garden was a bit too neat and tidy for Matheson's taste. Daffodils grew in square borders arrayed in lines like a platoon of soldiers. Other beds were less severe and blazed with wallflowers and early roses; it all smelt good. He saw Greta instantly, although her head was concealed in a bee veil and she carried a hive smoker.

'Frank, go in and put the kettle on,' she called.

The cottage was dark but cosy. The interior was furnished in minimalist severity. He glanced into Greta's study. "Order is perfection" was her motto. Two computers on separate tables stood adjacent to filing cabinets and perfectly arranged shelves of box files. There was still something very German about Greta, he mused. He boiled the kettle and found the coffee cups and the percolator. He knew that caffeine addiction was Greta's only admitted vice, and she liked her coffee ground and strong. He carried the brew on a tray into the sitting room. Greta entered the room pulling off the bee veil.

'Hi, Frank, sorry to keep you waiting. Caught a swarm over Hambledon – had to get the little sods into their new home.'

'You never get stung?'

'Thousands of times, but my immunity is good. Now what have you got for me?'

Simon Hexham had finished his shift at Solent Coastguard. Not much happening at this time of year. The weather was still lousy and that kept the yachties in harbour: or those who had actually launched their craft. The beaches were deserted which was just as well as the rain and mist would hamper the rescue helicopter. He had little to do except answer a few calls from incoming commercial ships, then read the inshore forecast before signing off pretentiously with his own name. He rather fancied the idea of being a TV newsreader or a disc jockey: help him pull the girls plus shorter hours and a bloody sight better pay. He looked at his car dashboard clock. So much lighter the evenings now that the days had moved to sensible summer time. He could go home to his shared flat in Lee, or maybe check on his own boat at Dell Quay. Yes, he had time to shoot off down the M27, check the boat and then make it home. It wouldn't do to be late. Leanne had agreed to a second date. He could take her to Vivs' Club in Lee, give her a good time and maybe he'd get lucky. First he would call Marcus and ask if they could meet by the boat. Marcus was a good crew who had almost agreed to sail with Simon this season. He put his mobile back in his pocket. No luck, Marcus had been helping at the boat yard with a messy diesel overhaul and only wanted to go home.

In a little over half-an-hour Simon reached Chichester and took the roundabout exit for Appledram. At Dell Quay his dinghy was as he had left her, although the cover bulged under an excess of rainwater. This little boat was his pride and joy. He had run up a sizeable debt to buy her, and there she was: a brand spanking new RS200. He had scored a couple of first places in club racing on the harbour, crewed by kid brother, then two weekends ago he'd won the open at Branham. Simon's best race had been watched by Steve Simpson, a man who had won an Olympic gold medal donkey's years ago. He couldn't quite visualise Steve as a super-star. The man was an amiable grey-haired old codger, but none-the-less a great coach and his few words of praise and encouragement had delighted Simon. It was low tide in the creek, which was now only a sheet of mud with a trickle of water in the centre. This probably accounted for the fact that no one was around the boat park. He laid the cover aside and sponged down the boat. He walked round her and stood back while he admired her lines almost as if he was undressing Leanne or some other tasty bird. He looked at his watch. It was growing dark, and he was due back at Lee in an hour. He replaced the boat cover and walked to his car parked on the grass inside the sailing club's boat field. A Land Rover had stopped next to him and a fat man in greasy overalls was struggling to lift a box from the wet ground into the open tail. He'd seen this guy around the harbour villages, on and off, but didn't know his name.

'Want a hand, mate?' Simon asked.

'Could do,' was the grunted reply.

Simon bent down and grabbed a rope handle. The iron bar smashed his skull with a single blow.

Greta adjusted her reading glasses and stared at her notes. 'Very well, I think we agree that all three of these killings are by the same hand.'

'But not Henry Preston's?'

'Of course not and I'll tell you why he was never involved in any of these killings. Inspector Le Bois is sincere but he has made the classic error of naming his suspect and then scratching around to find anything that fits his hypothesis.'

'That's obvious, but you'll have to explain your reasoning.'

'Psychopaths reveal their traits in little ways long before they begin to kill. Mr Preston is a highly regarded well educated professional...'

'So were Crippen and Shipman.'

'I cannot say about Crippen, but in Shipman's case the signs were evident for years, if only someone had had the sense to interpret them. As I say, Mr Preston is a well-liked professional. I've made my own enquiries and it seems he is not a man easily roused to anger, and it is unlikely he would have the physical strength to bludgeon a much stronger man.'

'I agree.'

'Good, because I work on the balance of probability. I don't believe this man would kill, and I don't believe his wife and friends would cover up a killing.'

'They might have known nothing about it.'

'Not so, Frank. The murderer would have arrived home with blood on him and in a shocked state. His wife would have seen instantly that something was wrong. In this case none of that did happen. The police will find no DNA link; the Crown Prosecution will decline to act and DI Le Bois will have to release him.'

'I agree; your science meets my own gut reaction. So what now?'

'Links,' said Greta. 'What do all these killings have in common?'

'All three slugged from behind.'

'Yes, of course but anyone can deduce that. No there's more – much more.'

'That Nadine was Evans' tame bimbo.'

'Obvious personal link but it's not enough.' She shuffled her notes. 'Frank, what about the schoolteacher, Zeigler? I understand she has an ex husband.'

'He's in the clear. Mr Zeigler is a Norwegian and he's never left Norway. Mrs Zeigler left both him and Norway at the same time. Fox told me this morning. But I found out today that Linda used to work out along the shoreline at Pagham. That's where Le Bois thinks Evans was battered.'

'Sorry, Frank, but you're still missing it.'

'All right, I suppose I'm not as sharp as I was – old age.'

'Right, I have two leads. One I'm not sure about and I'm keeping the theory under my hat, for now anyway. The other one is water – each body was left in water and that to me is a pattern.'

'I suppose so.' Matheson was interested now. He had huge faith in this amazing woman. 'Yes, you're right. It had occurred to me that it seemed odd.'

'Let's take that a step further. Three locations: Branham Lake, the central reservoir, the River Wey. Lots of water, but do you see the common link?'

'Our murderer has a penchant for the wet stuff.'

'Yes, but it's fresh water, not salt. Which leads me to my main surmise-the link that shouts at me.' Greta sat back.

'Which is?'

'It's so bizarre that I'm not going to put my neck on the block just yet, but if I'm right there are dozens of innocent citizens throughout these islands who could be next.'

'I've changed the filters, fitted a new impeller – full tank. Start her up and she'll sail away.' Peter Terring wiped his hands on a piece of towel.

Steve stood beside him in *Traveller's* central cockpit drinking in the scene. The ship looked magnificent. Chris the rigger had fitted new shrouds and halyards. Sails that he, Steve, had designed and helped to stitch were now bent on to the fore and main booms, although they lay concealed beneath customised sail covers.

'Water tank's full and we've put in some purifier,' Peter continued. 'It'll do you until you reach France. Your cooking gas is a bit low – I weighed the cylinders. One's empty and the other's light.'

'That's not so important, we'll replace them the day we go.' Steve felt the buzz he always did at the beginning of a summer season. He could dream of warm days to come, lazy days in the sun with the whole family, or challenging days with a full crew in a good force seven. *Traveller* was better than any conventional holiday home. She was a beautiful living being with a personality honed over a lifetime at sea.

'Thanks, Peter, we're in the water early and I appreciate that. You can take a trip with us if you like.'

'Maybe one day. I'm not too sure about all these sails – sooner have a good motor under my feet. And how do I fish with all this rigging?' Peter was returning to his habitual gloom; Steve was regretting he'd spoken.

'We could always trail a line and spinner off the stern – catch a few mackerel.'

'Where's the sport in that?'

Steve gave up. No doubt Peter and his friends found fishing relaxing and contemplative. Steve was conscious that at sixty, he was running out of years. While he still had body and soul together he wanted action. He climbed slowly back onto the marina pontoon and admired his ship, taking in the traditional varnished wooden spars, the gleaming white topsides and the two club pennants flying from the crosstrees: Branham and Itchenor Sailing Clubs.

The mobile phone in his pocket was ringing, bringing an unwelcome intrusion from the outside world. As Steve extracted the thing and put it to his ear he knew with a sinking stomach that this was more trouble.

'Frank Matheson here,' said the voice. 'I'm at the Crown and Anchor. Can you join me, there's been another one.'

'Another what?' Steve had to ask but he knew what was coming.

'Another killing, just like the others and it fits Greta's profile like a glove.'

'Phil Le Bois isn't going to like this one bit,' said Chief Superintendent Fox.

'What, this murder or me being here?' asked Matheson.

'Both in equal measure. The killing will blow his investigation sky high. The Crown Prosecution Service are not pleased with him jumping the gun and charging Henry Preston. All the evidence is circumstantial: no prints on the murder weapon. Forensic can find nothing DNA-related on Preston's clothes, or in his car and his house has been checked – nothing there. If Le Bois doesn't come up with something better then he'll fail at the next magistrate's hearing.'

'So he bloody well should. Preston's got nothing to do with it. Professor von Essens is convinced and that's good enough for me.'

'That woman won't impress Le Bois. He says your Miss Marple is a charlatan.'

Matheson followed Fox under the police tape and across the muddy field. He could see white suited officers quartering the ground and young Lucy the doctor.

Fox stopped and looked at the scene. 'Why can't these sick psychos pick on bank managers or tax men? Not poor young lads like this one. That's what winds me up – how can we expect to be objective? The victim was a cracking youngster by all accounts – his mates are devastated.'

'When was he found?' Matheson asked.

'Around six this morning – farmer calling his cows in for milking found him. But Hampshire say the victim's girlfriend had already made a missing person call and of course he never turned up for his work shift. We haven't touched anything, so see what you think.'

Inspector Le Bois met them on the edge of the scene. He looked harassed and unfriendly. 'Matheson, what are you doing here?'

'Ex Chief Superintendent Matheson is here by my invitation,' Fox was clearly bent on cutting Le Bois down to size. 'He also represents Professor von Essens who is helping with the wider investigation.'

'Sir, I must protest. I have this investigation under my control and near to a conclusion. I don't need that stupid Kraut woman and we don't need him.' Le Bois jabbed a finger at Matheson.

'I'm happy to hear it. Perhaps you can tell us why you consider you have a solution to a case that is baffling the entire nation and frightening every living soul on our watch.' Fox was becoming angry.

Le Bois looked around. 'All right, but not in front of that bimbo doctor and all these wallies.' He jerked a thumb towards Lucy and the forensic team.

Matheson and Fox followed him a short distance into the field. 'Right,' Le Bois began. 'Open and shut case now. The lad Hexham was just over the way looking at his boat. Apparently he phoned a mate of his at the boatyard next door to say he was coming. His mate works in the yard; we've seen him and he's already given a statement. Says he never saw Hexham – couldn't wait for him as he wanted to go home. He'd been all day helping an engineer with a diesel overhaul. We haven't checked it all yet but I'd say his alibi is solid.'

'So, why is the case open and shut – that sounds dramatic?' Fox asked.

'Hexham races little dinghies on the Harbour,' said Le Bois, 'and two weeks ago he went to an event at Branham. That's all the connections we need. Surrey are pulling in Preston's wife again and this time we'll charge the pair of them – conspiracy to murder.'

'Motive and firm evidence?' asked Fox.

'Well, nothing definite yet but there will be – just give us time and it'll all come good.'

'Well done, Phil,' Fox smiled. 'If it's all done and dusted there's no harm in Mr Matheson looking at the scene.'

Matheson noted that Le Bois failed to detect the irony.

'Yes,' said Le Bois. 'You can tell that interfering Kraut woman to sod off. We don't need her stupid theories. I don't like Germans – I've not forgotten the war.'

'Phil, you weren't even thought of then.'

'The Jerries kicked in my old Gran's front door and nicked all the food in the house. I'll never forgive the Germans for that.'

Fox sighed. 'It's a new world now; any German soldier who

mistreated your Gran, if not dead, will be in an Alzheimer's home.'

Lucy met them and waved toward a rectangular water tank. 'We've sent for the ambulance. I think you can lift him out now and put him on the ground. His skull's crushed – worse than the last one.'

Matheson felt sorry for the girl. She was young and he knew had only been in the district a few months. Now she had to work with these gruesome corpses. The body was clad in a uniform of some sort and lay floating face down in the water tank. The thing was a galvanised rectangular cattle drinker about ten feet long. It was strengthened with cross bars, and the body had been thrust full length and trapped beneath them. The water was discoloured from the congealed blood on the victim's head.

'Was he a Navy lad?'

'No, Coastguard service, but their uniform is similar,' said Fox.

'Did he walk here to be killed?' Matheson asked.

'No,' said Le Bois. 'A vehicle crossed the field. Heavy tyres – long wheel base four-by-four for certain. Surrey are checking on the Preston woman's car. Surrey toffs – they all drive four-by-fours. We'll take a cast of the tyres, they'll find the blood in the back and bingo we've a result.'

'So one slightly-built woman lifted a six foot male body and pushed it in there?' Matheson failed to restrain his sarcasm.

'The information I have,' said Fox, 'is that Mrs Preston was only released from police questioning at 1200 yesterday.'

'Point taken, but this killing was in the evening, she had plenty of time. And how d'you know she's a slight woman? Anyway she's a psycho – got super strength when they're gripped by madness.' Le Bois gave an impression of supreme self-confidence. Matheson, who had been in the business a lot longer, detected a scintilla of doubt.

The men had lifted the body from the water tank and laid it on a plastic sheet. Matheson moved closer and stood beside the doctor. 'I'm Frank Matheson,' he introduced himself. 'I'm not police any more – but I've been retained as a professional investigator.'

Suddenly she brightened. 'You did some work for my Dad,' she smiled. 'Tom O'Malley, remember?'

'The Girl on the Beach affair, of course: not that I did much beyond trace a few car registrations.'

'No, Mr Matheson, that was a key contribution at the end of the day.' She grimaced. 'You know my Dad found the girl just over there, the other side of those trees. It's one of the things that's shaken me a bit with this call out. I've bad memories of that business. I saw

42

men killed that day...' Her voice trailed away as Matheson saw the pain mirrored in her face.

CHAPTER 8

Liz Preston had had enough. Once again she had been taken to the police station. This time she was not distraught only very angry. She had a clear conscience as had Harry but this was too much. At least she would have the support of her son. Jeremy had phoned her from Gatwick. He had hired a car for the weekend and would be with her at four o'clock. That was assuming, of course, that the police did not intend putting her back in that horrible cell.

She still felt cold at the remembrance of last time. The police had called just as she was cooking a supper for Kirsten's two. Without explanation they had dragged her away from the children and driven her to that awful Gestapo style interrogation. The cell that night had been cold. No bedding was supplied for the hard bench, and the apology for a mattress stank. Only her own inner steel and the certainty of her innocence had sustained her.

The next day she had been returned home to face two shrewish officials from social services waving bits of paper, wanting to seize her children. What children? She had only one living child, Jeremy. She tried to explain but gave up when she found she was in a dialogue of the deaf. The women left muttering about legal proceedings and their intention to check school rolls. Liz had rung Jeremy before their car was out of sight. Good boy, he had dropped everything, including an important business deal and flown home.

This morning, the police attitude had been odd. The phone had rung, and a polite voice had asked if she wouldn't mind calling at the police station for a short discussion. With trepidation she had driven into town and arrived at the reception on time. The Gestapo had vanished. This time she was shown to a table in an empty canteen and given a cup of coffee and a piece of fruitcake. It gradually dawned on her that the officers were going through the motions of questioning her at the request of someone for whom they had no good opinion. Odd questions though: what cars did she and her husband drive? She answered correctly: Harry drove an Audi, she her new-style Mini.

She explained that Harry had the more powerful car as a tow vehicle for the family dinghies. Did she now, or ever, own a four-by-four? Well, not likely: horrible gas-guzzling beasts.

The questioner confirmed that her testimony agreed with official records. Then came a shock. 'Mrs Preston, do you know Simon

Hexham?'

'Yes, that is I know someone of that name.'

'Who is he?'

'Sailor from down the South Coast. He's good too – won our RS200 open meeting two weeks ago. Nice boy – had his brother crewing.'

'Have you seen him since?'

'No, he collected the cup, made a rather nice speech and went home.'

'Would it surprise you to hear that Mr Hexham is dead and that our colleagues suspect foul play?'

For the first time in the presence of the police Liz's reserve broke and tears tumbled down her cheeks. 'Why – why? He's such a nice boy, a bit cheeky, but everyone liked him. And he's good at sailing – could do great things one day.'

'Not any more,' the WPC smiled at Liz and handed her a bulging bin liner. 'Mrs Preston, these are your husband's clothes that we borrowed for testing. You are free to go home now.'

If things were not bad enough already, thought Liz as she came in sight of home. Another police car was parked outside in the lane and a police officer was standing with a disparate group of individuals: six men and two women. Three of them were waving cameras, and thank God, standing to one side was Jeremy.

'My son,' she shouted the words aloud although neither he nor the others could have heard her.

She stopped the car and leapt out leaving the engine running. A babble of shouting broke over her head.

'Mrs Preston, look this way…this way…'

'Mrs Preston, have the police charged you…?'

'Mrs Preston… Mrs Preston, is your husband a psycho?'

'Mrs Preston, are you a murderer?'

This last question had proved too much for Jeremy. Liz watched her son, fit and bronzed, eyes blazing, walk to the questioner and fell him to the ground with a single blow.

'That's assault, actual bodily harm!' The man prone on the tarmac looked up at the policeman.

'Oh, I'm sorry, sir. I didn't notice anything. I was looking at Mrs Preston's garden. What happened – trip up did you?'

Jeremy held her arm. 'Come on, Mum – let's get indoors and then you can tell me what's happened to Dad.'

45

Steve reached the Crown and Anchor at Dell Quay. The pub had opened, and in the bar as promised he found Frank Matheson and an elderly lady. Frank waved to him and Steve joined the pair.

'This is Greta, or should I say Dr von Essens,' Frank introduced his companion and Steve shook hands. Two blue eyes stared him down. Steve was startled; with no warning whatever this was becoming one of the most intimidating first meetings that he could remember. She was smartly dressed, still slim, with styled grey hair, less make up and no adornments apart from small diamond earrings.

'Dr von Essens has been working with me,' said Frank. 'Now she's had a call from Surrey's Chief Constable, so her presence in the investigation is official.'

'Has Mr Simpson been told about the latest victim?' the woman asked.

'There's police all over the place,' said Steve. 'They stopped me on the road into here.'

'A young chap's been murdered – in the same manner as all the rest. He's a sailor, and I think you know him.'

Steve again felt a sinking stomach.

'Yes, he keeps his boat by the water over the way – Simon Hexham.'

'Oh, hell – Frank are you sure it's Simon?' Steve took a huge gulp from his beer. Was the world going mad?

Steve didn't know Simon Hexham that well but he'd coached him and he had been impressed. Hexham was not without faults. He was cocky and laddish. He had a reputation for late nights, drinking and girls: all things that could damage a potential Olympic career. None of that mattered now, but why? What had the boy done to be killed – what had all of them done?

'Frank, are you sure this killing is connected to any of the others?'

'I can answer that,' said Greta. 'He was struck down from behind and the body was left in a tank of fresh water. It all fits my profile in every respect save one.'

Matheson looked at her. 'Which is?'

'Meteorology; was the boy interested in the weather?'

'Would you know, Steve?' asked Frank.

'Everybody who sails worries about the weather. Hexham was a coastguard, and I know he sometimes reads the inshore forecasts on VHF...'

'Yes,' said Greta. 'That's most interesting.'

46

'I was coming home anyway,' said Jeremy. 'I heard about Nadine on the BBC, but I had no idea that you were involved or that it happened here.'

'I thought it would blow over,' his mother replied, 'but it's getting worse and madder by the day.' She dabbed at her eyes again. 'I keep ringing the police holding your father but they won't let me see him.'

'They've got to – you've rights. I'll have a go at them now.'

'No, J, leave it. They keep saying I can't see him as I'm under caution.'

'But you're not – that copper at the gate says you're not a suspect – you're asked to stay around so that they can confer with you.' Jeremy poured himself another huge slug of scotch.

'I hope you're not going driving?' Liz couldn't help being motherly.

'No, I'd better stay here unless…'

'Unless what?'

'You could drive me to Tilford down by the bridge. I'd like to see where Nadine was found.'

'I'm sure I don't want to – If you're that keen you can walk, it's not far. Anyway, why do you want to see the place?'

'Well, I think I can prove I was in Spain all last week, but poor Nadine,' he paused and Liz was startled by the expression of pain on her boy's face. 'You see I knew her. We had a bit of a thing going once, before I went overseas.'

'It's time you made your mind up and found a decent reliable wife.'

'Yeah, Mum, I'm sure – I'll do it when I'm ready – promise.' Jeremy yawned. 'Who was the other man you told me about – how on earth could those stupid police think Dad could kill someone?'

'Arnold Evans.'

'What, the internet man?'

'We only know him as our landlord at Branham. The trouble is, your father was seen arguing with him down in Sussex at Pagham. Evans destroyed one of your Dad's pictures.' It was too much for Liz; she collapsed onto the settee.

Jeremy put a supportive arm around her. 'We'll go and see him tomorrow,' he said. 'I'll talk to the solicitor myself.'

The stairs would be too much effort, so the man decided to take the lift. The stress and emotion of the last two weeks had got to him big time. He carried a plastic carrier bag stuffed with that day's newspapers. The tabloids had gone mad with up to three whole pages reporting on their mission. Stupid stuff: strong on imagination and weak on substance. Wicked, evil, mad were the adjectives that spattered across the pages. Well they were wrong – they should be rejoicing. It had been such a well-planned sacrifice. Four workers for the wrong had been chosen: one major player, two acolytes and that girl. He regretted that it had been necessary to release the girl to the next life. She was not the primary target, and Mother, the Powerful One, was not pleased. Brother and he had spotted Nadine from the bar in the Lakeview. They knew her, of course, from way back when she was small child. Years later she had reappeared on television. Both brothers knew too well the damage she had wreaked on innocent people. On their initiative they selected her on the spot for the sacrifice. It had been a hard decision to separate the evil woman from the child. Who could say that they had not done good work? No, the Power had selected her and sent her to them. Now the Power was appeased, and already they could see the good results. The Power must be appeased, and it seemed only they were willing to do the appeasement. Were they to fail, the Power in his anger would consume the whole human race and leave their planet a barren desert.

The lift doors opened and the man walked down the long corridor checking the numbers on the apartment doors. He found number twenty and pressed the bell. Now he must make the mental adjustment to talk in Spanish, but that was not a problem once the first couple of minutes of speech were done.

Sid Everett, long-serving journalist and reporter for the *Daily Banner,* knew how to be pushy. He was ensconced in reception at the Headquarters of the Mid Southern Constabulary and he was not moving. In his briefcase were archive pictures from nearly three years ago, but now a red-hot bargaining counter. He had told them he had evidence and a statement to make and demanded to see the Chief Constable. The police had laughed, before suggesting he handed over the envelope to the desk sergeant. No way, he told them. He would part with them only to a member of the multi-murder investigating team. He didn't add that the favour would have to be two-way. Sid had glared at the lot of them, then sat down and began to read a book. Twenty minutes later DI Le Bois arrived, shook Sid by the hand and called him into an inner office.

'Here you are, Chief.' Sid tipped the contents of the envelope onto the desk; two enlarged photographs and a copy of a news report. 'Tanya, our gossip editor remembered this one...'

Le Bois picked up the news report. *Nadine's night out...Lovely weather girl Nadine was seen at Annabel's with suave property developer Jeremy Preston...*

Le Bois put down the paper. 'Preston, is this a connection to my suspect?'

'Too right, Chief. Jeremy is his son and what's more he's around and about in Surrey right now.'

Le Bois looked interested. 'Do you know any of this for certain? Social services say the Preston's two children are missing, or rather that they were taken away by a couple who weren't given permission.'

'I don't know about any younger kids, but Jeremy Preston is Henry Preston's eldest son. He was at his mother's house yesterday, and he assaulted my oppo, Kevin.'

'Did he now.'

'That's right, Kev says Preston came at him from behind with a wooden club, knocked him senseless.'

'Did he report this?'

'You bet he did. There were police all over the shop but they never saw anything.'

'Any other witnesses?'

'Yeah, five other journos, but none of them like Kevin, and they say there was no club and that Kev saw the man coming.'

'Hmm, perhaps your man has a journalist's imagination.' Le Bois looked at the photographs. 'If this younger Preston killed his ex-girlfriend, then it is certain that he is working in conjunction with his father. But, Mr Everett, I haven't enough here to add additional charges. Now, if you would like to do some freelance delving, as you call it, I'm sure we could come to a mutual arrangement when the matter comes to court.'

'You bet, Chief. *The Banner* stands for law and order and family values. We'll do everything we can – s'long as you keep your end of the deal...'

Le Bois interrupted. 'Evidence, Mr Everett, I want hard facts that will stand up in court before a jury.'

The man stood in his mother's presence. She alone was worthy of the title Powerful One. How he loved her: she was his world, his inspiration, their spiritual guide. One day he would die for her because that was right and proper – a fulfilment. His twin stood beside him, and he knew from the look of awe and wonder on his face that the love was mutual: mother and sons – brother and brother.

'You have done well. Good boys. Meanwhile no more release and sacrifice. We will wait until the Power instructs me. Now I want you to find me an old man and a child.'

'Yes, mother, we can do that – when do you want to know?'

'There is no hurry, as long as the Power is resting. An old man and a child; to be specific, I want an old warrior tested in combat, and a child in the stages of puberty – find them and watch them.'

'Yes, mother. I think I know the child.'

'I know. You told me of one that you do not like, but that is not sufficient motive and your brother has a different view.'

His twin who had been standing silent beside him spoke. 'I would be reluctant to choose that one and I would not willingly hurt her.'

The man was not having that. He would never normally dispute in front of Mother, she the Powerful One, but he had to have his say. 'They are an arrogant family – rich and full of deceit. That child fits our criteria in every respect. I say choose the wretched brat and have done.'

Mother spoke, reducing them both to their proper state of meekness. 'The child can wait, but you must find the warrior. The Power is resting but I may have other work for you. That meddlesome old woman; the one who is asking questions.' She paused and wrote a name and address. 'Do nothing yet – wait for my word.'

'Yes, mother, All Powerful.'

'You are my two good boys.'

'We're going to pick up Liz and Jeremy and take them to Branham,' Steve put down the phone. 'She's very nervous about facing club members.'

'What do the police say?' Kirsten asked.

'It gets more stupid every day. Liz is in the clear – no longer a suspect...'

'I should bloody think so – idiots!'

'The thing's taken another turn – now they're accusing Jeremy – seems he had a bit of a fling with this Nadine a couple of years ago.'

'I'm sure he did,' Kirsten was scornful. 'Jeremy is lovely; I bet he has a hundred girls like her. So they think he kills all of them – why?'

Her indignation was almost comic. 'Hey, you trying to make me jealous?' Steve laughed.

Liz met them outside her front door. She was dressed to go sailing. Although her face was lined, and she had clearly been tearful, she had found some composure.

'They're going to let me see Harry tomorrow – Jeremy's going to drive me there.'

'Those stupid police,' Kirsten spoke. 'Tell me they believe you.'

'Yes, I'm in the clear, not a suspect. I am no longer helping them with their enquiries.' The bitterness was there now. 'But I've got to face people – you know what it's like. They read the papers – no smoke without fire. And they'll all think Harry's a killer...'

'Come on Mum – face it – show those coppers what blind fools they are.' Jeremy had joined them and put an arm around his mother.

'They've been having a go at you?' Steve asked him.

'Sort of, we had a couple of them call late yesterday. I told them I was in Spain – showed them my airline ticket. They didn't push it too hard, but I've got to produce... "signed statements as to my where-abouts on the night in question."' He mimicked police speech. 'I gather there's another lot of police that want to link me to Dad.'

'If it's any reassurance, we have people working independently on your behalf.'

'Frank Matheson and his woman guru,' said Kirsten. 'Don't worry, Frank is the best...'

Steve turned the corner from the main road into Lakeside Lane; a few hundred yards and they came to the sailing club. He could sense Liz's nervousness. Something was different: the car park was full and a crowd surrounded the club flagpole, which was dressed overall as for a regatta. Steve drove the car to the space reserved for the commodore.

'What's going on?' Liz looked puzzled.

'It's all right, we know,' Kirsten spoke.

Liz climbed out and looked around with a bemused expression on her face. The buzz of conversation died as John Marriott, the Vice-Commodore, stepped forward. In his hand was a clutch of A4 paper. 'Liz, Madam Commodore, please accept this petition. We have here over seven hundred signatures from your members and from the community at large. We have every confidence in you and Harry, and whatever anyone says, we know you are good upright citizens.'

On cue a child stepped forward with a huge bouquet of flowers and handed them to Liz.

'Thank you all,' her voice was husky but controlled. 'Thank you –

Harry and I will never forget this day. Now, come on – let's get these boats launched and go sailing.'

Steve spent a happy day in the coaching launch working with twenty Cadet dinghies, among them the Simpson boat sailed by Emily and John-Kaj. The sun shone all day but it was windy with sharp gusts and a hint of breaking waves: rare conditions for Branham. All the experienced children coped well. Steve was delighted with Emily's progress at the helm – he began seriously to consider her future potential. In his heart of hearts he felt it unwise for children to try and emulate their parents. Thirty-five years ago, a young Steve had won Olympic gold in the Finn class. Twenty-five years later, at the advanced age of thirty-four, and not to be outdone, Kirsten had won bronze for Denmark in the women's windsurfer class. Sailing was a major sport in her country, and Kirsten remained a household name. In Britain, Steve had been forgotten within a month by the general public but never by the sailing community. Advancing years had taken their toll, but he had found a new and unexpected ability as a teacher and coach.

The kids were clearly tiring; capsizes were becoming frequent, leaving the two safety boats busy. Steve turned to his own boat coxswain. 'Ed, we'll call it a day.'

Ed Grogan nodded in agreement. Ed was a morose man of few, if any, words but he was a good seaman and a fine engineer who maintained the safety boat engines for free. They motored to the jetty to be greeted by Emily and John-Kaj. Emily's face was flushed and her eyes shone. Her hair was wet as was her dinghy dry suit but that mattered not – she had come through a tough afternoon and was ready for more. Steve felt a shared joy before he remembered: afloat, he was in a different world; ashore all their troubles were real.

'A word of advice,' Steve spoke to Liz and Jeremy. 'Photocopy those names in the petition and send them to me. I'll pass them to Chief Superintendent Fox. He's the top man in the district where Harry is being held.'

'Can't I hand them to him direct?' Liz asked.

'If he's there you can – mention my name. But if he's not there I wouldn't risk it – those papers could mysteriously vanish.'

'God, what have we done to be in this bloody mess?'

'You haven't done anything, nor has Dad,' said Jeremy. 'Steve, you ever read Kafka?'

'No, I haven't, but you're the second person to mention him in relation to this business.' He groaned. 'Jeremy, did you know that social services want you taken into care?'

Now Jeremy laughed. 'Too right – Mum told me. Let them, there might be a few half willing female teachers – whatever.'

They strapped the children into the back seat and set off for home, this time with Kirsten at the wheel.

She spoke. 'Do you remember the time I drove you home after you fell in the duck pond?'

'I'm not likely to forget.'

'Me too – that night we made love for the first time.'

'I heard that,' said Emily.

'You should be sleeping after a day like this,' Kirsten laughed.

'You still do it sometimes,' said Emily. 'I've heard you – you're noisy.'

'And you, young lady are cheeky,' Steve replied. 'I don't want another word out of you this trip.'

They drove home in contented silence until Kirsten spoke again. 'Do we ring Frank when we're home?'

It was strange how the two of them seemed to read each other's thoughts.

'I was wondering that myself, but I think it's better that we be patient. He'll contact us when he's ready.'

It was growing dark when they arrived home. Steve wanted nothing more than a bath and a hot meal. He was not pleased to see a familiar and somewhat battered Vauxhall Cavalier parked in front of the house.

'It's dozy Dolly and old Gerry,' Emily called.

'Oh, give me strength,' Steve moaned. 'I've had enough for one day. What the hell do those two want?'

CHAPTER 9

Greta was in her office at the university. Frank Matheson had received a call from her at eight that morning and had come running. Metaphorically of course, as at seventy-four he was past doing much running.

'Right, professor, what have you got for me?'

'Some progress, I hope.' She pointed to her computer screen. 'First of all, there is the pattern. Death by single blow to the back of the skull, in each case followed by deposit of the body in fresh water.'

'So it's a psycho – not much doubt about it.'

'That's an all-embracing term and I need to be more precise. A psychopath is a person devoid of any morality regarding life and death. He or she kills on momentary impulse, and they have no sense of guilt. Or they can be immunised from guilt by being members of some disciplined group. I remember interviewing many in Germany – old SS men and concentration camp guards. No, Frank, I find elements of both traits in this case.'

'Are you implying we've more than one killer on the loose? It had crossed my mind already.' At last, Frank thought, we are getting somewhere.

'Oh yes, there are at least two individuals, and they believe that they are working for a purpose. They are male, still young and strong, and have the use of a powerful off-road vehicle.'

'All right, you're implying barking mad but with a purpose – what possible purpose?'

'I need more input, but I would be very surprised if we do not find a semi-religious or cult motive.' Greta began to flick through an internet site.

'Greta, this is fantasy. I mean – what religion?'

'No, I'm not talking about the mainstream Abrahamic religions. I suspect something much older.'

'Druids – no Greta, they're daft old men in white drag.'

She looked away from her screen and picked some sheets of computer printout. 'Let's see what we know about the deceased. First, Arnold Evans. He's a very rich man – his company Maxstats.com is an internet giant. I use its sites all the time for my work.'

'I'm not a huge computer fan, but I understand it's different from

Google.' Frank knew he was in alien territory.

'Maxstats is a data bank of statistics. You can find almost anything there that can be compiled statistically. Sporting leagues in any country, financial indices of course, political and voting figures, journey distances in mileages or kilometres, but most significant I believe are the weather statistics. Maxstats' most accessed site is the weather forecast and past weather statistics for any country or region, recorded at six hour intervals.'

'Yes, that does ring a bell; my grandson was playing with that site on Sunday. I'm more concerned about the other victims. You know the weather girl Nadine was having a fling with Evans?'

'True, but that was common knowledge. The tabloid press are making a song and dance about it – saying it's a planned double murder.' Greta stuffed her sheets of paper back into a file box and opened a notebook, whose pages were covered in her own precise handwriting. 'I'm not being consulted by Mid-Southern Constabulary, but the Surrey Police have asked my advice officially.' She looked at her notes.

'Nadine Rotherton was killed in Branham Country Park around six forty-five on the evening in question. She had left her car at the Lakeview Hotel car park two hours before, and was seen drinking and socialising in the main bar. She mentioned that she was going for a walk, which it seems she did and fatally.'

'You're saying that this must have been an impulse killing – Nadine in the wrong place at the wrong time? That blows your religious cult theory.'

'No, not in my view – she was unlucky, and as you say, in the wrong place, but everything else about her fits my formula.'

'Have Surrey traced the people in the pub?'

For the first time Greta laughed. 'Frank, the Lakeview is not a pub – it's an upmarket Surrey gathering place for the rich and beautiful. They hold very elegant wedding receptions there.'

'Do they really? I'm a red blooded Hampshire hog – we don't go much on Surrey and even less on Sussex. Both seem up to their necks in this case.'

'Well, the Surrey police have been on the ball but it's not easy. There were at least thirty people in and around that bar – mixture of visitors and locals. They've given me a list and I'm working on it. I hope I can narrow it down, and then we'll go looking for details.'

'Evans was found in Branham Lake; Nadine was killed near the water – there's got to be a connection.'

'That is the one certainty that we have, Frank. Give me a few more days and I hope I'll have more.'

'But Greta, this religion or cult. Give me some sort of clue. If it's not the Jehovah's witnesses or the Priory of Sion – what the hell are we looking for?'

'I don't like to broadcast my suspicions without definite confirmation, but as it's you, Frank…yes I'll drop a thought, not a clue, only a thought. Have you ever been to Latin America?'

'Gerry – Dolly, you're late visitors,' Steve did his best to appear hearty and welcoming.

'Sorry to intrude,' said Gerry, 'but there's something we think you should know.'

Dolly spoke. 'We think we should warn you.'

'What about,' Steve was puzzled. Dolly in particular looked worried and she hardly tried to suppress her Australian accent.

'There's a simply ghastly little newspaper reporter asking questions about you,' said Dolly.

'Awful fellow – damned impertinent,' said Gerry.

'But what did he want?' Steve asked.

'He wanted to know if we knew where you all were on a couple of dates last week.'

'Well, he could have asked me himself. I can't see what his interest in me can be. For Heaven's sake I'm not a politician with my trousers down.'

'The little swine wouldn't tell us,' said Gerry. 'So I told him to go to hell. Then, would you believe it, he said you were hiding some children in your house and their mother was wanted for murder.'

'Oh …' Steve only restrained an expletive at the last moment. 'I hope you will accept that's pure fantasy. The lady he refers to was only called in for questioning, and she's been eliminated from police enquiries.'

'And she only has one son, and he's a big grown up guy,' Kirsten said. 'Who is this newspaper man?'

'He left a card – said he worked for that awful comic *The Banner*. Here's his card.'

Steve read the card and handed it to Kirsten. 'Sid Everett again. Thanks Dolly, thank you both – I appreciate the warning.'

As their visitors drove away Steve spoke. 'Get those kids to bed and then, late as it is, I'm going to ring Frank.'

Liz and Jeremy sat at a table with Harry Preston. Harry looked strained, as only to be expected, and he had lost some weight. His wife and son looked concerned and angry in equal measure.

DI Le Bois watched them through the one-way window. 'Now we may get somewhere.'

'Sir,' the young detective constable spoke. 'Can we really do this – I mean is it legal?'

'If it helps me put this man away then anything goes in my book.' Le Bois stared through the window.

'Yes, sir, but would anything we hear be admissible?' he hesitated. 'I'm new to the job, sir, and I want to learn these things.'

'That's a diplomatic way of putting it. No, son, it doesn't matter. It's leads I need, and admissible or not I need information.'

'I've brought you the clothes you asked for,' Liz began. Now she was here with Harry, it was difficult to know what to say.

'Thanks,' said Harry. 'If they let me, I'll change before you go, and you can take these away. God, they stink of sweat. They let me have a daily shower, but I have to put these on again and the underwear is foul.'

'How are they treating you?' asked Jeremy.

'It's hell being cooped up, but in a way they're a considerate bunch. I don't get much exercise, although I contrive a bit in the cell. The food's OK, they let me send out an order to a local Italian restaurant for a tasty meal, and I'm allowed a bottle of wine every three days.'

'That's encouraging anyway,' said Liz. 'I can tell you we are raising heaven and earth behind the scenes. There's all sorts of people working for you – so, chin-up as my dad used to say.' Liz bit her lip hard. She knew she was on the edge of breaking down in tears again.

Harry leant forward. 'I am innocent of any crime, you do know that?'

'Every one knows that, except your dumb police.' She told him about the petition.

'People have been very kind,' it was Harry now who had a tear on his cheek. 'You know, it's odd but I get the impression that most of the people in here are almost on my side. It's only that stupid interrogator. He's been trying to crack me open for session after session. But I've nothing to tell him. Yes, I had a run in with Arnold Evans. I was sketching wildfowl. The man must have been looking for a confrontation – can't think of any other reason why he should have been there.'

'Did anybody else see you?' Jeremy asked. 'Dad, this is vital – we've people working who could trace them.'

'There were people around, but I've told Himmler that already.'

'Who?'

'Heinrich Himmler – chief of the Gestapo. He's got a double who works the third degree and I'm not impressed. Funny thing is, I suspect the people in here know the man's a buffoon. They wouldn't be so nice if they really thought I'd done it.'

'Dad, please. Do you recall seeing anyone you know watching while you were at Pagham?'

'Believe me, I've been worrying over that night and day. It was rotten bad luck me running into Evans in the Seal pub. There were other people in there of course, but I can't say I knew any of them – I didn't really look. I think there were five people around the shore at Pagham. Remember, I was arguing with Evans at the time and I wasn't paying attention to anything else but there was the warden, he walked past; a couple with two kids and two chaps sitting on a bench. I rather fancy I've seen one of them before, but they wore sort of hooded tops so I can't be certain. But I really didn't take much notice. Evans trod on one of my sketches – nothing important. I'm sorry the man's been killed but at that moment I could have wished he would have a heart attack and fall dead.'

Jeremy spoke. 'What was it that Evans was so worked up about?'

'He'd heard that I was negotiating with the RSPB and the local council. We'd more or less agreed a deal whereby the council would compulsorily purchase Evans' holding at Branham.'

'Did he threaten you?' Liz asked.

'Oh, all sorts of threats and promises, but it was bluster. I'd had enough by then. I picked up the sketch, got in the car and left with Evans shouting and doing a sort of war dance.'

Jeremy had another thought. 'Was anyone sitting in a parked car?'

'There was only one other car. It was a Land Rover – big, long wheelbase sort. It followed me into the car park but I didn't notice the driver.'

'Dad, is it only about Evans that they've been questioning you?'

'No, the interrogator kept asking about some poor woman teacher that's dead. They say she was killed the morning after Evans. I can't help them: they wouldn't even tell me her name.'

'She taught at the local comprehensive – Linda Zeigler.'

'That's really dreadful – what are the police doing about that?'

'Not a lot from what we've been told.' Jeremy paused. 'Look, I'm sorry Dad, but the tabloids have been trying to link the two cases.'

Harry hardly seemed to hear him. 'My God – Linda Zeigler. I did meet her. She ran the youth art club in Havant. It's in Leigh Park, you know, that deprived area. I gave them a talk, a sort of master-class. She's a lovely girl and you say she's dead.'

'That's it,' Le Bois punched the air in triumph. 'He knew her – we've got him!'

'Sorry Phil, you've no case that we can put to a jury.' Chief Superintendent Fox tapped him on the shoulder. 'The CPS are not satisfied. Forensic have also reported that there's no DNA connection between Henry Preston and Arnold Evans' body or car. Preston's due before the magistrates tomorrow – after that your man's out on bail.'

'I don't like that, sir – he'll do a bunk for certain.' He looked craftily at his chief. 'We'll ask for conditional and a lump sum more than he can find.'

'We've been contacted by Frank Matheson. A mutual friend is standing bail and Preston will be directed to stay with the bail provider.'

'Matheson's a busted cop. He shouldn't be anywhere near this enquiry and who the hell is this bail provider?'

'It's two people, Phil, and they are both personal friends of mine and as honest as the day is long. They're Mr and Mrs Simpson, and they live at South Marshall in the north of the county but still on our patch.'

'I suppose I'll have to live with this,' Le Bois looked morose.

'Evidence, Phil, evidence that will stand up in court, and you haven't got it.'

'I'll get it, sir. I've people delving deeper than we can go. Sid Everett of the *Banner* – he swears he can find something.'

'I didn't hear that. We don't employ the likes of Everett, and if it's any comfort, we've taken on board officially someone who might give us real evidence: Dr von Essens.'

Fox left the room. Le Bois looked somewhat less than comforted. 'Buffoon.' He glared at the young PC. 'Who around here thinks I'm that?'

'I'm sure nobody does – sir.'

Fox heard the exchange and smiled; the PC's hands were behind his back, fingers crossed.

CHAPTER 10

Steve felt better. His phone conversation with Frank Matheson had lifted his spirits.

'Greta is on the case.' Matheson explained. 'Can't let you know too much yet, it's all confidential, but your friend Preston is definitely out of the frame as far as Greta is concerned. She's got her own ideas. I can tell you some of what she's suggesting would make your skin creep.'

'Will she find the killer, because the police haven't a clue?'

'I wouldn't say that,' Matheson sounded shocked. 'Both Surrey and Mid-Southern are engaging Greta as a profiler. The Crown Prosecution are not satisfied and Fox has overruled the officer investigating Henry Preston.'

'Thank God for that – will Harry walk free?'

'I'm glad you've rung me. You see, the bail will be conditional, and Preston will have to live within the county. They want a bail deposit of ten grand, and I'm not sure Mrs Preston can raise that comfortably...'

'But we can – no arguments. I'll write the cheque and Harry can live at our place. The kids can go sketching on the downs with him. That would be allowed wouldn't it?'

'Yes, not a problem. It's your responsibility to see that Mr Preston attends the police station when required and answers bail when a court summons comes.'

'That doesn't sound as if he's out of trouble.' Steve began to worry.

'No,' replied Matheson. 'If this was going to trial they'd never release him on bail. It just wouldn't happen if they really thought he was a psychopath, with two murders to his credit.'

'What about Sid Everett?'

Frank laughed. 'I will seek out that little weasel and he'll wish he'd never been born.'

Steve climbed from the marina pontoon onto *Traveller's* deck. Yes, what a relief, he felt almost happy again as the hot May sun shone down on the beautiful scene. Blue sky, boats moving on the harbour, trees in leaf. This was his world. He might move around arthritically, but he was a fortunate man with this lovely yacht and a full summer season ahead.

Even the lugubrious Peter Terring looked cheerful. What might almost pass for a smile creased part of his face.

'I've installed your new holding tank and pump,' he said.

He meant the tank for holding the waste from the ship's toilet. It was no longer permissible to pump this dubious mix of liquid and solids into the sea, and certainly not into any harbour or marina. Exorbitant fines were levied on those who did so.

'Thanks, Peter, to tell the truth it was one thing I'd forgotten and the old tank was beginning to stink.'

'Puts me off living aboard a boat,' Peter replied. 'Living within four foot of a load of piss and shit – not my idea of fun.'

'Don't be such a negative misery,' Steve laughed. 'Anyway we can pump it out at the waste station as soon as we get to France.'

They could hear the drum of heavy diesel engines. Both men turned to watch a huge motor yacht, a real gin-palace, move through the entrance lock.

'You know whose that was?' said Peter.

'Not sure, but she looks familiar.'

'That's the *Extravaganza,* she belonged to Arnold Evans – he got his comeuppance all right. Deserves to for calling a ship by a name like that.' Peter stared at the gleaming white super-yacht.

'I must say I never liked the man,' said Steve, 'and he's left a bundle of trouble for some people I know.'

'I did ten hours work on that generator system for him, and the bastard never gave me a tip. Not so much as a fifty pence piece. While look at old Ted over there – scrimps and saves all year to keep that fishing boat in the water, and he always gives the lads a tenner each.'

'I suppose that's life,' Steve agreed. 'But no doubt he's answering for that in heaven.'

'Heaven is it?'

Steve went below into the cool of the saloon and then forward to inspect the new toilet system. After one unfortunate accident last season, Kirsten had set to and trained the children to use the complicated pumping system. Peter had certainly done a first rate job with the new holding tank. It sat on its location, pristine and new, with that distinct scent of glass fibre and resin.

'Ahoy there, sailor,' a familiar voice roared from the dockside.

'Come aboard, Frank,' Steve called back. 'I'm down here.'

'Thanks, I've brought a visitor and we'd like to talk to you.'

61

Matheson cautiously descended the three steps to the cabin followed by Greta von Essens. Matheson glanced warily at the deck beams and flopped down on the starboard settee. Greta looked around with interest that went beyond the casual. 'I say,' she said, 'what a lovely ship: she's got to be a Hillyard.'

Steve couldn't hide his surprise. 'That's right; built in 1935 – she's a real classic. How do you know about boats?'

'My parents had a boat on the East Coast at Pin Mill. We went for lovely trips when I was young. Our boat was wooden, a lot smaller than your one – a Harrison Butler twenty six footer.'

'Oh, God,' Matheson grumbled, 'I've blundered into a convention of yachties.'

Greta ignored him. 'Oh, this makes such a change – I'm so nostalgic. You wouldn't have room for an extra crew member some-time?'

'Of course we can, in fact my wife and I are going to have a try out sail next week and we could do with an extra hand. How about it?'

'You're on,' she smiled happily.

Frank spoke. 'Can we return to the subject in hand?'

'That's what's known as coming down to earth with a bump,' Steve replied. 'I doubt you came here to talk boats – what's the latest?'

'Mid Southern Police and Surrey Police have established a joint incident room and they are holding a press conference tomorrow. Best news is that Greta here is now an official consultant profiler.'

'That means there's a limit to what I can tell you people,' said Greta.

'But between the two of you there must be something you can say,' Steve felt disappointed. 'You haven't come out here just to tell me that.'

'Steve: may I call you Steve?' Greta asked. 'Thank you. This criminal investigation is just about as challenging as anything I've been asked to undertake. Steve, I think you can help me. You know people. I believe from everything Frank here has told me that you observe people. You have connections with both locations. For better or worse, you knew two of the victims, and your daughter was taught by Mrs Zeigler. Your friends have been falsely accused. I need you to help me.'

DI Le Bois was not in a mood to give up. His chief suspect was loose, worse than that the man was free to kill again. And, in Le Bois' experience, that was more than likely and then what? He would be proved right. While his superiors dabbled with that fraud of a German woman and co-operated with Surrey police, another poor sod would be dead. It seemed incomprehensible to him that Surrey would drop charges against the Preston woman and this alleged son. The Prestons were clearly implicated in three of the four killings. As for the odd one out, the Zeigler girl, well, he himself had heard Preston admit to knowing her. Yes, there was evidence out there, evidence probably staring him in the face.

He had ordered a covert surveillance on Henry Preston. It worried him that Preston was being placed in a house with young children. The man was unstable, an artist. Yes a painter and dauber of pictures. If Le Bois were to be honest he would have to admit that was the reason for his intense dislike of this man.

Artists were drunkards and adulterers, or homosexuals – notorious for it. Artists were known practitioners of every vice with no respect for the decencies. The man might be married, but who could say he was not a potential pervert? Placing him in a house with young children seemed the height of irresponsibility. What did he know about the parents of these children? The man, Simpson, ran some sort of boatyard, but the finance for this came from his wife. The wife was a foreigner, another bloody German more than likely. That he would have to check. Worse, much worse, the woman was a nudist. The local police in the north of the county said that the people in those parts knew all about that. The woman made no attempt to be modest in her garden during the heat wave. The locals were tolerant; more amused than outraged. In Le Bois' book nudism, equated with paedophilia, and he would hear no argument to the contrary. Now he was certain that placing Preston with this family would end in tears.

Once more he opened the Preston file box; Le Bois was not one for computers. What had he missed? He had the instrument that Preston had used to kill Arnold Evans. It appeared to have been the tiller of a Folkboat; a sort of wooden yacht, he had been told. His officers had found the boat laid up in the Chichester Marina. The owners had replaced the artefact some weeks before and thrown the murder weapon, the old one, in a skip. Now, wait a minute, the skip was outside the premises of Easterbroke Sails. He leapt to his feet and almost sprinted down the corridor arriving breathless in the office that stored the court files. Easterbroke Sails was owned and managed by Stephen Simpson, and Mr and Mrs Simpson were the bail providers for Henry Preston. DI Le Bois returned to his own office with a smile of satisfaction. He had his breakthrough and he had more. He picked up the internal phone.

'Can you help? Social services were searching for a house where some children had been taken... Yes, two children, surname Preston and they were removed illegally by...? Ah, thank you, that's exactly what I wanted to hear.'

Le Bois put down the phone and punched the air. 'Hallelujah!'

The man took the exit from the M3 at junction six and headed into Basingstoke. A few minutes on and he was past the Black Dam roundabout and out on the circular ring road. He often wondered why Mother, the Powerful One, had chosen to live in this ridiculous place, the roundabout capital of Western Europe. One of those great conglomerations of housing estates and small industries peopled by sad persons eking out their petty lives with no hope and no religious faith. Even in the cathedral city where he lived the majority of the people believed in nothing but money and vanity. And only when their lives turned sour did they turn to their God and plead for his help and mercy. Why should their God help them when they did nothing to appease him? They built mighty cathedrals to their God just as his Yucatan ancestors had built their pyramids. His people didn't have to pray; they could use practical means to appease the Power – that Power that all could see above them in the sky. He felt nothing but cold anger for those who sought to interpret the Power and Its ways and foretell its whims and moods. They were ripe for sacrifice and did not the results prove the merit of his actions and those of his brother? Brother was not with him today; mother had commanded that he visit her alone. He knew they were both concerned about his brother. The man had shown weakness about the obvious choice of a child for sacrifice. Likewise he doubted his brother's loyalty and commitment were he to discover the identity of the next persons for release: persons that he himself had selected following conversations he had overhead.

He parked in the residents' area and took the lift to his mother's floor. Once again he must readjust to speaking Spanish. Mother, the Powerful One, never bothered now with English, although she could speak it and understand it as well as he could. Sadly, her family had lost their native Mayan tongue. Since she had married their Basque refugee father she had lived in England and adapted well to the climate and culture. Her faith in her ancestors and in the Power had inculcated the whole family, father included. Father and children never thought of themselves as anything other than British. They held total belief in the Mayan culture and Sun faith, but did not many indigenous British people practice religions imported from far away lands? The difference was that his faith was scientifically credible. Sacrifice brought tangible results to the benefit of all.

'My son, how are you?' Mother hugged him.

'I feel inspired, Powerful One – have I done well?'

'You have done everything that the Power has asked for. Now, one more mission.' She picked up a package from the table. 'You say you know the day the German woman will put to sea. Your brother has made this device, now it is for you to use it well.'

'If you say so, Mother, but if we release this woman the others will die, and the consequences could be bad for us.'

'I know that, but this is too good an opportunity – you must use it. The Power will protect us. After all it will be an accident and,' she looked quizzically at him, 'you need not tell your brother where you have placed the device, nor the names of the people it may harm.'

'That is good. I am tired of his weakness.'

His mother rested a hand on his shoulder. 'When you succeed the Power will reward you.'

'This place is much too big anyway – too big just for us,' Steve stood in front of his house with Harry Preston.

It was two-thirty in the afternoon. Harry had been released from police custody an hour before, and Steve had driven him straight to South Marshall. 'Liz is going to bring a stack of your things and Jeremy is driving her. You're all to stay here until we've some sort of resolution.'

'I feel embarrassed,' said Harry. 'You've been too good – I must repay this bail money.'

'No you won't, as long as you don't abscond we'll get it back.'

'I wouldn't want to run away from a place like this – it's magnificent. How did you find it?'

'Not long after Kirsten and I married. We'd been commuting between Copenhagen and the bungalow in Fishbourne, but we wanted a real home somewhere to raise kids.'

Firs Farm was a beautifully proportioned Georgian country house in the shadow of the South Downs, not a mansion, but a comfortable five-bedroom home. The place had been in a state of disrepair when they bought it, but that had suited Kirsten. For six months she had stood over the builders encouraging and sometimes bullying. The men had taken it in good part. Steve suspected that they regarded this mad Scandinavian woman as a mildly comic figure to be distracted and appeased, while they got on with the job in hand. The one thing that had worried Steve was cost. His entire life had been a struggle to lift himself from his humble roots to some comfort and security. Kirsten's inherited fortune was something outside his experience. Kirsten saw much of it as her grandmother's ill-gotten loot. Creating a family home and a peaceful garden was her attempt to bury the past. Having refurbished the house and completed the purchase of Easterbroke Sails, there was little capital left and that suited Steve. From now on it was back to long hours and hard work in the world he knew best.

Jeremy Preston arrived with Liz and carried her luggage into the house. 'Can't stay long,' he said. 'I want to talk to a mate of mine in London – he used to work with Nadine.'

'You'll stay for a coffee?' asked Kirsten.

'Yes, thanks.' He pointed towards the turn in the drive. 'Hello, what have we here?' An elderly man with a labrador was walking towards them.

'Hi, Gerry,' Steve said. 'You look fit.'

'Ah, Stephen – I hoped you would be in. There's something we think you should know. The Rozzers are watching your house.'

'The what?'

'The constabulary, the boys in blue – what have you done?'

Steve was not entirely surprised but he was still angry. 'Gerry, are you sure?'

'Oh yes, three of them came yesterday. They wanted to put a camera in our spare room – you know, that window.' He pointed towards the gable end of his own house, visible across the fields at the back.

'Why?'

'They said you were giving house room to some wild desperado.'

'That's rubbish.'

'Told them so,' Gerry agreed. 'I told them find somewhere else.' He turned and looked towards the front door, and then dropped his voice to a conspiratorial whisper. 'Better tell your wife to stay indoors. I'll lay odds they're trying to catch her in the nudd so they can prosecute. Three men working in shifts, for God's sake; is that what we pay our taxes for?'

'Thanks, Gerry, we appreciate that.'

'I told them to go stuff themselves. If your wife wants to trot around in her birthday suit, who cares? Three men round the clock, when they should be out catching the villain who killed that poor little school teacher.'

They ushered Gerry Pembelty plus dog into the house, and refreshed the man with a cup of coffee and the dog with a bowl of water. Steve was now thoroughly alarmed. The police, short of evidence, were clearly determined to build a case against Harry. They would all need to be very careful.

Greta examined her computer program for the tenth time. She needed to be certain her timings were right. Arnold Evans had been beaten to death on Wednesday 3rd of May. According to the police forensic people, that death had taken place at Pagham nature reserve around four pm. Some sixteen hours later, on Thursday, Evans had turned up in his car in Branham Lake. Almost to the hour, Linda Zeigler had vanished, leaving her abandoned car at West Ashling, near Chichester. The car had been sabotaged, and skilfully so, by tampering with the ignition disabling system. At two o'clock the following afternoon, Friday, Linda's body had been found in the reservoir about ten miles away. In the intervening hours, Nadine Rotherton was killed by a blow to the head somewhere within walking distance of the Lakeview Hotel at Branham. Her body had been found in the afternoon of the next day, Saturday, in the River Wey, six miles from Branham. That evening, the young coastguard Simon Hexham had been clubbed to death and his body deposited in a water tank. Four violent deaths within seventy-two hours and the bodies disposed of in fresh water. The killers were making a statement there – no doubt of that.

How could she take this one stage further? She was clear in her mind that these killings had a ritual purpose. They were not the work of a large group. Her estimate was two active killers working in conjunction, more than likely with a mastermind or planner. Mercifully, all four deaths had been instant. Greta had had a quiet word with Dr Lucy Watts, the police surgeon. Lucy was convinced that all the killings had been executed with a metal bar. She doubted that the bloodstained yacht tiller found at Pagham had been the instrument that had killed Arnold Evans. Greta accepted that, so clearly the tiller had been soaked in Evans' blood and left as a distraction. This was the only time that such a ruse had been used – so why?

Obviously, the killer or killers had a plan to kill Evans. By chance they must have seen the confrontation between Evans and Harry Preston. The chance to finger the unlucky Preston must have been too good to resist. So the killers were covering their tracks, and that was strange. A ritual assassin often courted discovery and a chance to posture in front of a baffled world. If these people were covering their tracks it meant only one thing. They planned to kill again, and more than likely in some spectacular way. Dr Lucy Watts had also told Greta that none of the bodies had shown a sign of violence or bruising, only the single fatal blow. One thing she did know was that it was unlikely a killer would creep up behind a victim unheard. In certain circumstances, if the victim was distracted and in a noisy situation, it might be done. It was far more likely that all the victims knew their killer and had no reason to distrust them. Evans had been killed in daylight, maybe within minutes of Preston's departure from Pagham. Someone with mechanical skills had disabled Linda's car, leaving her isolated in the middle of nowhere. Speculation again, but in Greta's view it was likely Linda knew her killer and had accepted a lift. Now, what was the link between all four killings? Greta was fairly certain that she knew the link, but that was merely from experience and what might be called gut feeling. But this was not a scientific judgment, and she would put it aside for now. She shut down her computer and went to the kitchen to make a cup of tea.

Tomorrow was the day of the police press conference. Superintendent Fox was not only insisting she attend, he was adamant that she should sit on the platform with the investigating officers. His thinking had some logic. The media circus would certainly notice her and ask questions, most of which she would be unwilling to answer. Fox believed her presence would unsettle the killers and maybe impel them into an unwise move. Greta had her doubts. If the killers were the kind of people she suspected, then they would not be easily panicked.

Kirsten had collected the children from school. Her car pulled up in front of the house just as Gerry was leaving. Emily bounded out of the car and ran towards her father; face alight with excitement. She was literally dancing with joy.

'What's all this about?' Steve asked.

'I've done it – I'm in the team!'

'Well done – good girl. You mean the big team?'

Emily danced a couple of steps. 'Yeah – Southern Schools against Birmingham – eight hundred metres.' She began to dance again, while the adults laughed. 'Oh hello, Mr Pembelty and hello, Clancy' she rushed across and began to hug the Labrador.

Kirsten, having put the car in the garage, joined them. 'Gerry, they've started digging up your aeroplane. We stopped and looked.'

'Not my aircraft,' Gerry laughed. 'We think it's a German 109; maybe I put it there – 428 Squadron, my crowd, were operating over that part of the county in July of Forty.'

'Where is this?' Harry had joined them.

'In a field outside Walderton,' said Emily. 'Mr Cotton says the Ancient History Group can go and watch the digging – just like we did with that old Roman villa.'

'Ancient history…' Gerry exploded with mock indignation. 'Romans! Am I that ancient?'

'Yes,' said Emily. Smiling sweetly, she sprinted indoors.

The brothers worked through the night in the dimly lit workshop. It was not easy to operate silently and both were aware of the hazards. Drilling through the outer casing was easy but it wouldn't do to penetrate too far and blow themselves to smithereens. Doing so would be to fail the Power. They laid the circle of metal beside them on the bench before sliding the tiny mobile phone through the aperture. The explosive followed and lastly the chemical compound.

'Will that phone stay charged?'

'For a week at least – that's enough.'

'It's an elaborate trick – where did you discover it?'

'Got it off an Islamist website.'

'Muslims are no different to Christians. They both reject the Power. Have you tested it?'

'Three times – three successful firings – it was a dream.'

'When should I activate?'

'Anywhere within the mobile's range, but I suggest you don't activate too early. We want all to vanish without trace.'

'All right, let's seal her.'

They took the metal circle and replaced it. By the time they had finished the casing was restored without blemish.

The police press conference had been arranged for eleven o'clock in the morning. The venue had not been easy to agree. Two major police authorities were directly involved, each with two murders on their territory. Both would have preferred to hold the conference in a prestigious venue on their own ground. In the end a compromise had been reached. Guildford, Chichester and Brighton were ruled out and the mass media of Britain, with some from beyond, descended on the

Angel Hotel in Midhurst. The citizens of that town woke up to find themselves in the grip of an invading army. Reporters and paparazzi swarmed everywhere. Satellite dishes were set up at the most inconvenient places, while outside the venue a clutch of presenters, male and female, spouted in front of television cameras. As Greta looked at this mob the scene only confirmed her original opinion. Far from inciting the killers into some premature mistaken action, the contrary was a certainty. They would be viewing this mayhem and revelling in it.

Superintendent Fox saw her and waved. Greta wended her way through a sprinkling of reporters, all taking a last drag on cigarettes.

'Glad you could come,' said Fox. 'Have you anything you can tell this lot?'

'Very little I'm afraid, at least not at this stage.'

'That's our problem too. We're anticipating a rough ride in there, and all we can do is play a straight bat and block the bowling.'

Greta tried to encourage. 'I'm not saying I'm getting nowhere. I've some useful findings already, but I can't go public. I can tell them that your Inspector Le Bois' suspect had nothing whatever to do with anything.'

Fox frowned. 'My advice is be noncommittal on that one. We've enough trouble with Phil Le Bois. Is there really nothing you can give them to bite on?'

'We'll see how things go.'

The room was crowded of course, with seating for less than three quarters of the accredited reporters. The remainder pushed and jostled at the back, irritating the battery of TV camera operators. Greta joined the police spokespersons all sitting at a cloth-covered table. This party included two assistant chief constables as well as Fox and another senior officer from Surrey. At the last moment, Greta spotted Frank Matheson standing near a fire exit. It was reassuring to see him, and she felt less nervous.

From the police point of view the meeting started badly. Both the assistant chief constables made short, platitudinous statements that told the gathering nothing. Next was Fox's turn to speak. Unlike most policemen, Fox had an educated well-modulated speaking voice, that clearly surprised those present. In other circumstances he could have been taken for an old-style consultant surgeon. Many witnesses had been questioned, he told them, and much useful information had been compiled. No, he regretted that he could not confirm any early arrests.

70

At this point things began to go downhill. A little man in a leather jacket stood up.

'Sid Everett – *The Banner*. You had a clear suspect in custody and now you've let him go – why was that?' A disquieting rumble of agreement spread throughout the room.

Fox chose to answer. 'I think you have been misinformed, Mr Everett. Certainly we questioned a man, but we found no substantive evidence to hold him.'

'All right,' Everett was on his feet again. 'What has Dr von Essens got to say about that?'

The local assistant chief constable nodded to her. Greta eyed Sid. She knew all about him. The man had been around as a crime reporter for almost as long as she had been a profiler. 'I have been retained to study the bigger picture. In my view the investigation has not yet interviewed anyone directly involved in this conspiracy.'

The result of this statement was uproar. Sid Everett sat with arms folded and a stupid grin on his face.

As the hubbub died, another man, younger and balding, stood up. 'Holdcastle, BBC. Conspiracy, Dr von Essens – can you substantiate that?'

'I cannot reveal details of my work, but I think it is obvious that these murders are the work of the same person or persons. The motive is not a rational one and that, of course, makes the work of our police harder. I leave further comment on fact to them.'

Greta left it at that. For the next half-an-hour the police represent-atives stonewalled heroically before the Surrey senior officer called time, and the whole assembly filed out into the sunlight. Greta made a quick getaway, but not before she managed a word with Fox.

'I think we've bought ourselves a little bit of time,' he said. 'I'm afraid the ball is in your court now, Doctor. Frankly we haven't got an idea about this, and that bloody shower know it.'

'You're a great one for sporting metaphors, Superintendent.' She smiled at him. 'Don't worry too much. I have made some progress, but this one is not easy. I'll put in a report tomorrow.'

'Can't you give us anything now?'

'The killings are ritual. They will stop for the present and will not start again as long as we have this rather nice sunny weather.' She waved goodbye to Fox leaving that officer with a bemused expression on his face.

She drove back to the faculty in Portsmouth, feeling less confident than she had first thing this morning. She wondered if she had given away too much in that last comment to Fox. She had no wish to set the police harassing obscure religious cults. Certainly, the Le Bois man would enjoy that, and it would deflect him away from the Preston family. Just give her a few more days and she might have a definite profile that would yield genuine names. At least she had a relaxing day to look forward to. Steve and Kirsten had invited her to join them for a new season shakedown trip on *Traveller*.

'Watching us – really?' Kirsten was not surprised.

'Yes,' said Emily, 'but there's two lots. There's the blokes under that thorn bush up there, and there's another man with a tripod for his camera and he's on the edge of the old chalk dell.'

'Gerry said the police were watching us, but I can't say who the second man is.' Kirsten filled the kettle.

Emily looked thoughtful. 'Is it true that we'll be in trouble if we swim in the pool nude?'

'No, Gerry's got that wrong. Even in England we're allowed that in our own gardens. No, it's your Uncle Harry they're after – idiots.'

'Poor Harry, it's not fair.'

'Darling, there are lots of things in life that are unfair. Anyway it'll be a week before we fill the pool again.'

Emily sniffed. 'Sod the bloody police, they're not making me wear a horrible, itchy wet swimsuit when it's hot.'

'Don't let your father hear that language. He'll only want to take you away from the comprehensive and send you to some boarding school for young ladies.'

Emily's face twisted in disgust. 'He wouldn't – would he?'

'Be a good girl and I will protect you.'

'Why can't we come with you on *Traveller*?'

'Because we're going on Friday, and you'll be at school.'

'Why can't we all go on Saturday?'

Kirsten sighed. 'Because this is a trial run, and Daddy doesn't want the ship crowded with kids. Also, we're taking Dr von Essens with us, and she's not used to the likes of you.'

'Will we go to Branham on Saturday?'

'If you want to, of course.'

Kirsten began to fill two large Thermos flasks with coffee. She put them in a wicker basket with mugs, a plastic milk bottle along with biscuits, and a little jar of sugar.

'Come on' she said. 'How about another walk on the hill.'

'Why?' Emily looked puzzled.

'I expect your watchers are getting thirsty. So I say we take them coffee.'

'Wow,' Emily giggled. 'Good thinking, Mum – that'll shake them.'

The two of them returned an hour later. Emily looked subdued, and her mother looked flustered. They found Steve with the Prestons in the sitting room.

'What's happened?' Steve asked.

'We took those camera people some coffee,' said Kirsten. 'The police are the ones hiding in that bush, the one in the chalk dell is a bastard little newspaper shit.'

'Not Sid Everett by any chance?'

'No, I remember him. I'm not likely to forget. This was a young guy and he called me...he called me...' Kirsten spluttered.

Steve was concerned now. His wife had a temper with a notorious short fuse but he had rarely seen her in this state of cold fury. 'It's all right, love – tell me what he said.'

'Not in here and not in front of Em and our friends.' She beckoned him to follow her out of the room.

Outside in the entry hall she told him. 'He called me a dirty slapper...said he knew all about me.'

'Christ!' Steve was outraged. 'Nobody gets away with talking to you like that. What did you say?'

'Say? I didn't say anything: I tipped his stupid camera over and threw it down the hill. Last I saw he was scrambling after it.'

'Oh no! Sweetheart when will you learn to control that temper?' He felt worried now. 'Did those police see anything?'

'They cheered,' said Emily. She was leaning through the half-opened sitting room door.

'No they didn't,' Kirsten replied. 'But when I went over to talk to them they thought the thing was funny.'

Steve continued. 'Did they threaten any charges?'

'God no – they said if the little shit reported me they would have been looking the other way.'

'What brought all this on and why is that man there anyway?' Steve was puzzled.

'He asked me if my name was Rachel,' said Emily. 'He didn't make sense.'

'In what way?'

'He asked me if I wanted to be in our house, and had I been forced to come here. Why, Dad?'

'You mustn't mention any of this to Liz and Harry – OK? They've been through enough already.' He looked his daughter in the eye; she stared back unflinching.

'Rachel was Liz and Harry's little girl, and she died years ago. Some people in social services thought she was still alive, and they wanted her taken into care. That's all I'm saying and it will go no further – right?'

'Sure, Dad.'

'It's to be between us. You are not to tell anyone.'

'Can I tell John-Kaj?'

Steve reached forward and grasped her shoulders. 'The answer is no. Not a word to anyone.'

Emily nodded with a solemnity that didn't fool Steve for one moment. He could only hope that she would keep her mouth shut until the weekend.

'Come on,' he said. 'While you've been trotting around the countryside I've been cooking. Go and tell the others that supper is ready.'

They had almost completed their meal when the front door bell rang. 'I'll go,' said Steve. A young man stood in the porch holding a wicker basket.

'Mr Simpson?'

'Yes,' Steve waited while he looked the man up and down.

The stranger held up a police ID card. 'I'm Detective Constable Baird. Could you give Mrs Simpson this and thank her for the coffee.'

'So you are one of the people watching us. May I ask why?'

'We've been ordered to. It's one of these boring surveillance jobs. But I've nothing against you, sir. I sail on the harbour and I know you're a great guy.'

'Thank you – I appreciate that.'

Greta pulled up a file on the computer screen. 'These are the names of persons who were present in the Lakeview Hotel at the same time as Nadine Rotherton.'

Matheson peered at the monitor; his short vision had deteriorated since his younger days, but the lettering was in a font size he could cope with. 'They just look like names to me. Good old Anglo Saxon local names – no sinister Chinese mafia.'

Greta smiled. 'You are skating on the edge of political correctness, Frank.'

Matheson shook his head. 'After all my years in this business the only race I know is the human race – good, bad and indifferent, and most of them the last two.'

'It's not a definitive list,' she continued. 'Surrey police cannot guarantee that it's complete, but it is a starting point.'

'How many can we eliminate?'

'Good question. All section A. They are the hotel staff, and they were all on the premises at the time of Nadine's death. Section B are the guests and bar drinkers or as many as the staff could name.' Greta handed Matheson a sheet of A4. 'Take this, it's the print out.'

Frank adjusted his reading glasses and studied the list.

Cynthia Gllidings age 47 – divorced – three children – resident of Churt, Surrey. This lady reported as consuming seven large glasses of gin. Too unsteady to drive home – stayed the night at the Lakeview.

Barry Whitering age 29 – married – one child – travelling salesman, resident in Sunderland – staying overnight at the Lakeview with lady, age around 18, claiming to be Mrs Whitering – hotel manageress suspects latter untrue.

Edward Grogan – age 45 – unmarried – local resident – was present with another unidentified male – hotel manageress thinks the couple were gay.

'Christ,' Matheson exclaimed. 'That place is a den of iniquity.'

Greta smiled again. 'This is Surrey, Frank. Nothing as pure and unsullied as your Pompey.'

'Point taken – what about this one: *Ricardo Standfast* – he's got to be dodgy with a name like that?'

'Come on, Frank, you sound like Inspector Le Bois. But you've a point; it's a strange name and the police have been unable to trace anyone with it anywhere in the UK. He stayed overnight, and the address he gave doesn't exist.'

'And these other four – your Section C?'

'Committee meeting of the local bowls club. The Manageress can vouch for all of them at the time in question. We've one more list to come – all people who signed in at the hotel's gym that evening. But I doubt that'll help us much.'

'Then it's find Mr Standfast – why does that name ring a bell?'

Greta smiled again. 'Literature, Frank – John Bunyan's Pilgrim's Progress, and Standfast is also a code name for a character in a John

75

Buchan novel of the same name. Anyway, ours went out for a walk about twenty minutes before Nadine did the same. And, Frank,' Greta's smile had extended to a hearty grin, 'the hotel manageress says the man was dark skinned and spoke with a dastardly foreign accent. But, as that good lady wants to protect her establishment and needs to point the finger, I will treat her testimony with caution – so should Surrey police and so should you.'

'I suppose so.'

'Is there anyone on our books who knows about art?' Inspector Le Bois was addressing his morning briefing.

The plainclothes officers looked at each other. 'WPC McGregor, Sir. She paints some good pictures – I've seen a few.'

'All right, Alkford, we know about you and Sam. What sort of pictures does she draw?'

'She's done a course up the art school before she joined the force, she's drawn some great life studies.'

Le Bois eyes narrowed. 'Does that mean naked pictures – that's disgusting.'

DC Alkford looked agitated. 'Not just that, Sir, she's done beautiful landscapes, some of them around the harbour with all the boats.'

'That's better, much better,' for the first time Le Bois looked happy. 'Where is the lady?'

'What, now Sir?'

'Yes, now.'

'Last I saw she was downstairs doing her paperwork.'

Le Bois relaxed. 'You lot get back to work. Alkford, go find young Sam and bring her here – pronto.'

'Constable,' Le Bois addressed Sam McGregor, 'I understand you've an interest in joining us in CID?'

'Yes, Sir.'

'I don't know about a permanent position, but I have a temporary assignment which should suit you. Do it well, and that could lead you to better things.'

'Really, Sir?'

'I understand that you are a talented artist?'

Sam was surprised. 'I paint pictures. I find that relaxing after work, but I don't claim to be talented.'

'This is no time for modesty, McGregor. You know about art and you can identify painters?'

'Yes – I suppose so.'

'I will allocate you a budget. Now, this is your assignment and it's undercover. You will at no time identify yourself as a police officer.'

'Is this dangerous, Sir?'

'In the final analysis it may be. In fact I expect it could be, but you will be wired, and I will have armed back up if needed.'

'Sir, if I'm to be in the line of danger – I must know what this is about – all of it.'

'All right, McGregor. You are interested in art,' Le Bois could not hide his disdain. 'We recently released a suspect, against my advice, who is an artist. Your assignment is to approach this suspect, Henry Preston, on the grounds that you wish to buy one of his pictures. You will use every opportunity to get to know this Preston and report his moods and movements.'

Sam was interested. 'If I buy a picture can I keep it? A Preston could be worth a lot of money now and a lot more in ten years time.'

'In ten years time the man will be inside doing life, if I have my way.'

She was worried now. 'Sir, how well do you want me to know this man?'

'All right, McGregor, I'm not asking you to go to bed with him, but I do want you to flatter the bastard; get to know him; clean his bloody studio anything reasonable he wants.'

She smiled at him mischievously. 'If I'm wearing a wire Sir, I'd better not strip off for a life study.'

'That's quite enough of that, McGregor. Go buy some suitable clothes and research your part. Come back tomorrow for a briefing.'

CHAPTER 11

'I think we've got everything, but I'll check the list again,' Kirsten stared into the back of the car: not her Megane but Steve's larger Volvo.

Steve spoke. 'We're not sailing a trans-Atlantic; we're only going for twenty-four hours.'

'I know, but I'd like to have the tinned galley stores aboard for the next trip.'

'I'm loading the GPS as well as the French charts.'

'We'll need to be moving soon,' said Kirsten, 'or we'll miss the tide.'

'Which reminds me,' said Steve. 'I'm not sure I put the almanac in with the charts. I've got the local tide tables, but we'll need the book later.'

Steve returned to the house. Harry was using the telephone with Liz standing beside him. She followed Steve into his study. 'I'm worried,' she said.

'It'll be all right,' Steve said. 'The kids will behave. We laid it on the line before they went to school.'

'Oh, I'm sure they will. No, it's not that, someone wants to buy one of Harry's pictures. I thought our being here was secret.'

Steve was surprised. 'Only the police and the courts are supposed to know. Fox promised me that.'

'Someone's broken that confidence,' said Harry. 'It's some woman called Samuels; wants to buy one of my watercolours of Branham Little Lake. I told her to ring my agent, but then she started on about being my greatest fan and always wanting to meet me.'

'What are you going to do?' asked Liz.

'I've said she can come over and talk. Steve, is that all right?'

'I'm sure that's fine as long as she's not one of those demonstrators from outside the court house.' Steve remembered the scenes on the television.

'She sounded all right, and she knew her stuff – a lot of details about my work, and she said she's studied at art-college – named her tutor.'

'Well I hope you make a good sale.' Steve picked up the almanac. 'I suggest you fetch John-Kaj from his school first, and then you all go on to fetch Emily. She'll be fine waiting – you'll find her in the gym.'

'It's their last day before half-term isn't it?' Liz asked. 'I'll cook something special.'

Sam McGregor could not honestly say that she was looking forward to this assignment. Yes, she wanted to progress to plain clothes and CID. The uniform branch was part of frontline policing but so much of it was boring and repetitious. Her station alone must have used a whole forest of paper to record minor incidents and petty offences. And she'd had just about enough of abusive motorists and foul-mouthed teenagers of both genders. Her attitude to people had changed. She had been unaware of this, but her civilian friends had noticed. They told her how her voice had hardened, and how she seemed suspicious and distant. This worried her, but worse; she knew she was smoking more cigarettes and sleeping less well. After nearly eight years in the job she needed a change and a challenge.

She wished she could share DI Le Bois's unshakeable conviction that Henry Preston was a psychotic killer. She knew from the files that the inspector had found little supporting evidence against Preston, and it was not surprising that the CPS had intervened and had the man released. She wondered how much of Le Bois's obsession was grounded in the man's hatred of art and artists. For an elderly police officer the Inspector was broad minded when dealing with blacks and Asians, even though he detested European foreigners and gays. Sam knew all about Le Bois's prejudices and had never previously dared to admit her delight in painting.

Two miles short of the village of South Marshall she pulled her car to the side verge and began to will her mind into the part she was to play. She had never met Preston face-to-face, but she had been to one of his lectures where the man had spoken about his philosophy of painting. He seemed a gentle, focussed individual, wholly committed to his work. Nevertheless Sam would do her best with the assignment and use her skills, perception and feminine intuition to root out the truth.

She found Firs Farm without difficulty. The building was a magnificent Georgian farmhouse, on the edge of the village, in the shadow of the downs. Looking upwards, she could see sheep on the hill and figures in silhouette walking along the footpath. She had sketched on that hill, a glorious spot with a view of rural Hampshire to the north, and across Sussex to the sea and the distant Isle of Wight to the south. As she turned right into the driveway Samantha McGregor ceased to exist. The only connection was the transmitter concealed in her clothing and the listening van parked one hundred yards down the road. Now she had become Ellen Samuels, artist and devoted fan of Henry Preston.

'Hello, you must be Ellen.' A middle-aged woman waved her through the open front door. 'I'm Liz, and Harry is my husband.'

Sam tried to adjust her eyes to the dark entry hall. 'You've a beautiful house, Mrs Preston.'

The woman laughed. 'Not ours, worse luck. We live in Surrey but we're staying with old friends, and this is their house.'

'Hello, there I'm Harry.' Sam knew the man already, not only from the lecture, but from her view of the tense interview session with Le Bois three days earlier.

'Mr Preston, it's a real honour to meet you.' She could say that with total honesty. 'I've had a small legacy, and I want to buy one of your paintings.'

'Thank you, I'd be delighted, but you'll have to talk to my agent.'

'I know, but that's money; I've always hoped I could meet you.' She must not go over the top and play the hysterical groupie.

'Unfortunately I'm only staying here temporarily. All my work is in my studio at home.'

Sam did her best to look disappointed. 'Your wife told me…'

'However,' Preston smiled at her. 'I have some prints and my catalogue. That will give you an idea of my work at present.'

In the end the visit was a pleasant experience. Henry Preston did more than show his work, he gave Sam paper and an easel and conducted a sort of master class. She had felt nervous at first but then entered into her part with gusto. Preston had complimented her and also added some useful criticisms. Liz Preston had given her lunch, and she had left the house with an invitation to visit the studio in Tilford. Sam was very aware that she had seen nothing whatever to confirm Le Bois's view of Preston. What could she tell the inspector?

The bad moment came only as she was leaving. Liz Preston confronted her. 'May I ask how it is that you knew we were staying in this house?'

Sam knew only a version of the truth would serve. As the expression goes she needed to think on her feet and fast. 'A friend of mine, Paul Baird, he's in the police, and he told me he's called here and seen you.'

'You knew the telephone number when you rang Harry.'

'Paul said this was where Steve Simpson lives. People still talk about what he did with sailing.'

Liz stared at her for a good twenty seconds. Sam was not sure if she was believed. If Henry Preston was a likeable, if untidy artist, his wife was too sharp for comfort. If Sam were to be allowed near Henry Preston again she would have to have a watertight cover story.

'Come on, half-an-hour and they'll open the lock to freeflow.' Steve carried the last of the bags and boxes off the pontoon onto the deck of *Traveller*. 'Just time to stow this lot and we'll go,'

Traveller motored down Chichester Harbour with Kirsten steering while Steve pulled off the sail covers. He could only rejoice that they were doing this trip on a perfect spring day with a warm sun and a moderate southwesterly breeze. Greta sat on the starboard cockpit seat. Steve was surprised that the lady's whole demeanour had changed the moment she stepped aboard ship. She was dressed in several layers of clothing over a tracksuit with an old-fashioned oilskin top. Kirsten had giggled at the sight and whispered to Steve that their crew looked like an advertisement for Fisherman's Friend lozenges.

Half an hour from leaving the marina they reached the point where the channel divided north for Emsworth and south to the open sea. Steve returned to the cockpit and took the helm. The next two miles would be painful for both of them and especially for Kirsten. Fifteen years ago, the pair of them had nearly drowned in this place in their last desperate chase to save Kirsten's Uncle Kaj. They had been plucked to safety by the rescue helicopter: Kaj had died as he had always intended, with his dark family secret remaining hidden to this day. If they passed the place with the children aboard, Kirsten would fall silent with a masterly display of self-control, although God knew what was going through her mind. Today, Steve realised would be different. As the inner entrance beacon came in sight, she bolted below decks and threw herself face down on a settee. Greta had been warned, and tactfully said nothing as she looked at the Hayling shoreline.

Now, with the outer beacon behind them, Steve went forward to hoist sail. *Traveller's* wooden masts were the same ones that had served her well since she was refitted following World War Two. Steve's preferred rig was a large Bermudan mainsail on the schooner's main mast, with a staysail from the head of the main to a point aft of the foremast. Ahead of the foremast was a short bowsprit carrying two roller-furled jibs. He inserted the handle in the sail winch and started to raise the mainsail. Kirsten, emerging on deck, took control of the jib furling lines. Steve set the main and then hoisted the staysail. Kirsten unfurled the foresails and turned off the diesel; the ship was sailing now on a reaching leg towards the Nab Tower, visible in front of their bow.

The three of them looked at each other, faces alight with an almost childlike delight in the moment. Suddenly it was so quiet – only the sound of the water rushing past the wooden hull and the creak of the spars as an extra strong puff heeled the ship and sent her surging forward.

Where shall we go?' Kirsten asked.

'Can't do Cherbourg this trip,' Steve replied. 'Tide's right, wind's great, let's go south of the Island and see how she goes.'

They cleared the Nab, avoiding the big ships in the main channel and sailed on south. As they cleared the land, *Traveller* felt the full force of the westerly breeze. Steve left the cockpit and wound down a reef in the main. The ship, more comfortable now, began to revel in the conditions.

'Greta, your turn to have a go on the helm,' Steve called.

She took the spokes of the wooden wheel in her hands. 'Our old boat had a tiller,' she said. 'This is new to me.'

'It's direct steering, like a car,' said Steve. 'Watch the compass and steer as near 160 degrees as you can.'

'It's easy,' she laughed. 'What a lovely ship.'

'The motion's better now,' said Kirsten. 'I'll make us a cup of coffee.' She pushed open the sliding hatch. Instead of descending into the cabin, she stopped and bent forward. With an alarmed expression she turned round and shouted one word. 'Gas!'

Now Steve could smell it too; the scent of Propane cooking gas. The one substance aboard that could bring complete disaster. Steve froze mentally and physically. For ten seconds he could neither move nor think coherently. What had gone wrong with a safety system he had designed himself? Then he moved; he knew that unless he did something positive in the next five minutes the ship and all in her could be lost in an explosive inferno.

He seized the lid of the cockpit locker that contained the gas bottles. Oh shit, the bloody thing had been padlocked. 'Kirsten, the bolt cutters, in the emergency box, port side!'

He saw her take a deep breath and scramble down into the cabin. The emergency box lived under the navigation station and contained tools to cut away a fallen mast. 'Got them,' she called.

'Bring'em to me but don't bang anything – no sparks!'

82

She handed the heavy bolt cutters to him through the hatch. Steve fixed them on the padlock. He was taking a risk with generating a spark, but there was less smell of gas out here in the wind. He sheared the lock with one swipe of the cutters and lifted the locker lid. The rush of gas that met him was almost overpowering, although cooking gas was heavier than air and always sank to the lowest point. Steve had designed this locker to be sealed, with drains through the hull to the outside. As an extra precaution he always insisted that the gas bottles be turned off when not in use. Everyone in the sailing community had seen the results of gas explosions that had destroyed craft and inevitably taken lives.

Steve seized the valve knob of the nearest cylinder. It was closed, and so was the second one of the pair. Then he saw something he could not comprehend. The drain holes were blocked; not accidentally but sealed with plastic filler compound. And fresh holes had been drilled, and these holes led directly into the main cabin. The truth filtered into his mind. Someone wanted them dead and their lovely ship destroyed. There was no more time to think; explanations were for later and the truth for the police. Steve struggled to undo the fly nuts that held the wooden frame containing the bottles. He could see the bottle that was causing the leak. The outer casing had split and was hot to touch. Age and arthritis forgotten, Steve grabbed the bottle and lifted it from its mount. Damn, the bloody thing was still retained by the copper delivery pipe. It wouldn't spark would it? Too late to worry about that – with brute force he no longer knew he had, he pulled the bottle, snapping the pipe and staggered with it in his arms onto the aft deck. Raising it to shoulder level he heaved the thing overboard and into the ship's wake. Utterly exhausted, he sagged to his knees on the unsteady deck and watched the red object bobbing as it disappeared astern. Two minutes later it blew. With a thump and a tongue of flame the cylinder exploded.

Steve slid back into the cockpit. He was filled with weariness and he felt sick and of course he knew the danger was still with them and still desperate. He saw the forehatch open, then seconds later the skylight hatch in the centre of the cabin roof. Kirsten's head appeared. 'Shall I start the pumps,' she called.

Steve was alert now. 'No, nothing electric – it'll have to be the hand pump and buckets.' He flung open the locker lid opposite the gas and found the handle of the manual pump.

'I'll work that.' It was Greta. He had forgotten her.

'Thanks, please do. Work the handle all you can until I give the all clear.'

She turned a wan face towards him. 'That was meant to get me – wasn't it?'

Steve didn't know what to reply. Instead, he entered the cabin and grabbed a large plastic bucket. The heavy gas had by now sunk to the lowest part of the hull. The hand bilge pump would extract much of it, but more would remain in the cabin. Steve began to scoop with the bucket, then lifting the thing through the open hatch and making the invisible contents blow away on the wind. To any onlooker the action would look comic, but it was for real, and the only thing they could do. Kirsten worked for half an hour in the forecabin with another bucket. Then, as the smell of gas decreased, she took a turn with the hand pump relieving Greta who looked close to collapse. Steve noticed that throughout the crisis *Traveller* had continued lumbering along on a broad reach with the helm unmanned. He took a couple of seconds to whisper a word of thanks to his ship. Irrational, he knew, but the old ship had a personality stronger than many people. They worked on for another hour until Steve was satisfied that the last trace of gas had been dispersed.

'All right, you can stop now,' he called. 'Just be careful. No electric switches and no cooking, of course.'

'Sod the bloody cooking' Kirsten snapped. Her voice was squeaky and unreal. Throughout the crisis Steve had heard her muttering and shouting in Danish.

'We turn round and go home.' For the first time he tried to rationalise what had happened. 'Someone wanted us dead. Why us – why?'

'No, it was me they wanted dead,' said Greta. 'But I don't know if it's revenge or whether it's because of my work now.' She spoke quietly, but still loud enough to be heard above the wind and waves.

'I shall have to report this,' said Steve. He went below and fetched a small hand-held VHF radio. 'I dare not use the main set, but this should be safe out here.'

Steve called Solent Coast Guard and reported a version of the incident. 'Chances are someone's already seen that last bang and reported it. We don't want the lifeboat launched for nothing.'

'Steve, darling, for God's sake someone's tried to kill us – all of us.' Kirsten had flopped down on a cockpit seat and was sobbing and shaking.

'It's got to be me they're trying to kill,' Greta's face was strained but controlled. 'It happened once before. I was profiling a terrorist cell two years ago.'

'Look,' said Steve. 'We call the police when we're ashore, but now we are going home. This little cruise is over.'

Two hours later they passed the entrance beacons to Chichester Harbour. This time Kirsten stayed on deck, oblivious to old memories. She sat hunched in the cockpit, taking no part in handling the ship. Steve was only thankful he had Greta's help and good support it was. This lady academic was also proving a good seaman.

'Steve,' said Greta. 'Do we have to go back to the marina? That's obviously where you were tampered with.'

'Agreed, we'll pick up our own mooring at Itchenor. We can either walk back to our cars or hire a cab. After this I'm going to find a security firm to have someone sleep aboard and keep watch through twenty four hours.'

'How are we going to get ashore?'

'No problem, our inflatable is stored down below.'

'Steve,' Kirsten spoke. 'I've noticed something is missing.'

'What is?'

'The life raft.' She pointed to the lashing point on the aft deck.

'That I've also noticed. I didn't give any precise instructions, but I would have expected the yard to have shipped it aboard. In any case, I let my guard down; sort of didn't think we'd need it on a day trip. That's one lesson I've learned the hard way.'

They sailed in silence the remaining distance up the harbour until Steve furled the remaining sails. Judging that by now the gas must have dispersed he started the diesel. At five o'clock that afternoon they secured to their swinging mooring in the Itchenor Channel.

'I'll report this to the police right away,' said Steve. 'But I will make my own enquiries in the morning. I ordered those two gas cylinders from the local suppliers, so they've got some explaining to do.'

'What about the other one,' Kirsten asked nervously.

'I've checked it and turned it on for a minute, and it looks safe and normal. All the same we'll lower it overboard on a line.'

Steve extracted his mobile phone from the cabin and thought long and hard. He knew that their story was so bizarre he doubted the local police would believe in criminal intent. In the end, he dialled Norman Fox, and fortunately that officer was at home.

Fox was sceptical as Steve had expected. 'Why is anyone going to blow up you two?'

'Not us, they were out to get our crew person if you ask me. She's

Dr von Essens.'

'Bloody hell, Steve. If this is a consequence of our present enquiries I'll have to tell DI Le Bois.'

It had been a sombre gathering at Firs Farm that evening. They had walked to the marina and recovered the two cars. Not an easy trip for Steve who was in pain and feeling the after-effects of the day. Kirsten had asked Greta to stay with them for her own protection, but the lady declined. She needed to return home and work. Also, the police had promised her around the clock watch on her cottage.

Steve was beginning to feel the full horror of the experience, and he was concerned for Kirsten who seemed to exhibit early signs of posttraumatic stress. Liz and Harry were also badly shaken and inclined to blame themselves: an idea that Steve dismissed out of hand. How much should they tell the children was their next worry. In the end Steve told them an edited version of the truth, making out that the gas leak had been an accident. The two were packed off to bed, though far from distressed they seemed excited by the event. Then Steve had poured everyone a stiff drink.

He looked at Harry and Liz. 'How was your day?'

Harry spoke. 'Not long after you left I had a nosy press reporter around.'

'I was out shopping,' said Liz. 'A couple of little news creeps walked in uninvited. Asked personal questions.'

'I can guess which paper,' said Steve.

'It was the Daily Banner,' said Harry. 'I didn't give them anything.'

'Good.'

'I'm afraid we also had a visit from a spy,' said Liz.

'Eh?'

'I thought she was rather a nice girl, and she's talented,' said Harry.

'She pretended to be a fan of Harry's work,' said Liz.

'She can draw,' said Harry. 'She's amateur but a good draughtsman, I was impressed.'

'Oh, I don't doubt her ability,' Liz was scathing, 'but she was playing a part and when I challenged her she admitted she had found this address via the police. And playing a part is the right word, it stood out a mile.'

'I think,' said Steve, 'that the police would be a lot better off if you were in charge of this investigation and not some sort of suspect.'

The next morning DI Le Bois called Sam McGregor into his office. 'Constable, you will remain attached to my group, so you're still CID. How do you like that?'

'Very much, Sir – thank you.'

'Good. Today you are liaising with Surrey police. You will go with PC Baird to this address and witness a search of the garage and outbuildings.'

'Yes, Sir,' she paused respectfully. 'Wouldn't that be a uniform job?'

'Surrey uniform are searching but you will represent Mid-South CID.' He stared at Sam coolly. 'Well, McGregor, don't you want to know what this is about?'

'Of course, Sir.'

'Yesterday, Henry Preston sabotaged a sailing yacht and nearly killed everyone aboard.'

'Sir, I saw Preston yesterday and he was at the house in South Marshall.'

'I know that, and much good your probing told us. Never mind, I'm not saying he laid the explosive charges himself but someone did, and Preston's the man to gain from the killings.'

'Can I know who was the target of this alleged murder attempt?' Sam, whose doubts about Le Bois had been increasing for days, could not hide her scepticism.

'The yacht was called *Traveller* and she belongs to the same couple who are harbouring Preston right now.'

'Mr and Mrs Simpson? Oh, come on, Sir, you know they've been speaking up for Preston...'

'No, McGregor, they weren't the target, they had a passenger – Dr von Essens, that useless bloody German woman. She's part of our investigation worse luck, and Preston knew it. He a psycho – wouldn't think twice about killing his friends if it got rid of that kraut.' Le Bois took a huge gulp from his coffee mug. 'Funny thing is that Preston has no idea that the stupid woman hasn't produced a single valid piece of evidence.'

Sam's respect for Le Bois had turned to irritation. She knew of the muttering among fellow officers about this man. Too old, prejudiced, paranoid and over-promoted into a difficult job that had ultimately overwhelmed him. She didn't care for the thought that her blundering new chief was patently making an idiot of himself. Her boyfriend had whispered that some of his colleagues were referring to Le Bois as the

Sussex Pink Panther.

'Which is Dr von Essens worst fault, Sir? Being a stupid woman or a German?'

'McGregor, when you've had a little more experience you may begin to see things clearly…' Le Bois paused as his desk phone rang and he picked up the receiver. 'Put him through.'

Sam watched as her chief listened with unusual intensity. Then with a satisfied smile he spoke. 'Well done, Sid, come on in and bring that tape.'

Steve, in his own words, was up for a confrontation when he walked into the warehouse. He had waited outside the gas suppliers before they opened shop at seven a.m.

'Who delivered the propane to my boat?' His rasping tone surprised the two men in the room.

'It's Mr Simpson, isn't it?' The young man was polite but puzzled.

'Someone fitted a dodgy gas cylinder to my boat that damn near exploded and killed me!'

'Which boat, sir?'

'*Traveller 3* – she was on a pontoon in the marina.'

'But you cancelled that order. I know – I took the call.' This time it was the unit manager, an older man who had emerged from his glass fronted office.

Steve began to understand, but he was not going to make things easy. 'If anyone cancelled the order it certainly wasn't me.'

'Come to think of it, Mr Simpson, the man didn't sound like you. I did wonder at the time.' The manager turned round and shouted for someone called Tony. A fourth man, wearing green overalls, walked through the double doors. 'Tony, you delivered that load to the marina on Thursday. We're worried about the quality of the gas delivered to Mr Simpson's *Traveller*.'

'Yeah, I saw that delivery. I was pissed off about us losing the business and then this bloke comes up says he can't find *Traveller*. Well, everyone around here knows *Traveller*, she's a beauty – stands out from the crowd like.'

'Was this man delivering gas?' Steve asked.

'Yes, but he didn't say it was gas, but that's what I saw in the back of his wagon.'

'Wagon?'

'Not a proper delivery truck – just a battered old Land Rover.'

Steve strove to stay impassive. 'We think there may be something criminal about that gas delivery.'

'I agree about that. The bloke was a hoodie – you know like one o'them yobs around the town centre, but he wasn't no yob, he was a grown man. Tell you something else. I think he knew bloody well which boat was *Traveller*. I think he wanted me to see him as an outsider. Anyway, I didn't like it so I took his number.'

'Car registration?' Steve could have shouted with excitement.

'That's right – I wrote it down. It's in the Toyota glove pocket; I'll get it if you like.'

'Thanks, please do,' Steve replied trying not to let his voice sound too eager.

Two minutes later the man returned and handed Steve a scrap of paper. 'That's it.'

Steve copied the number on the back of an old envelope and handed the original back. 'You must keep that for the police. I'd better warn you now they will be round to talk to you.' He left feeling relieved and rather pleased with himself. The staff looked correspondingly gloomy.

Sid Everett and Andy Ikes, his photographer, had watched the family leave Firs Farm on the Friday morning. Both had been standing in the bus shelter opposite the driveway entrance. Earlier, at nine o'clock, Sid had walked unseen into the grounds and stood within listening distance of the front door. He had returned to Andy wholly satisfied. Had they reached the house an hour earlier they would have seen Kirsten take the two children to school.

'The whole lot of them are off for the day on some boat,' he said. 'Preston and his wife will be alone.'

'Fuck them,' said Andy. 'I want the bitch who wrecked my camera. Five hundred quid digital long zoom.'

Sid snorted. 'What's worse, Andy, hurt camera or damaged ego, eh?'

'Dirty little foreign slapper – they know her around here.'

Sid gave up. 'I want to get Preston on his own, and I want you to stay with me should he turn violent. Don't bother with pictures – just keep the tape turning.'

They sat down on the wooden bench and waited. This was no particular hardship; both were inured to long sessions of observation, an activity in which they took professional pride. Their victims would probably label it as snooping: stalking even. Ten minutes later a car passed them and turned into the Firs Farm entrance.

'Woman,' said Sid. 'I recognise her – she's a copper but I don't know her name. She's in plain clothes this time but I'm sure it's the same one.'

They waited for a further two hours before the car left the drive and turned south towards Emsworth and the coast.

'That was a nuisance,' said Sid. 'I need Preston on his own.'

A few minutes later they were rewarded. Liz Preston drove out through the gates and turned north towards Petersfield.

'Right, that's it,' said Sid. 'In we go.'

The pair climbed over the perimeter fence and ran across the lawn, stopping behind a border full of tall flowering shrubs. They halted while Sid removed binoculars from a case and began to survey the house.

The main door was shut but several windows were open and a wisp of white smoke trickled away from a chimney. Sid swung the binoculars to focus on the long conservatory, and there he saw his target. Harry Preston had set up an easel and was busy sketching.

'The door's open,' said Sid. 'We can go straight in and corner him – all completely legit.'

They reached the actual threshold before Harry even noticed them. He seemed oblivious to everything outside his own world. Sid tapped lightly on the glass door and Harry turned towards them. 'Hello, who are you?'

'Sid Everett, Daily Banner.' Sid advanced holding up his press card.

'I'm afraid I don't read your paper – how can I help you?'

'We're interested to know how your recent problems affect your work.' Sid moved round to look at the sketch. 'That's a very peaceful scene if I may say so.'

'Thank you, but my wife has insisted that I work as usual and not brood.'

'It must be comforting to have a partner who stands by you in trouble – mine never did.' Sid sighed.

Harry favoured him with a wan smile. 'Thank you for your interest, Mr er…?'

'Everett – Sid Everett.'

'Thank you for your interest, Mr Everett, but I doubt you came just to commiserate with me.'

Sid looked around; the conservatory was equipped with smart top-of-the- range garden furniture, while early spring flowers brightened vases at other points around the room. 'This is a great house – very tasteful.'

'Not my house, alas, but my friends have made it special.' Harry had returned to sketching.

Sid could not understand the attitude of the man. Normally he would have expected hostility and abuse from someone into whose presence he had intruded unasked. Now he wondered if this mild-manner was a front that concealed the mental instability that had made this man a killer. It was time to push a little harder.

'Four people are dead, Mr Preston. All murdered in identical circumstances. You know what the local CID chief thinks.'

Harry shrugged. 'A man I intensely disliked is bludgeoned just after I spoke to him. I can't deny that. I met the young man murdered at Dell Quay briefly and I once helped the teacher with her art class. The weather girl I have no knowledge of. I might have cheerfully killed her if it brought better weather.'

This man is so laid-back he's creepy, Sid thought. Perhaps Le Bois is right. Time for a change of tactics.

'Where's Rachel today?' Sid stared at Harry and was rewarded. The man's face twitched to be replaced with a look of deep sadness.

'My little Rachel is no more. Weren't you told?'

'Told what – I mean she was here…'

'She was here only once – now she's dead…' Harry had put down his pencil.

Sid was surprised. He was no shrinking violet, and long ago sensitivity to his target's feelings had ceased to be a factor. It had to be so if he was to win a result and have a story. 'How did she die, Mr Preston – did you kill her?'

Harry gave a long audible sigh. 'I will always have a conscience about her death. What was it Oscar Wilde wrote? "All men kill the thing they love." Others may dispute that, but in my heart I know I did it. Yes, I killed her…' Harry slumped on a garden chair. The man was crying now and mopping his face with a huge white hand-kerchief.

'Thank you, sir, I'm sorry we intruded.' Sid jabbed a thumb towards the garden door. Andy walked through it and Sid followed.

'Jeez, he's admitted killing her. God almighty – he killed his own kid. Christ, Le Bois is right, the man's a psychopath. Did you get all of that?'

Andy held up the pocket recorder and grinned. 'To think, I only saw that poor little mite Rachel on Wednesday evening. It's too late now, but no wonder social wanted those kids in care. They must have known something. What do we do?'

'My editor has first listen, but then we take that tape to Inspector Le Bois.'

CHAPTER 12

'Did it happen?' he asked his brother.

'I think so. An explosion was reported south of the Island, and the yacht never came home to the marina.'

'Let's hope it worked. Mother says it's best we release that psychologist to death. That woman is clever, and she could ruin everything.'

'If it didn't work we shall have to be a bit more direct next time. There's too much at stake for us to fail now. I'm sorry if we killed the yacht owners – they are nice people. I wish you had told me before. I would have found another way.'

The man was irritated. Why did his brother sometimes seem to lose faith. 'Well I've never liked them, and they will die anyway like we all will. We'll all be shrivelled, and only we can stop it. Man, the Power is out of control with anger...' he put a finger to his lips. 'Quiet now – she's coming.'

Both men stood up as their mother, the Powerful One, came into the room.

The whole family, with Liz Preston, had a happy day at Branham. The sun was shining on the lake when they arrived. The car park was full and boats were busy launching for the handicap timed event and the race for mini-keelboats.

'Shall we sail today?' asked Kirsten.

'What, you and me and the RS200?' Steve felt dubious. 'I'm especially stiff in the joints today, and after nearly being murdered I'm not feeling that competitive. I don't fancy coming last.'

'Go on, Dad, it's your duty to come last. Then all of them, even old Charlie, can say they beat the Olympic Gold winner.' Emily began dragging the cover off the dinghy.

'All right, we'll give it a go.'

To sail a race in a high performance dinghy was exactly the tonic Steve needed to raise his spirits. Kirsten lost much of her moodiness crewing for him. They didn't win, nor did they disgrace themselves. In the excitement of that hour, Steve forgot his arthritis and blocked out the pain in the excitement of a race. He knew he would pay dearly for this, and his medical advisers would be horrified; he didn't care. Following a fierce battle with the Marriott family's boat they just scraped a fourth place, rounded down to sixth on corrected time. Emily and John-Kaj had sailed in the morning but followed their parents' race sitting in one of the rescue launches yelling encouragement.

Steve came back to earth literally and mentally when he crawled painfully out of the boat and back onto the jetty. 'God, I feel stiff.'

Emily appeared holding two mugs of coffee. 'Well, done, both of you. Jane says you can have these cups on my tab.'

'Very generous of you, I'm sure,' Steve laughed even as he grimaced with pain.

'Don't forget to sign off or you'll be disqualified,' said Emily.

'And you, young lady, can go suck eggs.'

Steve delegated Kirsten to drive home. He felt tired and stiff and not up to the journey, even with the automatic gears that he'd lately been forced to use. The roads were reasonably clear, and they did the trip in half an hour. It was only when they reached Firs Farm that they could see something was wrong.

A police car was parked on the verge opposite their entrance. Then, as they turned into the drive, two policemen moved into their path waving them to a halt. Kirsten wound down her side window.

'This location is barred to visitors,' said the policeman.

Kirsten began to bristle. 'This is our house, what the hell are you doing here?'

'Can you produce identity?'

'You can go piss yourselves.' Kirsten eased the car slowly forward until the luckless PCs gave ground and jumped aside. She then drove the last twenty yards in a fury.

'Mum, cool it – cool it,' Emily shouted.

Two more police cars were parked in front of the house, plus a red Mondeo that Steve didn't recognise. All this was irrelevant in his eyes. Two police constables were escorting Harry, in handcuffs, from the house. Standing to one side were three men. One, middle-aged, looked vaguely familiar although Steve could not place him. A second, younger individual, broke away from the group and ran towards them. In his hands he carried a camera.

'That's him,' Kirsten shouted. 'That's the little creep on the hill with the camera.'

'Nasty man,' Emily joined in. 'He asked me questions – I bet he's a paedo.'

Steve admitted afterwards that all this had rendered him speechless. Not Kirsten though. She had leapt from the car followed closely by Emily. The sight of these two had an extraordinary effect on the cameraman. He stopped running; he halted abruptly, staring open mouthed. 'Rachel, it is Rachel,' his voice faltered and he moved forward and touched Emily on the shoulder.

'Keep your hands off me – pervert,' she hissed.

'But, you're dead – he admitted it. He killed you.'

'What's all this?' A second man wearing a blue suit had joined them, followed by the familiar man: grey haired and wearing a leather jacket.

'And who the hell are you?' Kirsten was looking increasingly dangerous.

Blue suit replied by holding up a police warrant card. 'I, Madam, am Detective Inspector Le Bois of Mid Southern CID. And you are?'

Steve had painfully extracted himself from the passenger seat. Kirsten was clearly about to go ballistic. It was time for him to intervene. 'We are Stephen and Kirsten Simpson. This lady is Elizabeth Preston who is a guest in our house, and these two are our children.'

'But, no,' the cameraman pointed at Emily. 'She's Rachel, that's Prestons' kid that he murdered, except she's alive.' He seemed close to tears.

Leather jacket seemed faintly amused and now Steve recognised him. 'You're Everett.'

'That's right, squire: Sid Everett – Daily Banner.'

'Liz,' Harry called across from the police car in which he had just been seated. 'Liz – Steve; tell them how Rachel died. They've got this all wrong. They think Emily is Rachel. It's all the fault of those social services people. Please both of you put the record straight.'

'Well?' said Le Bois.

'Steve,' said Liz, 'can you explain – I don't want to talk about it.'

'Rachel Preston died of leukaemia when she was ten years old,' Kirsten intervened. 'The medics got the diagnosis wrong, and the condition became terminal. Liz and Harry have never got over her death. Harry thinks he was neglectful, and he always says he killed her, but that's the most stupid nonsense.'

'Is this true?' Le Bois looked at Steve.

'Yes it is. I think you owe these people an apology. If you won't, I personally will take the matter up with Chief Superintendent Fox and if I don't get satisfaction there it will be a matter for the Police Complaints Commission.'

95

The car carrying Harry was already moving away down the drive. Le Bois glared at Sid Everett. 'Thank you for nothing. This enquiry is going down the shit hole.'

'Then I suggest you follow it there!' said Kirsten.

'You really did have a close call,' said Frank Matheson.

'I know, and this time whoever it is meant to kill us.' Greta von Essens opened a window in her cottage. 'That's better – it's hot today.'

'You'll have to take precautions. I doubt they'll leave it at that.'

'The police are taking this seriously, even Le Bois is. They're patrolling down this lane and I've been given an alarm.'

'That doesn't mean they'll get here in time.' Matheson was worried. 'I think you should shift out of here until we've settled this case.'

'I'll think about it.'

Matheson let the matter rest. 'Have you any more for me?'

'Yes, I think I may have. I've been trawling the internet trying to find support for my theory. Well, I've found something. You see the only clear link I have is that each murder victim has a weather connection, and each body was left in fresh water. That means we are looking for a very small highly-motivated group of disturbed people who are convinced they are acting for the public good. My first thought was misguided individuals blaming the weather forecaster for bad weather. We must all have felt an irrational urge to thump some of them.'

Matheson grinned. 'You recall that Martin Herring a few years back? I remember that bastard. Every evening for weeks he was smirking on the box. Multiple depressions and gales in the North Atlantic – complex areas of low pressure all coming straight over us during school holidays. And the bugger was pleased. It wouldn't have surprised me one little bit if we'd investigated his murder.'

'Would that have changed the weather?'

'It might have if Nadine had strutted on in that bikini.'

'I think that would have been a triumph of hope over experience.' Greta pulled two sheets of A4 from a filing tray. 'I picked this up from the internet on Thursday.'

Matheson fumbled for his reading glasses, took the papers and frowned. 'What's this – *Children of the Sun Power – False Earth Faces Vengeance.* Greta, is this something to do with your supposed cult?'

'Not only that, I've been talking to Howard Fulzeimer, he's my opposite number at Princeton. There have been similar killings to ours: seven in Montana and two in Arizona. He's convinced that these are ritual murders, and he has connected them to this Mayan sun-god cult.'

'Montana?' said Matheson. 'That's where a lot of these cults are based, I understand, and in Oregon too. You remember the Girl on the Shore case? Tom O'Malley and his wife were nearly killed by some group of loonies there.'

'That group were neo-Nazis, ridiculous and nasty in equal proportions. The people I'm looking at are much more obscure but are beginning to establish a pattern.'

'Right, what are they all about?'

'I think one might call them fundamentalist sun-worshippers.' Greta picked up another clutch of A4 sheets. 'There have been other killings: one in Canada; two in Australia and maybe up to fifteen in Guatemala, but I can't quantify these accurately because murders there are a daily occurrence.'

'What is this pattern?'

'In every case that we've identified so far the murder is by a blow to the back of the skull, and the body is left in a river, lake or some other fresh water source. You had better read all of this.' She passed him her remaining papers.

Matheson read with increasing bewilderment. *People of Earth you are about to pay the penalty of your false religions. You foolishly are blind to the Power. You worship false and imaginary gods while you cannot see that the only Power is that true Power that warms the seas ripens the crops and sustains all life. The Power is angry and he shows his anger and his quest for vengeance every day, every week and every year. The Power will shrivel your puny planet until the seas dry and all your soil becomes desert...*

'Greta, what is this stuff? It's barking.'

'It makes complete sense if you are of that turn of mind. Sun worship used to be the world's dominant religious faith. It had millions of followers in the Americas, and it's a key influence in the Shinto culture of Japan. And you can see why. The sun is the power that sustains all life, and it's not a concept, it's visible every day.'

'Except when Martin Herring was around – we never saw much of it then. Greta, are you trying to tell me that these nutters think that they can change the weather by disposing of Arnold Evans and a bimbo like Nadine Rotherton?'

Greta replied, 'Howard Fulzeimer says sun-worship cults have been reviving in the Americas and throughout the English-speaking world, and that includes India and even places like the Philippines. The cults are growing and multiplying. Fulzeimer says it was all harmless and eccentric to begin with...'

Matheson interrupted. 'What time scale is this – when was "to begin with"?'

'These cults in their present form date back to the 1930s on the back of Nazism and Fascism. Then in the 1950s there was a revival of interest in Central American civilisations, in particular the Mayans and Incas. Did you ever see 'The Royal Hunt of The Sun'?'

'The what?'

'It was a stage play about Pizarro's conquest of Peru. I saw it at Chichester Theatre in the Sixties. It certainly made an impression on me.' Greta picked up a book from her desk and handed it to Frank. 'Here you are: *The Highest Altar by Patrick Tierney*. I read it last night – fascinating and horrifying. The author has made a detailed investigation of current human sacrifice in Peru and Chile. The book is controversial but an awful lot in it reads true.'

'Greta, you forget you are dealing with a simple copper. I don't buy all this intellectual chattering-classes stuff any more than I buy sun gods burning up the good Lord's earth. This is crap; nobody is going to believe you. Are you seriously suggesting telling Le Bois his murder victims died to stop global warming?'

'Oh, Frank. Have a bit more faith in my good sense. I'm disappointed in you – you've always trusted me in the past.'

'No, Greta, I'm sorry but on this one you are wrong. I'm not saying that Le Bois is right about Preston, well he isn't. No, somewhere out there we have a lunatic, or I give in to you when you say there's two working together. We're looking for a Shipman or a Neilson. There's no religious cult and no rational explanation. They are psychopaths. We've seen them before, and we'll see them again.'

'Frank, every psychopath I've ever profiled has had a motive, however crazy. Inside their heads they think what they're doing has some logic. I am profiling these people in the same way, and with the same programs I always use and this is the result that keeps coming up every day, louder and louder.'

'All right, Greta, I know. I should take you seriously and I do, but it all seems so crazy.'

'These are crazy people.' She took the papers and returned them to the filing tray.

Matheson remembered something. 'I think I'll make my own enquiries into Ricardo Standfast. Have the police any news of him?'

'Yes,' Greta frowned. 'The news is that MI6 have told us to back off – Mr Standfast, whoever or wherever, is off-limits.'

'Not to me he's not – bloody spooks.'

CHAPTER 13

The family did not go sailing on the Sunday. Steve had suffered the after-effects of Branham the day before and was disinclined to repeat the experience. He still had nightmare visions of the day on *Traveller*. He had reported the incident to the police and had made a statement. Officers had gone out to the Itchenor mooring and seen the blocked locker drains and the holes into the main cabin. He understood that they intended to interview the gas suppliers, and Steve had passed on the registration number of the suspect Land Rover. So far he had had no reaction. Harry had been released after another savage hour of questioning by Inspector Le Bois.

'He kept asking me how I'd passed messages out of custody. How often had I been on your boat? Did I know where the gas was stored? The answer to that was definitely no – I love *Traveller*, but I've never asked where the heat for the soup comes from.'

'Will they leave Emily in peace?' Kirsten asked.

'I told them that Emily is a lovely feisty little girl, a bit too out-spoken for her own good, but a sweet girl. I said I would be very proud of her if she was mine, but she is definitely not.'

'I hope that's the end,' said Steve.

'I wish it was the end of all of this nonsense, but I doubt it. Worse than that, I know that man Le Bois is not convinced.'

At lunchtime they had visitors. Gerry and Dolly, plus Clancy the labrador were standing on the doorstep. Kirsten invited them in and poured glasses of sherry. Clancy slumped to the floor and luxuriated in front of the log fire.

'Where's young Emily?' Gerry asked.

'Upstairs, I think,' said Steve. 'Shall I call her?'

'In a minute, but I've some news,' said Gerry. 'Her headmaster, what's his name, dear?'

'Cotton,' Dolly replied.

That's it, well done. He says that he wants the Walderton excavation to be an educational history thing. Can't get my head round that myself. That bloody battle is like yesterday to me: some bad memories – still dream about it a lot.'

'I remember,' Kirsten handed Dolly a sherry glass. 'Emily said it was her ancient history society.'

'Don't blame her,' Gerry laughed. 'When I was Emily's age we thought any adult was ancient history. Later, when we were fighting, we thought our station commander was a doddery old woman. He was only forty-six; been a top flyer in the first war.'

'Gerry,' said Dolly. 'You're losing the plot – tell'em what's proposed.'

'Yes, of course. Well it seems they've located the cockpit area of this 109, and they want me and a pupil from the school to be there for an open day next Friday. You know, crossing the generations and all that sort of thing. I thought it might suit young Emily. She knows me, and she's a bit of an actress. There'll be press there and the telly – she'll revel in it...'

'And you can bore the pants off all of them,' Dolly smiled.

'I'm sure Emily will be game,' said Steve. 'I'll call her down.'

'Gerry, just a moment,' Kirsten looked anxious. 'Will there be a dead German in the thing when they dig it up?'

'Good heavens no. In fact they found the serial numbers in the fuselage and the engine and the pilot is still very much alive. He baled out and spent the war as a PoW. Decent fellow by all accounts, and he's coming over for the day if he feels fit enough. The idea is that we're filmed shaking hands, and a child from the school stands with us.'

Kirsten looked thoughtful. *"We're fools to make war on our brothers in arms..."* she quoted.

'That sounds profound,' said Gerry.

'It's only a line from a song.'

'What do you think, darling?' Steve looked anxiously at Kirsten. Steve's own father had been killed in the war, but Kirsten's family had the most ambivalent connection to that event, and he knew the memories hurt.

'I think it would be very good for her,' she replied.

Steve looked his wife in the eye. 'What about meeting this German?'

'I know that in Denmark we still do not completely trust them, but then my own father was a German.'

'Really?' said Gerry.

'Before I married this big ugly man my family name was Schmitt.' Now she laughed.

'How much do you trust this man Simpson?' Inspector Le Bois glared at his chief.

101

'I've known him and his wife for as long as I've been in this division. My wife, Carol worked for him at one stage. I've told you before, the man is as honest as the day is long.'

'Sir, I mean no criticism but could you be letting personal feelings get in the way of objectivity?'

'Le Bois, could your fixation be getting in the way of your objectivity?' Fox was not offended. He looked at his subordinate and almost felt sorry for him. Le Bois sat at his desk, clothes rumpled and tie loosened. He looked tired and his features hollow and lined.

'God, Sir,' Le Bois voice had lost its usual bluster, 'I know everybody says I've got this wrong but you have to go by intuition sometimes – I mean gut feeling. Preston's the only lead I have, and he did know three of the four victims. Then Everett comes in with that tape and that seemed the final brick in the wall and now it's back to square one again. But I've only got the Mr Simpson's word for all this and now Preston's free to kill again.'

'Any developments over the yacht *Traveller*?'

'Another dead end,' Le Bois looked even more depressed. 'The Land Rover seen at Chi' Marina had false plates of course. There is an old Land Rover with that number, but it's on the Isle of Wight and hasn't left the island for five years. Their police confirm it. Then the gas suppliers can't identify the driver because he wore a hood.'

'Stephen says they told him the driver was a grown man not one of our yobs.'

'And the gasmen confirm. So that's it Sir, we're no further forward and that means I've got to stick with Preston. It could have been him with that gas. He must have killed Evans and even if he didn't actually do the other three, I reckon he ordered their deaths.'

'Dr Watts says all four were hit from behind with metal – she doubts the Pagham tiller would have done such a clean job. Apart from that could Preston have had the strength to kill with a bit of wood?'

'If he's a psycho of course he could, and that young doctor didn't examine Evans: it was the Surrey police.' Le Bois sounded desperate.

Fox looked at the man with genuine compassion. 'Phil, I think you should have a spot of leave.'

It was Monday, and Steve's first opportunity to corner all of Easter-broke's employees. He had wondered how many rumours concerning *Traveller* might be circulating, and he was relieved to find that there were none. Better than that, no one on his staff seemed to have heard a thing about any explosions or gas leaks. However, he guessed that his employees would be meeting the gas supplier's employees in the pub or around the village, so Steve gave them a cautious and edited version of the truth. He told them a rogue supplier had installed a faulty cylinder that had leaked and could have caused an explosion. He would be obliged if they could keep a lookout for these people and report to him if any other marina customer had seen a Land Rover and its driver around the time in question. He had then gone into the office and ordered the best and most expensive paraffin cooking range on offer. He knew that he would be forever nervous of bottled gas, and that Kirsten would probably refuse to step aboard the ship while it remained.

Greta had once more logged onto the sun-worshipper's internet site. She could understand Frank Matheson's incredulity. Frank was no longer a police officer and his attitudes were more flexible than most, but he was still an old copper and tended to think in straight lines. Her work was different in so far as she came at these problems from a fresh perspective. To Frank, villains were villains and motives were part of evidence needing to convince a jury. Police officers were not required to comprehend the minds of disturbed individuals. It would be wrong if they were. Frank had not given her the chance to show him the itemised information that the American academic, Fulzeimer, had emailed her, but every one of the murders in the United States had a weather forecasting connection, however vague. But the two in Arizona were the most revealing. A man and a woman discovered dead: naked in a garden hot tub. Both had been struck in the back of the skull. That man was a senior executive of Maxstats.com and the woman was the weather girl from the local TV station. The girl killed in Canada worked for a meteorological department, although she was only a secretary. Fulzeimer had yet to complete an analysis of the Guatemalan killings and Greta had agreed to follow up the murder in Australia. She knew that the victims were a man, an elderly veteran of Viet Nam and his young daughter. Some of the features were the same, but there was no traceable connection with the weather.

Greta was not an expert in Central American sun cults, but she remembered that the Mayan civilisation was said to have collapsed through successive crop failure. The Mayans had sacrificed to their god, but he had not been appeased. Finally, the people had killed their priests. Global warming, whatever its cause, would not be halted by any number of ritual sacrifices. Greta knew that unless she could put

103

the puzzle together soon there would be more futile killings. The police, or at least the likes of Le Bois, would still be trying to make square pegs fit round holes with unlikely suspects. Unless she could fit her profile to the right target she would have more blood on her head.

Frank Matheson sat in the glass-fronted dining room of the Lakeview Hotel. Although he regarded this as a professional assignment he was enjoying himself. The sun was shining on Branham Lake as the cold easterly wind rippled tiny wavelets over the surface. The ducks were clustering around the water's edge on the off chance of a feed from picnickers' sandwiches.

'Good morning, sir – you asked to see me.' The hotel manageress had walked up silently, disturbing his reverie.

'Thank you,' Matheson put on his most disarming grin. 'A friend of mine stayed with you ten days ago, and he said he lost something here which was supposed to come to me.'

'Who was this?' The woman looked puzzled.

'Ricardo Standfast – he's in a similar business to me and he had a document report which he can't find. Thinks he may have lost it here.'

'I remember him – Spanish gentleman was he?'

'Yes, that's the man.'

The woman was looking at him in an odd way. Matheson stared back; he had years of experience in soothing witnesses even if this one looked sharper than most.

'Mr Matheson, may I ask if you are a policeman?'

'Used to be one – but I'm a private investigator now.' He passed her his business card.

'Is this friend of yours one as well?'

'Not private exactly – he's an officer from his country's investig-ative force.' If not an exact lie this was an audacious shot in the dark.

'We've already had the police all over us on account of that poor man in the lake and the girl, Nadine Rotherton.' The manageress looked much less friendly.

'Oh, that's just a coincidence,' Matheson lied. 'Arnold Evans had enemies.'

The woman relaxed. 'This could be very bad PR for us, we don't want any more trouble. The police arrested Harry Preston, but we think they're wrong – he's harmless.'

'My friend is following a totally different investigation.' He leaned towards her and beckoned in his best conspiratorial manner. 'Standfast is not his proper name.'

'We guessed that. What's he up to?'

Matheson looked grave. 'He's working undercover, I can't tell you more.'

'What is it you're looking for?'

'Brown A4 size envelope.'

'I can't say I remember seeing anything like that, but I'll ask my staff.'

Matheson took a further chance. 'Does my friend, Ricardo stay here often?'

'It's funny you ask that, but he's been here once a month since February.' She paused. 'Look, Mr Matheson, I've only your word for what you've been telling me. I don't think I should be gossiping with you about our guests.' She stopped speaking while the waiter cleared the table. 'I've already been asked by the local police and as I say, it's all bad PR.'

'Yes, Ma'am, of course you're right. However, if I were you I would take precautions.'

'What does that mean?' She was all frost now and also nervous.

'I'm sorry, no offence meant. I'm only advising watch strangers. This is an excellent hotel and your reputation is beyond reproach, but your speciality is business and not all business is as white as the driven snow.'

Matheson caught the frisson of alarm on her face. 'Criminals?' she whispered.

'That's overstating it. Look, you've got my phone contact. Could you call me if Ricardo comes here – I'll stand him one of your excellent dinners.' He smiled.

Matheson took time out to walk around the lake. It was a cold but crisp morning and a delight to walk, even though at seventy-four he was slower than of old. He certainly wouldn't catch a villain in a foot chase. The police tape around the crime scene had long since gone. He had never met this Nadine but still felt a regret; she had always seemed such a happy, bubbly girl as seen on TV. Back at the Lakeview he was just about to collect his car when a voice hissed at him in a deafening stage whisper. 'Mister, I've got something – what's it worth?'

Matheson swung round. It was the man who had waited on table that morning. 'What's what worth?'

'I've got this; it's mail for that Standfast. Look if that guy's a drug dealer, I want him nicked – you're a copper aren't you?'

'Indeed I am.'

'My kid brother died of heroin – I owe those bastards…'

'You're still trying to sell me evidence,' Matheson confronted the little man with his sternest expression.

'I could lose my job here, nicking guests mail – what's it worth?' The waiter looked shiftily around.

'Let me have a look first.'

'Three letters – twenty pounds each.'

'You're on.' Matheson pulled out his wallet.

'What's the big deal about old Gerry and the German?' Emily looked less than overjoyed.

'It's history – don't you realise that Gerry fought in the most decisive battle of World War Two?'

'No.'

'Doesn't Battle of Britain mean anything?'

'Never heard of it. Anyway Ms Flotton says wars are all caused by men and if there were no men there'd never be wars and everyone would be happy.'

'Is she your history teacher?'

'Not likely – history is dull. Ms Flotton says we don't need to know anything that happened before we were born and it's the future that matters.'

'If all men have to be done away with what'll happen to that boyfriend of yours?'

'Jamie's different.'

Steve gave up. One thing was definite. Emily was going to the Walderton dig with Gerry, Dolly and the German, and before that she would have a crash course on the events of 1940. Who was it said: "Those who forget their history are condemned to relive it"?

That evening Jeremy arrived to be greeted ecstatically by his mother and with obvious pleasure by his father.

'Are you in the clear?' Jeremy asked.

'I'm in complete oblivion at the moment,' Harry replied. 'But the answer to your question is no. That policeman Le Bois is paranoid, but I think the others have given up on me.'

'What did you find out in London?' Liz asked.

'Tell you in a minute – first a drink. I had no idea the traffic was like it is these days.'

'Dinner in twenty minutes,' said Kirsten. 'You can tell us then.'

Jeremy eyed the main course with almost childish delight. 'Sausages and mash, onions and thick gravy. This is food to die for – bit of a change from sardines and prawn paella. I like the Spanish grub, but this is good old England.'

'Oh really?' Kirsten smiled. 'You are eating one good old Danish recipe as it happens.'

'Don't care – it's great stuff.'

'Thank you. Now, did you find out anything about that Nadine?'

'Lots, but I'm not sure it will help. My mate introduced me to her a couple of years back. He'd known her all his life – used to play with her when he was a kid. The interesting thing is that they all lived in or around Branham, not a stone's throw from the lake, and Nadine came from nearby as well. He said they used to roam all over the common, and they had a little lugsail dinghy on the lake: sort of Swallows and Amazons boat. They used to play pirates.' He laughed. 'Dominic, my mate, said the boys used to sail into a little landing place and then throw the girls in the water. That couldn't have been easy with Nadine. She could pack a punch.'

Steve spoke. 'I think this could be relevant. It means Nadine had a nostalgic reason to stay at the Lakeview. Dr von Essens says she was killed by someone she recognised.'

'Did your friend give you the names of any of these children?' Liz asked.

'No – I didn't ask. Wait – the other girl they threw in the water was Lela or Lisa, something like that and Dominic mentioned some twins. I assume they were boys who were a few years older, but maybe a bit backward mentally. I think there were one or two others on the periphery of the gang so to speak, but those were the ones he talked about.'

'I think Frank should try and find them,' said Kirsten.

'Might not be so easy,' said Jeremy. 'I expect they've all moved on. Like me they could be living anywhere in the world.'

'But it is exactly the sort of thing that Greta likes, or I gather so,' Steve was becoming excited. He didn't know why, and after all he had no sleuthing skills. 'Does anyone remember a Swallows and Amazon boat on the lake?'

'That would be before our time,' said Liz, 'but I'll ask around the club.'

'Whatever made me pay forty quid for these?' Matheson placed two envelopes onto Greta's desk. 'I've been conned.'

'What are they?'

'Holiday brochures – not even addressed to the man.'

Greta examined the two letters. 'Junk mail, they probably receive a pile of the stuff and bin it.'

'That little runt of a waiter must have known. He conned me well and true. Greta, I'm losing my grip.'

'Not this one,' Greta held up the third envelope. 'This could be most significant. There's no stamp, it looks as if it was hand-delivered.'

To Ricardo Standfast.

Mae fy mechgyn yn dweud eu bod wedi dy y lle hwn. Rwyf angen siarad a thi am yr hen ddydiau.

'It's written in Martian,' said Matheson. 'We'll need to find a Martian to translate it.'

'Not as far away as that. You know, I think it's Welsh.'

'That's even worse than Martian – who knows that in these parts?'

'Don't be so negative, Frank. I'm sure we'll find someone who can.'

'We can always ask at the Rugby club,'

'I have a friend in BBC Cardiff. I will email her and we will have an exact grammatical transcript.' Greta looked smug.

'This Standfast is supposed to be Spanish – that's what I was told. Who ever heard of a Spaniard speaking Welsh?'

'No, Frank, I think we may have struck lucky here. There are Spanish speakers who also speak Welsh, some few thousand as I've been told.'

'Oh God, I get you – we're back to bloody South America again. Anyway even if you're right I expect all it'll say is: "don't forget to feed the cat".'

'Frank you are reverting to the pessimist policeman again. Do you want to turn into DI Le Bois?'

'My boys,' Mother spoke. 'You have only ten days left, and you say you have the child but not the warrior, also Signora Essens is still alive. You tell me the police are involved.'

The man was disconcerted. Mother, the Powerful One, was angry with them and it hurt him. His brother, standing beside him, seemed almost tearful. He must take the lead.

108

'Dearest Mother, the police are stupid, they think Henry Preston planned it and I heard one of them say so. As for the sacrifice: what you ask is not easy. Those who have been tested in recent conflict do not advertise the fact and the men from World War Two are old.'

'Use your wits, boys. Age means nothing if the man was brave. Think, and trust the Power. I will do my best for you, but I cannot get out much these days.' Now she smiled at them.

The man felt a surge of relief. How wonderful she was, how he loved her. It was one of those sacred moments when he could have recalled every day of their lives together. Sitting by the campfire as five-year-olds while she filled them with her knowledge. The night had been cold, but they knew that in a few hours their loving god would rise out of the east to warm and caress the earth. He remembered so well her kindness when he had been sent home from school for challenging the Christians' god in the nonsensical religious studies class. She had put her arms around him and dried his tears. The moment had confirmed his certainty in all that she had taught them. He knew without a single doubt that everything she had inculcated into them was the truth. He loved the Power. Every morning he would stand face uplifted to the sun and be filled with love and joy.

'Don't worry, Mother. All the main preparations are in hand. It will be a day to remember.'

She smiled again. 'Boys, you will be recorded as great men after this. You, with all the others, will have saved our miserable world.'

It was time for him to raise the one thing that worried him most. 'I think we should be careful. There are men asking questions. Not police, but others.'

She nodded. 'That is to be expected. Where was this?'

His brother spoke. 'In the Lakeview Hotel. The other day, a large man whom I didn't know and another. He was the one who was in the hotel the night we liberated Nadine from this life. I still wish we had not done that.'

'Have faith,' said Mother. 'What's done is done. Now, tell me about this other man.'

Emily had never felt so subdued. Her parents had compelled her to watch that DVD and it had made her sick. It was history of course, a preparation for Friday and this stunt at Walderton with Gerry and Dolly. If she knew nothing about that war then wasn't it partly the fault of Mum and Dad? Mum in particular would never tell her about her side of the family. If she asked, Mum would snap angrily and say all her family were dead. She knew her Danish granddad had been part Jewish but he hadn't died in that place the DVD had shown. He had died in an air crash thirty years ago and Grandma Schmitt had died of cancer not long before Mum and Dad met. John-Kaj had been named in honour of an uncle who had died in an accident at sea. There had been something odd about that accident that no one would talk about. But there were other things she hadn't been told, and they were connected to that same war. Whispered things, secrets between adults, because they thought she was too young. Something to do with this Uncle Kaj, something terrible about him that she was too young to know. How dare they think that – she had a right to be told.

The DVD had opened her eyes in the way her parents had intended. She had seen views of Auschwitz, deserted but still sinister. Then she had been shown the black and white shots of the victims, the starved survivors, and then piles of naked bodies, skeletons covered by loose skin. Some of them were children of her age. She felt sick. The film had shown piles of children's shoes and the skeins of hair taken from them alive before they were marched to the gas chamber. She had heard of this, but to see the reality was something she could not get her head around. It was horrible, but what was the point? It was cruel of them to make her watch this stuff.

'Emily,' her father had looked her in the eye. 'Sweetheart, had it not been for Gerry and his friends, it would probably have happened here as well.' He paused while he watched her absorb this. 'Those men will not be around much longer. To learn from them on Friday will be a privilege.'

The following day Steve drove to Itchenor intending to move *Traveller* up channel to Chichester Marina. Kirsten refused to come with him; evidently their narrow escape still haunted her. Emily and John-Kaj had no qualms: both were excited and intrigued to see the damaged gas locker. The children would not be enough to handle the ship through the marina lock, so Steve press-ganged Jeremy Preston and two young employees from the workshop. The new cooker had arrived and Steve was in a hurry have it installed. Without it there was no chance of Kirsten accompanying the children and him on their holiday cruise to Cherbourg.

On arrival in the marina he was pleased to inspect the new galley range, while the children spent a happy quarter of an hour freeing it from its cocoon of cardboard and bubble wrap. Steve was less pleased to find that Peter Terring had reported sick with some mystery virus.

This was doubly annoying as the man was needed to do the install-ation and he had never been ill before.

'He's a misery guts, I hate him,' said Emily. 'Can't we find someone else to do it?'

'You mean someone cheerful?' Steve grinned. 'Very few of those in the engineering branch – gloom and despondency goes with their territory.'

In the end, with the assistance of Chris the rigger and a couple of bystanders, they manoeuvred the awkward lump of metal on board and down the companionway steps. Steve borrowed a cordless drill and a set of spanners and removed the old propane galley range. With Jeremy's help the new cooker was slid into place and bolted down. Steve, with memories of old-style primus stoves, had been doubtful about this object although he had been assured that its modern design eliminated any chance of paraffin odour. Time would tell. Lastly, they removed the remaining intact gas bottle and returned it to the supplier.

'We're sorry to lose your business, Mr Simpson,' said the manager, 'but it really wasn't our fault.'

'Of course not,' Steve was reassuring. 'But my wife was very distressed by the whole episode.'

'We've had police all over us; terrible for business.'

'I take it they don't blame you?' Steve was concerned.

'I don't see how they can, but we had this inspector bloke round twice. Kept asking if we'd done business with someone called Henry Preston. In all honesty we've never heard of him, but the policeman wouldn't take no for an answer – got quite stroppy.'

Steve glanced across to Jeremy who was busy helping another arrival with their lines.

'Then we had another one – foreigner. Spoke good English but I reckon he could've been an Argy.'

'A what?'

'Argentinian – I was in the Falklands in '82 when I was in the marines. After the Argies jacked it in we found some of 'em spoke good English.'

'What did this man want?'

The manager looked around before adopting a conspiratorial voice. 'Asked too many questions in my opinion. He asked about you and your boat. But I didn't tell him much – you've got to believe me. We don't gossip about our customers.'

Steve was more puzzled than alarmed. 'What did he look like?'

111

'Just like an Argy. Biggish guy with a moustache – bit like old Saddam.'

'You're sure he wasn't an Iraqi?' Steve smiled.

'No, Mr Simpson. He told us to call him Ricardo – that's an Argy name if ever I heard one. Said he was an insurance man but that I doubt.'

'Probably just some nosy parker, but thanks all the same.'

'One more thing, he wanted names of people who work for you in your shop. I told him to take a running jump. I promise you that is the honest truth.' The gasman looked anxiously at Steve.

'I believe that. Let's hope all this dies down. I don't want you to lose any business or me sleep for that matter.'

As Steve returned to the car his mobile phone rang. It was Kirsten. 'Frank Matheson wants to talk to us. He says he will call this evening around six- thirty.'

Frank drove in as promised, and Kirsten invited him to eat supper with the family.

'How is Greta?' Kirsten asked.

'She's fine, but a bit too confident in my opinion. Won't leave that cottage, although the police are keeping an eye on her.'

'Between you, is there any progress?' Steve asked.

'Yes, I think there may be. Greta has some theory about religious cults. I thought it was rubbish, but on reflection, I think we should go with her. The lady has an impeccable record with this sort of thing.'

'How do you see things?' asked Kirsten.

'Both Greta and I suspect a link to both Sussex and Surrey. Greta is convinced our killers have an intimate knowledge of Branham and the area around it.'

'I guessed that already,' Jeremy spoke quietly in a voice unlike his normal banter. 'If you must know I rang my mate Dominic again today. You see, I've been doing a bit of the Sherlock stuff myself.'

'Jeremy,' Liz spoke. 'Are you sure that's wise? If we hint at Branham that'll only excite the Le Bois man and make it worse for your dad.'

'No,' Frank held up a hand. 'Let's face it, Mrs Preston, there is a Branham connection; the police are right about that. Not about Mr Preston or Phil Le Bois's daft ideas, but three of the four dead have a Branham connection. Not the young sailor Hexham so much, but Arnold Evans yes, and Nadine spent her childhood there and met her death there. Then there is the matter of the yacht club gate code. The

112

police are right to take that seriously, so do I and so does Greta.'

He looked at Jeremy. 'All right, young man. What have you found?'

'I met Nadine three years ago through a mate of mine who grew up with her near Branham. They were all part of a little kid's gang and they roamed the heath and sailed on the lake in a little boat that Nadine's father bought for them. I think you or the law should track down those other kids.'

'Can you give me names?' Frank asked.

'Dominic Kelly, Leila Brent and two older boys that Dominic calls the twins. Dominic said they called them "Mike and Spike" but their dad called them some names in Spanish. Dominic says they were older than the rest but didn't seem to mix much with their own kind. Their father was a naturalised Brit – a refugee from the Spanish war. Interesting guy by all accounts. Arrived in the UK with nothing and built up a thriving business.'

'What about the little dinghy?' asked Steve.

'Nadine's dad gave it to her.'

'Have you any name for this Spanish man?' Frank had been listening so intently that his forkful of pasta had remained poised halfway to his mouth throughout Jeremy's speech. 'This is important. You may have given us a breakthrough.'

'Dominic says their family name was Larranaga, here you are: he spelt it for me.' Jeremy handed Frank a slip of paper. 'I gather the business is still going but it's under a different management. It's a motor firm, apparently they used to have a franchise to repair and service utility trucks for the MOD.'

'Would that include long wheelbase Land Rovers?'

'No idea, but I imagine so.'

Frank stared at Jeremy. 'Contact your friend again and get the full names of this Spanish bloke and the name of that motor firm.' He looked apologetically towards Kirsten and then to Jeremy. 'Do it now please!'

'The man was called...' Matheson adjusted his glasses to read from his notes. 'He was called Francisco Larranaga y Terra – What a mouthful!'

'Not really, if you work it out,' said Greta. 'It tells me the man was mixed parentage – Basque father, Castilian mother. Larranaga is Basque country and the Spanish often put the mother's family name as a courtesy: hence y Terra. Francisco is Castilian. That was Franco's

113

first name, which would have irritated our man somewhat, I guess.' Greta looked pleased.

'Like you, I was over the moon when young Preston came up with that name, but does it get us anywhere?' Frank still felt out of his depth. Greta's form of investigation always baffled him at the midway stage.

'I don't feel inclined to involve the police.' Greta was busy with her computer keyboard. 'I can't find any Larranagas in the motor business on this search engine.'

'No, Greta, this is one for old fashioned leg work and ancient as I am I can still do that.'

'I agree, but at the same time I'm going to find out all I can about this man and his family. If he was a refugee from 1930s Spain, I should be able to track him down.'

Acting Detective Constable Sam McGregor was tired. It had been one hell of a day, and in her opinion a waste of time. Once again she had been sent to Surrey with DC Baird to conduct another search of the empty Preston house. DI Le Bois had agreed to take a month's leave starting this coming Monday. That left the man with four days to chase his obsession. The Surrey police had refused to raise a warrant to dig up the whole garden; they clearly regarded Le Bois as an irritation. Sam, who retained a residual loyalty to her force, had part resented this while secretly agreeing with them. So she had spent the best part of a day ranging over the Preston garden with a metal detector. Her efforts had yielded no hoard of golden coins, only a 1920 penny and bits of rusty debris. Nothing she found could conceivably be a murder weapon. Simon Baird had made one more desultory search of the garage and outbuildings.

Le Bois had insisted that they report to him in person on return and Sam had been dreading the moment. She was shocked at the Inspector's appearance; the man sat at his desk head in hands with his jacket and tie removed. His lack of sleep showed in hollow eyes and the stress lines on his face.

'It's bloody obvious,' said Le Bois. 'The killings have stopped and for one reason – Preston is under observation twenty four seven. He can't kill anyone and if he tries we'll get him. It's those two kids that worry me – Surrey social services rang me this morning. They've crashed their computers again. There's not a trace or any reference to the missing kids. We really need to dig up that garden.' He gave a groan of exasperation.

114

Sam's own thoughts surprised her. She felt pity for the man and she could find nothing that would give him a crumb of comfort. Had there been anything at the Preston house that she could give him as encouragement? On the first occasion, at South Marshall, she had spent a happy couple of hours in Henry's temporary studio. Preston was a fine landscape painter and well worth his reputation. Surrey had been keeping an eye on the Tilford house, suspecting that thieves might help themselves to a few of his canvasses. However, her Inspector's phobic hatred of artists had warped his judgement in the Preston case. She remembered the one thing that might cheer the man up and send him on leave in a better mood. She was clutching at straws but what the hell...

'Sir, there is a small development. We made another check on the outbuildings, and this time we concentrated on the garden shed. It's crammed with rubbish and throwaway stuff – we could hardly see a thing. But at the back under a sheet we found a couple of gas cylinders.'

'What colour were these cylinders?' The Inspector showed less interest than Sam had hoped.

'Blue.'

Le Bois looked even more gloomy. 'No, should be red; anyway someone else organised the boat attempt. Preston's got associates and we need to locate them. In the meantime...'

'Yes, sir?'

'Find those children, alive or dead. They're probably dead, poor little sods.'

Sam left the station and drove home. Three more days, assuming what was left of her chief's sanity would survive that long.

The derelict cottage had a forlorn look that surprised the man. He remembered it from former times when the family had rented it to that young dentist and his wife. Now it stood crumbling with smashed windows and a rotting doorframe. They had replaced this and removed the shattered windows, cementing iron bars in their place.

His brother had told him that the local authority had condemned the house and that any request for planning permission would be refused. That did not worry the brothers. The cottage so far off the beaten track was ideal for their sacred purpose. The forestry workers had departed for the rest of the summer, and no one else came here. The Land Rover wouldn't do for this job so they were using the tractor and trailer. Apart from anything else, the loads of straw bales and fuel drums would attract no interest. His brother used the tractor and trailer several times a month, and the locals, who knew him well, would never question its use.

This would be their final mission. They expected to be exposed afterwards and indeed it was Mother's wish that the world should know the truth. But they would not wait for arrest by those slow-witted police. It would be their own final moment and they too must die. He did not fear this, death was a release, but on a day like this he could feel a twinge of regret. The Power diffused its warmth over the gentle landscape. A benign Power today, but what if their mission failed? It was one of some twenty similar missions worldwide, but all must succeed if the sun's mood was to be appeased.

They unhooked the trailer and used the tractor's front loader to stack the heavy straw bales outside the building, concealing the fuel drums behind them. The man examined both of the tiny downstairs rooms and the brick cellar. He had spent an hour cementing in window bars and that would require a few days to harden.

'Five more loads of the same should do the job,' he remarked as much as to himself as to his brother.

'Agreed,' brother replied. 'Then we report to Mother, the Powerful One.'

CHAPTER 14

Frank Matheson had been searching for his man all day, and now he'd run him to earth. Sid Everett was drinking in the Barley Mow, beside the picturesque Tilford village green. Frank spotted him at once, sitting alone and watched by a quartet of suspicious locals.

'Found you, Sid. Now you can buy me that pint you owe me from six years ago.'

Sid looked at Matheson with that shifty, ferret like expression. 'It's you that owes me all the favours, Matheson.'

'What favour?'

'Fifteen years-ago. I gave you that tip-off in the Lindgrune case – exclusive rights to the story you promised. You never delivered.'

'Oh come on, Sid. I promised you an inside view if Lindgrune came to trial, which he didn't. Justice was served when he fell out of that helicopter.'

Everett grimaced into his beer glass. 'All the main players died that day and you never told me the full story. There was unfinished business from the war that my public had a right to know.'

'Well that's all dead and buried years ago,' Matheson had no intention of discussing the Elgaad family. He needed to deflect Everett onto the matter in hand. 'You can tell me why you're hanging around these parts.'

'What d'you think I'm doing? Listening for news of course.' Sid looked indignant.

Matheson paid for two pints and carried them back to Sid, who was looking shiftily towards the outside door. 'Sid, are you still Phil Le Bois' jackal?'

'The DI is pretty confident that Henry Preston is his man,' said Sid. 'But there's Preston's two young kids missing and that's the real story that my readers will want to know about. Social services can't find them. Le Bois is convinced Preston's killed his own kids. That's news – big time.' Sid drained his glass and looked at pleadingly at Matheson. 'Then it might be the kid's elder brother. You know he assaulted Kevin from our paper?'

'Are you getting anywhere?' Matheson had no intention of telling Sid that his missing children did not exist outside the minds of small town bureaucrats.

'Nowhere, I don't mind telling you. I've been staying in the

117

Lakeview Hotel. None of the locals will talk to me. Then I went to the Duke pub, just up the road near Preston's house. Nobody has a word against him – same in here. This is exactly what happened when we covered Shipman. Nobody would believe a word against him either at first. I never understand how these psycho killers can charm their way like that...' Sid paused in mid flow. 'Matheson, how did you know I was here?'

'I am a detective.'

'A retired one. Go on; how did you find me?'

'Your mate Andy Ikes has been hanging around the Simpson house, and when he's not there he's been watching outside Dr von Essen's place. The police moved him on yesterday afternoon. Anyway, Andy said you were on this upper class Surrey pub crawl so I followed.'

'Why – what do you want?'

'What I want is your co-operation.'

Sid's facial expression was even more ferret like. 'What's it worth?'

'It's worth privileged information that I will give to you now if you play ball.'

'That depends what you want.'

'I would like you to keep an eye on the Lakeview Hotel. I can't do this myself. My boy's too busy with regular work and the police aren't interested.'

'All right, I'm there for another night. What do you want to know?'

Matheson noticed that two of the locals had moved within earshot. He stood up. 'Come on, not in here, come outside.'

The bright sun was almost blinding as they emerged from the dark interior of the pub. Matheson smiled. 'I'll give you a clue; or rather, a conundrum. This investigation has something to do with the old man up there.' He pointed skyward.

'I don't believe in God,' Sid was dismissive.

Matheson grinned again. 'I'm talking about someone else's god.'

'What are you on about?'

'Work it out for yourself.'

They crossed the road and stood on the edge of the green.

'I played cricket here once,' said Sid. 'The Street against the TV execs. Funny ground though – all hills and bumps.'

'Who won?'

'Who won? We did of course.'

118

'Now, Sid, to business. If you are going to be an unofficial sniffer dog you'd be much better off working for me. If it all comes good there'll be a nice little backhander that you won't have to declare to the taxman.'

Sid looked around and returned to Matheson with an even shiftier look. 'Go on.'

'You want information. First, Henry Preston never killed anyone in his life...'

'Yeah, but DI Le Bois...'

'Phil Le Bois is near to a nervous crack up. Superintendent Fox has sent him on a month's leave while they sort out some sanity into the investigation.'

'But Le Bois is a good bloke, I thought. He caught the Crawley rapist and the Bognor drug bust and the Sussex car jackers...'

'Yes, I know. Straightforward stuff he's good at, but this is baffling; esoteric is what my daughter-in-law calls it, and the case has just about tipped Phil off his trolley.'

'All right, how much is this backhander?'

'The Simpson family are offering twenty thousand pounds for information leading to a conviction. I personally will see that your share is paid in a brown envelope.'

'Matheson, this sounds really dodgy. What do you want me to do?'

'Keep an eye on the Lakeview and surroundings. I want information relating to twin brothers aged mid to late fifties, name of Larranaga. Secondly I want to talk to a man calling himself Ricardo Standfast...'

Sid smiled happily. 'That's easy, he's staying there now.'

Matheson returned to his car and phoned Greta. Unusually for her Greta was excited and Matheson was hard put to get a word in.

'Frank, I've just received the translation of that message...'

'It is in Welsh then?'

'Very much so. My friend has given me a verbatim translation. What it says is this.

My boys say they have seen you at this place. I need to speak to you about old times.'

'Greta, is that boys plural?'

'Definitely – it didn't say twins but we could have hit a hole in one. That is what you golfers say?'

'Correct, although I've never gone close to one myself. Now my

119

news. That little weasel, Sid Everett, says the man Standfast is staying at the Lakeview now. He's some explaining to do.'

'Frank, not so fast. Remember MI6 have told the police to stand off. If this man is working for them we don't want to blow his cover.'

'I am well aware of all that. Believe me, I shall approach this assignment with pussy foot stealth. But I do intend to watch the man and see who he talks to.'

The wall of straw bales was three parts complete. The brothers concealed the effect by spreading a large blue tarpaulin over the whole house. No one unfamiliar with this remote site would realise that within the neat rick of straw was what had once been a dwelling. Together, they sealed the entrance with four small bales wedged tightly and concealing the doorframe.

They stood back and admired their handiwork. 'Two more trips should finish it,' the man said to his brother. 'Should go up like a bomb and be all done before the fire fighters even reach this place.'

'We've just got to find the warrior that Mother specifies. Then we've got to bring them here. None of it will be easy.'

'We'll do it, we've got to, we're on a sacred mission. But we don't bring them here until we're ready for sacrifice.' He glanced at his watch. 'Look at that, it's seven-thirty and I've still got two jobs to do.'

Frank Matheson signed the register and waited while his bag was collected and taken to his room. The Lakeview Hotel appeared to have few guests, although their staff seemed busy dusting and vacuuming as well as shifting furnishings. Matheson gathered they were preparing for a plush stockbroker's wedding tomorrow, Saturday. He found a comfortable chair in the lounge, opened a newspaper and settled down to listen and watch.

It turned out to be a long wait. Matheson was not too worried about that. Years of this work had inured him from boredom. He had a mental picture of Mr Standfast, based on the description that Steve Simpson had been given by the bottled gas employees. Swarthy, with a Saddam moustache, he'd been told: not much to go on there. An Argentinian with a knowledge of Welsh – so presumably one from that bleak region opposite the Falklands. That aroused a distant memory from the days when he was a Detective Inspector working his patch around Portsmouth's Royal Navy dockyard. Could it be the same man?

Age was definitely catching up with him, or at least a strong call of nature was. Times were when he could have handled a stakeout for hours on end and not wanted to relieve himself, but at age seventy-four the body had other ideas. He was achieving nothing sitting here. He rose to his feet and went in search of the men's toilet. As he was in the process of re-zipping his trousers the door of a cubicle opened and a man emerged. He was dressed in a nice tailored blue suit typical of a denizen of well-off Surrey. But there was nothing obviously Home Counties about his features. Frank saw a swarthy, dark-haired man with a bristling moustache. Here was certainly Mr Standfast, and Matheson knew him. Had he not been thinking of the man ten minutes ago? He watched as the other, seemingly oblivious of him, washed his hands and dried them under the hot air blower.

Matheson spoke, keeping his voice to little more than a whisper. 'Blow me down – Costas the spy.'

The other turned quickly and stared. His face transformed into a smile. 'Mr Matheson, I thought it might be you. Always I hope we might meet again. You were kind to me then, which is more than I can say about your Navy.'

'They were a bit rough with you...'

'Rough – what do you mean by rough. Blindfold – no sleep – made to kneel for hours...'

'Well, you shouldn't have been nosing around a dockyard facility when our two countries were at war.'

Standfast shrugged. 'You English are always at war – always you invade other people's lands. Then it was our Malvinas, now it is Iraq – what changes?'

'We could argue all night about who did the invading in your case. How are you these days, Costas old son?'

The other smiled again. 'I saw the name Matheson in the register and I guess we may be on the same side this time.' He quickly walked along the line of cubicles checking the doors. 'All is clear. Mr Matheson, if you are doing here what I suspect you are we should talk about it. I suggest we walk outside along by the yacht club.'

'Good thinking – lead on.'

'It's going to be quite a day out,' said Steve. 'Apart from Gerry and Dolly, we're going to have a whole tribe of Dolly's relations. What is the collective noun for a lot of Australians in one place?'

Jeremy replied. 'I should think that would be: an "attitude" of Australians.'

Steve called up the stairs. 'Emily are you ready? We're off in ten minutes.'

This was Friday morning and the day of the family's visit to the archaeological dig. The remains of the Luftwaffe aircraft were in a field near the village of Walderton a few miles north of Chichester Harbour. Steve was flattered that the local television station had remembered that Emily was the daughter of two Olympic medallists.

John-Kaj had appeared, washed and dressed and looking rather smug. Of his sister there was still no sign.

Steve turned to his wife. 'Go and see what Emily is up to and bring her down. I want to be on time for once.'

Emily was peering over the banisters. 'Is it going to be hot today? Do I wear my new sundress or jacket and jeans?'

'Jacket and jeans,' said Kirsten. 'It could be muddy.'

Steve studied his watch and made an exasperated groan.

They reached the dig site on time. Steve was grateful to find that the last mile had been marked with crude signs right up to the point where they had bumped down a long farm track. In the field stood a small mechanical digger surrounded by a crowd of people. He parked the car on a grass verge, and the four of them walked across to the scene. Gerry and Dolly left the group and came to greet them.

'Hello,' said Gerry. 'They've started the day's excavation, and we should be seeing what's left of the cockpit in an hour or so.' He looked like an excited schoolboy.

Emily was jumping up and down while pointing. 'Look – that's Sam Wantage. Wow, I'm going to be on the telly again!'

Steve had already noticed a man shouldering a heavy camera followed by a colleague with a sound boom. Strolling in front of them, smartly dressed and balding was the genial Sam Wantage. With Sam was an old man dressed in a long coat, his head topped with a soft felt hat. The two men stopped in front of the camera while Sam began what was clearly the interview.

'That's our German friend,' said Gerry. 'Spry old fellow – a lot fitter than me.' He sighed. 'How young we were in those days – it seems like yesterday.'

'Is this his plane?' asked Emily.

'Yes, he was the pilot. He baled out – broke a leg on landing and spent the rest of the war in a prison camp. That's why his English is so good.'

Emily looked troubled. 'Did you shoot him down?'

122

'No, but if he'd crossed my gun sight I'd have killed him without the slightest regret, in fact I'd have celebrated.'

'Why?' Emily's lower lip trembled.

Good, thought Steve – maybe she's learning something.

Dolly spoke. 'Gerry, tell her about the Heinkel.'

Gerry shook his head. The old man seemed to have visibly aged in the ten seconds.

'Go on,' Dolly persisted. 'It needs telling and it'll be an object lesson for this young lady.'

Gerry took a deep breath; suddenly he smiled. 'In the early days of that battle I admit I was scared. I even wet my pants a couple of times. I kept wondering what the hell I was doing there. How had I come to be flying and fighting? Then something happened...' He half turned away as he fumbled in his jacket pocket finally producing a white handkerchief. 'You see I loved flying and I loved my aircraft...'

'Was it a Spitfire?' John-Kaj interrupted.

'Oh no, boy. It was a Hurricane – lovely aeroplane, steady as a rock could soak up punishment and if she was damaged the fuselage was mainly wood and canvas; the boys could fix it again overnight, and she'd be good to fight again next day. Spitfires were great too, but you couldn't fix them that way when they broke.'

'Gerry,' Dolly glared, 'get on with it.'

'Oh yes, you mean the Heinkel. It was in late August 1940 – can't remember the date but it's in my logbook. I don't suppose the technicalities will mean anything to you people but it changed me for ever.' Gerry looked troubled.

Dolly glared at him. 'Just tell them.'

'We'd been in action – lost two of our chaps. I only had a few seconds of ammunition left and then I saw this Heinkel One Eleven. I hated that aeroplane – resented it being here – looked like a big fat slug. Then something flashed through my mind: a vision I would call it.' Gerry was mumbling as they all strained to hear him above the distant chatter and the wind in the trees. 'You see, you have to blank out everything when you're fighting. Yes, everything connected to the ground and ordinary life. If you don't have a total fixation you're very soon dead. But for just a fraction of a second I saw them: the Goldman children. One of them was Emily, like you, and her brother Joe. I played with them when I was a child in Shropshire; their parents ran the jewellers shop in our street.'

Steve watched awed as he saw Gerry dab at the tears. All of his audience were silent; Emily stared at the ground while John-Kaj looked mesmerised.

The old man spoke again and now his voice was clear as if he had returned physically sixty years. 'I knew then that I had to kill that Heinkel. There's no logic to this, you'll think it sounds crazy, but I just knew that if I smashed that aeroplane then we would win and the Germans wouldn't come and kill Emily and Joe and Mr and Mrs Goldman.' Gerry stopped and turned away from them staring skyward.

Dolly put her arm through his. 'Tell them what happened – everything.'

'I knew I was higher and faster than him and he was dodging and weaving. I overhauled him, turned and took him head on. It was the only way. I had hardly any ammunition but I knew that if my guns didn't do the job I would take him out and me with him.'

'But you didn't – you're here,' said Emily.

'Yes, I'm here and that's good.'

Dolly stroked her husband's arm. 'The Heinkel exploded; fell apart in the air all the crew killed.'

'But what happened then?' John-Kaj spoke.

'I flew back to base, and then I drank a couple of beers. But I was cured of funk. I knew what I was fighting for and Emily..?'

'Yes?'

'Tell that teacher of yours that I knew what I was fighting for and it was worth it.'

The children were sombre for about five minutes. Then the whole party watched the dig. Emily was unimpressed, but John-Kaj was fascinated as he watched the bits of metal that emerged, some in an amazing state of preservation. Sam Wantage and his TV crew had interviewed Gerry and Emily. Then she had stood with Gerry and the old German while their pictures were taken for the local press. Finally, at midday, Steve and Kirsten had collected the children together and said farewell to Gerry and Dolly. Gerry by now was in deep and surprisingly convivial conversation with the German. The family drove home for lunch.

Emily and John-Kaj were still talkative when they reached home. Both children were in a state of suppressed excitement and were counting the hours until the six o'clock local TV news. Sam Wantage had assured them that the dig with their interviews would be featured.

The Prestons were not happy. Liz had driven Harry to the police station to answer his conditions of bail. Although the hostile police inspector was nowhere to be seen it had been a humiliating experience in front of total strangers.

'They still won't let Harry go home to Tilford,' said Liz. 'I don't know how long we can go on imposing on you like this.'

Kirsten was impatient. 'You're not imposing; you are our friends and welcome guests. You will stay here until this nonsense is sorted.'

At six o'clock all were gathered around the television. The Walderton excavation was the third item. The scene in the field with the mechanical digger opened the feature. Gerry and Dolly were shown, with the German staring at the objects extracted from the hole in the ground. Dolly's relations explained how they had flown half way round the world to be there. Following this, Sam Wantage had interviewed the German veteran who told of the day he was shot down and his narrow escape by parachute into the arms of the local Home Guard. He spoke good English, and Steve thought that for a German, the man had a passable sense of humour.

Then Emily appeared with John-Kaj and the interview began.

SAM WANTAGE: "Emily, I gather you are something of an athlete and a sailor?"
EMILY: "I'm running the 800 metres for Southern schools and I'm in the RYA national squad for Cadet dinghies."
SAM: "Did you learn something today from these airmen?"
EMILY: "I think Mr Pembelty is a very brave man and we should all learn what he did for us."
SAM: "I think we would all agree with you there. What are your goals for the future?"
EMILY: "I want to sail in the Olympics like my mum and dad did and be famous like my mum is in her country. Then perhaps I might become a pilot like Mr Pembelty but not be in any wars or nothing like that..."
SAM: "Oh the exuberance of our youth..." (turning to camera) "If the youngsters today have all the confidence of Emily here we've nothing to worry about."

At this point the camera switched to Gerry and Dolly. Gerry repeated his story about the Heinkel and his split second vision of his childhood Jewish friends. He concealed his emotions well and the story gained

125

in power with the telling. Lastly, Gerry and the German shook hands with the two children standing beside them. That was the end of the Walderton feature. The next item was about some planning dispute in Crawley. Emily scrambled with the remote control and ran the preset recording.

Steve and Kirsten looked at each other. 'What arrogance,' said Kirsten.

'All that stuff about your mother being famous and not your father,' Steve gave her a mock glare.

'Well, it's true,' said Emily. 'Sailing is big time in Denmark.'

'Exuberance of youth and our future safe in the hands of the young – I've never heard such a lot of piffle,' Steve replied.

'Well, I won't ask too many questions,' said Matheson. 'Knowing what you people are like I wouldn't get much for my money.'

'No need to ask questions, Mr Matheson,' Costas replied. 'Tell me where you come into this problem.'

'Answers in a minute. Last time I saw you was when we handed you to MI6 and they slung you out of the country. Now I'm told on good authority that you are back working for MI6. Explain the contradiction please.'

'We say we have a just cause with the Malvinas but war is stupid. Two stubborn dictators: our general and that woman of yours – so many young men killed for nothing, when all could be solved in peace.'

'All right, we've heard all that a hundred times – so why are you here?'

'I think you know that already, Mr Matheson.' Costas' stare was inscrutable,

'Typical spook,' Matheson muttered. 'All right, I take it there are crazy people killing innocent victims in pursuit of some religious cult. Our profiler has worked that out already. We also suspect that there is a link to this benighted corner of posh-toff Surrey. And I have something of yours that I will give back to you if you play ball with my investigation.'

'What could you have that is mine?'

Now Matheson laughed. 'All in good time. Twins – boys. What have they to do with this?'

'You know too much.' Costas's tone was hostile.

'Now come on,' Matheson retaliated in kind. 'MI6 are refusing to co-operate with the local police. I am conducting an independent investigation in collaboration with our top profiler. Now it's like this, old mate. If we don't share information quickly I would bet good money that more innocent people will wind up with smashed heads.'

They had paused beside the gate leading into Branham Sailing Club. Matheson's new companion seemed deep in some world of his own. 'Very well, I will share some knowledge with you on condition that you do not communicate it to the regular police.'

'The regular police are getting nowhere and they wouldn't listen to me anyway. But I will report to Dr von Essens – she's the profiler.'

Costas nodded. 'Very well, first you may call me Standfast or Costas, but my real name is Juan Gryffydd – that is John Griffith in your language.'

'Welsh?'

'My great-grandfather was Welsh but I am also a loyal son of Argentina.'

'Were you expecting a message in Welsh?'

Costas, or Gryffydd, for the first time showed some emotion. 'How could you have known that?'

'I know all sorts of thing – I am a detective.' Matheson pulled out his wallet and handed over the slip of paper with the original message.

'You have no right to steal my personal letters.' Costas looked more anxious than affronted.

'We have every right. We are investigating four linked murders, and you have been acting suspiciously. MI6 have ordered our police to back off. But I am working for Dr von Essens and I don't give a monkey's for MI6 or your Argy secret police...'

'Can you read this?' Costas was definitely worried.

'No, but we know a man who can and in fact already has. So who are the two boys and who is it who wants to talk about old times? And this had better be good, because spook or not, you give me a truthful explanation or you are in deep shit.'

The brothers were jubilant, their great problem solved. Mother, the Powerful One, was also pleased, and that delighted the man more than anything else could in this decaying world.

He opened the newspaper and spread it on the table. 'You see, we could hardly have found two more suitable choices. I doubt any of our brethren around the world will better these two.'

'I agree with you – good boys. I always knew you would succeed. Now tell me of the preparations.'

'We finished them two days ago,' his brother answered. 'It's a good site in wooded country but open to the rays of the Power. So we can start the final conflagration with a burning glass. I know our friends in America and in Peru are doing the same.'

'What of the interfering German woman?'

'Mother dear, I feel if the woman had discovered anything we would have had the police looking towards us. But they have not.'

Mother nodded. 'We are so close to the day now I think we can ignore her. The police are stupid, especially that inspector in Sussex. I really believe that the Power has addled his brain.'

There was one thing left that still worried him. 'There is a man staying in the Lakeview. We believe he is a Spanish speaker, and when I drove home last night I saw him by Branham Lake talking to the same old man we've seen before.'

Mother only chuckled. 'He is a relation of ours, one of our cousins from the Chubut Valley, but he is not to be trusted; he is not a friend. Do not worry, he will learn nothing of our secrets and when I meet him I will speak in his native patois.'

'You mean Welsh, mother?'

'Oh yes. For six years I lived in Chubut and spent a year in the Cymraig boarding school in Puerto Madryn.'

'I know that, mother. You told us before, but I did not know that you learned the language.'

'I know twenty languages. My boys, if there is still time you should learn them. The Power is merciful towards those who strive for knowledge. With such knowledge we may conquer the world.'

'I've got to hold my hand up, Greta.' Matheson looked rueful. 'It seems you're right. These sun-worshipping nutters are looking to do something spectacular on five continents. Costas says his intelligence service is watching three groups in South America, and of course there's others in the States as one would expect.'

'Why is he here?' Greta asked.

'That is the weirdest thing of all. I don't know what to believe.'

'That's for me to judge,' said Greta.

'This is the bit that I'm not to divulge to the regular police. MI6 have a block on it so Costas is taking a chance talking to me.'

'He must have amazing confidence in you. You say you know him from the past.'

Now he laughed. 'Believe it or not I arrested him for spying. That was in '82 during the Falklands shindig. He's grateful because I rescued him from the Navy who'd been giving him a rough working over.'

'We could hardly blame them for that; the Navy had men fighting and dying. He's asking a lot if we're not to report to the police. Neither of the forces involved seem to be getting anywhere.'

'I know. Le Bois has been sent on leave. His superintendent says the man's storming around like a castrated rhinoceros.'

'All right,' said Greta. 'Then if anything goes wrong MI6 will take the rap. So what is your friend doing here?'

'You will tell me I'm a cynic. Costas says the high priest cum co-ordinator of all this murderous lunacy is based right here somewhere in the UK.'

'I agree,' Greta sat back grim faced. 'I'd already deduced that myself.'

'Have you and all.'

'Every program I've set up and everything I've learned from overseas points to the epicentre of this movement being in the Southern counties of England. Doctor Fulzeimer says there are references to a leader, a sort of priestess – "the All Powerful One" who allegedly lives in the UK.'

Matheson had to agree. 'That's what Costas said. That's why he's here, and the good news is that he's set up a meeting with one of them.'

'Will he confide in you when he does?'

'Highly unlikely. We can only hope the spooks will do so when the time comes.

CHAPTER 15

'I don't think there'll be much sailing today,' Steve said. The thought was unnecessary as they could all see the broad waters of Branham Lake gleaming mirror-like in the warm sunshine. Around the edges the treetops were still, and not a zephyr touched the water.

'What are we going to do?' John-Kaj spoke for both children who were staring at their dinghy.

'We'll go into the clubhouse and see if Jane can make us a few things for a picnic.' Kirsten, decisive as ever, had taken command.

'I ought to go for a training run,' said Emily, 'but I haven't brought the right shoes.' She stared moodily at the tiny flipflops on her feet.

'Nothing so energetic,' said Steve. 'It's too hot. Your mother is right. Let's rustle up something to eat and then drive over to the Little Lake and have a nice relaxing family time.'

'I'll put on weight,' said Emily.

'Stop whingeing, girl,' said her mother. 'You can run it off the whole of next week.'

Steve drove the Volvo along Lakeside Lane and out onto the main road. Six minutes later they were stopping in the car park beside Branham Little Lake. Steve and Kirsten had discovered this tiny piece of water the previous year, and had been entranced. Boating activity was banned here, the whole place being a designated nature reserve. The Lake lay in a hollow surrounded by heather and pine tree covered hillsides. Today, in the sunshine, the water and its surrounds had a special magic and the children soon forgot their disappointment at missing sailing.

Kirsten spread a large blanket on the sand by a little inlet in the bulrushes. Helped by the children she began to spread out plates and cutlery plus the sandwiches, pies and crisps. 'I've promised Jane that we'll wash up all these plates and bring them back next Saturday,' she said. 'Any breakages come out of your own money.'

'Does that include me?' Steve replied as he set up his folding chair.

'Too right it does.'

'Then we shall all have to be careful.'

'Dad's asleep,' said Emily. Steve had relaxed into his garden chair and his head was definitely nodding.

'No I'm not.' He looked up at them. 'It's having you two around – you drain all the energy out of your poor parents.'

'Can we go for a walk?' Emily asked.

'Of course, good idea,' Kirsten replied. 'Walk round the lake and see how much water is running through the dam.'

'Are you coming with us?'

'No, we'll stay here – you go, both of you.' Kirsten waved to them as they set off in the direction of the stone dam.

The children walked round the lake past the warden's house and along the foot of the dam wall. Water was sluicing through the gate and tumbling down into the brook below.

'Harry told me they drained both these lakes once. It was during that war that Mr and Mrs Pembelty keep banging on about.' Emily addressed her brother with an air of authority she hoped would impress.

'Why did they do that?' asked John-Kaj.

'To stop the Germans finding their way around the sky. Harry said it was marked on their maps.'

'On their charts you mean.'

Emily glared at her brother. 'All right, charts then – clever clogs. Come on let's walk all the way round.'

The sandy track ran alongside the water a few feet above the shoreline. They sat for a while on one of the little park benches, and saw a lady watching a spaniel swimming, both children laughing as the little dog shook its wet coat all over the devoted owner.

'Come on,' said Emily.

They walked on until they came to a parting of the ways. On the right the path led deep into the marshy nature reserve and the little wooden causeway that led back to other shore. Emily ignored this and looked towards the wide track that led into the tightly packed firs of the forestry plantation.

'Let's go down there for bit,' she said. 'I've never been that way.'

'It looks spooky,' John-Kaj replied but there was a grin on his face.

'I'm not frightened of ghosts and anyway it's daylight. Come on, let's explore.'

They walked on down the track. It was rutted with signs that a heavy tyre vehicle had passed that way not long before. The trees to either side were densely planted and neither of them felt inclined to plunge into their dark interior. A few hundred metres and the track became soft and boggy with wide puddles. Emily, carrying her sandals, padded barefoot through the morass. John-Kaj removed his trainers likewise and followed, complaining.

'Shut up a minute and listen,' said Emily.

She froze and gripped her brother's arm. They could both hear it distinctly now: the drumming of a powerful diesel engine. 'There's a big tractor coming,' said Emily. 'Come on into the trees – hide!'

A minute later and they saw it: a massive, green-coloured tractor with four heavy treaded wheels, towing a long trailer. 'It's a John Deere, a big-un, and look who's driving – it's Ed, Mr Grogan from the garage over there.' John-Kaj pointed towards the outline of the King's Ridge. 'Shall I give him a wave.'

'No – no way – hide!' Emily was not sure why, but suddenly she had an overwhelming urge to be away from this gloomy place, and above all she didn't want them to be seen by Ed Grogan. She knew she wasn't making sense. Ed was a large gloomy man who did odd jobs around Branham Sailing Club. He spoke in monosyllables and grumbled about the club's children.

She kept hold of her brother until the tractor was not only out of sight, but until they could no longer hear the engine. Emily breathed a sigh of relief; she still didn't know why she had been frightened but she wanted to be away from here and back at the picnic with Mum and Dad. At that moment something walked across her bare foot and then rubbed against her leg. Startled, she looked down to see a dishevelled black cat, its coat splashed with mud.

Both children smiled, and Emily bent down to stroke the furry creature. 'Hello puss – where have you come from?'

The cat mewed and rolled on its back. Emily was aware enough to notice that the creature was male and entire. On impulse, she knelt down and picked up the cat, cradling it in her arms.

'Let's take it home,' said her brother.

Emily was tempted but good sense told her no. 'Mum wouldn't like it and the poor thing's probably got a home somewhere around here.'

'How do you know that?'

'Because he's so friendly, and look.' She pulled back some fur to reveal a well-worn tartan flea collar.

She replaced the cat on the ground. 'Goodbye puss.' She pulled again at John-Kaj's arm. 'Come on, you. Shoes on again – let's get back to the picnic.'

The family drove home in high spirits. For Kirsten it had been a day to remember. It was so rare to have all her family together relaxing and enjoying themselves just for the sake of so doing, with no organised activity to intrude on the day. Tomorrow was Sunday, and once more the whole family would be together on *Traveller* while they took the boat for a trip down Chichester Harbour and then back to her home mooring at Itchenor.

On arrival at Firs Farm they found Liz and Harry busy weeding the vegetable plot in the garden.

'You don't have to do that – you're our guests,' Kirsten had protested.

'No,' said Liz. 'This is by way of a farewell present. With a bit of luck we'll be back in our own house on Monday evening.'

'That's great, but what's changed?'

'It's this letter,' Harry replied. 'It came in the post after you'd started for Branham. We've a magistrate's hearing on Monday and our solicitor says it should be a formality. All charges dropped, no bail required – we can go home.'

'Oh, that's fantastic,' Kirsten hugged both and then stood back laughing in relief. 'I tell you though, in any other circumstances we'd have welcomed you. We don't really want you to go but I'm so happy for you.' She ran across the lawn to find Steve and the children.

'Thank God for some good sense at last,' said Steve. 'But it may only be the start of their troubles long term.'

'I know,' Kirsten felt sombre. 'People will talk – no smoke without fire and all that sort of bullshit.'

'That's exactly it,' said Steve. 'We've got to rely on Frank and Greta to catch the real killer. If they can't, I don't see the police getting anywhere.'

They both walked across to where their two guests were still busy digging and weeding. 'You do know,' Steve spoke, 'you know that you can rely on our full support in the weeks to come.'

'I know that,' Harry replied. 'You're such good people. I don't know where we'd have been without you. I tell you something else. That awful man Le Bois had been mooching around the village pestering your neighbours.'

'I hope they told him where to go.'

'Your Group Captain Pembelty did. He was so abusive that Le Bois tried to arrest him for threatening a police officer. Old Pembelty told him to shove off as he knew Le Bois was on leave and off duty. Well, Le Bois didn't like that one bit.'

Steve groaned. 'What is wrong with Le Bois? He's like a dog on a false scent. Surely to God he must know you've nothing to do with any of those murders.'

'Not a bit of it, Pembelty says the man lost his cool completely and shouted that I'd murdered my own children and that he was going to find their bodies.'

Steve had an idea. 'Harry, have you considered talking to your solicitor? You must now have good grounds for an action for slander, particularly as the man was shouting his mouth off when he was on police leave.'

'No. I don't want to spin this thing out any more. I want the truth discovered – nothing else.'

'I will do it – it means nothing to me,' the man spoke to his brother. He was concerned; he had to admit it. His brother was showing weakness at a time when success was almost within their grasp. 'I have no soft spot for this child, in fact I've always disliked her. The girl is insolent to her elders and richly deserves her fate. There can be no turning back now and anyway Mother, the All Powerful, has named her.'

His brother nodded. 'If it's got to be done we'll do it, but I can't agree about the girl's manners. I've seen her sailing, and she seems a nice happy kid.'

The man thought for a moment. 'If it helps I will see that the child is drugged before we fire the house.'

'That I agree with – thank you, brother.'

Sunday began badly for the Simpson family. Their arrival at Chichester Marina was met by an unfriendly reception. Steve was cornered by a series of angry boat owners wondering why their engine overhauls were incomplete.
Steve used all his tact and diplomacy to cool the situation. His chief engineer was ill and had been off work for over a week, he explained. The mechanics, and even some office staff, were struggling to complete the jobs on time but Mr Terring was the man with specialist knowledge of all the different makes of engine, and until he returned to work the difficulties would remain.

'I can't understand this. Half those people are threatening to leave us and go over to the shop over there and I can't say I blame them. Personally, I'm fed up with the engineering side of the business. It's profitable but without Peter Terring we'll be in deep shit.'

'Have you spoken to Peter,' asked Kirsten.

'I can't, he's vanished. All we've had is an email saying he's ill. He won't answer phone calls, and we sent someone round to his lodgings and he wouldn't come to the door. In fact the guy reckoned the place was deserted.'

'Has he been offered a better job?' asked Kirsten.

'Running out on us won't do him any good long term. We hold his employment and social security documents.'

They noticed a diminutive figure waving from the far end of the dock. 'Hi there, Greta,' Kirsten called. 'Were you looking for Steve?'

Greta von Essens tripped along the pontoon looking breathless. 'I've been looking all over for you people,' she said. 'I've news.'

'Now you're here you had better come with us on *Traveller*,' said Steve. 'You can tell us your news there.'

An hour later Steve and his crew were anchoring *Traveller* off the sandy beach at East Head. The anchorage was already crowded with boats swinging at different angles to the wind and tide. Steve needed all his skill and concentration to find the exact spot to drop the ship's main anchor. At forty-five feet length *Traveller* was by far the largest sailing yacht in the anchorage, but with a mere four feet in draft it was possible to anchor within swimming distance of the beach. It was close to low water with very little current running. The children had already donned their swimming costumes. Kirsten gave permission for them to bathe, and within minutes they had dropped into the water and swum ashore. They watched the pair of them set off round the headland towards West Wittering.

The adults remained sitting in the central cockpit drinks in hand. It was peaceful but the tensions were still there. Steve watched the children out of sight; then he turned to Greta. 'I think it's time for your news.'

'I've been wondering how much to tell you,' said Greta. 'But I think we owe you some explanations in view of what happened to this yacht and the police persecution of your friends.'

'We feel a sort of connection,' said Steve. 'Linda Zeigler's funeral is tomorrow. Emily is among the kids who have been invited to go to the church.'

Kirsten spoke. 'We knew Simon Hexham, not well, but we met him at Branham, and of course, Arnold Evans. Are you certain that they were all killed by these mad people?'

'Yes, every case has the same characteristics. They were all

135

weather forecasters except for Evans and he controlled a world wide forecasting site. The profile fits in every case. I looked further afield and I find there have now been sixteen identical killings in different parts of the world.'

'Have you any idea who is doing it here?' Steve was becoming impatient. 'This is what affects us. Until those people are caught Harry and Liz won't be free from innuendo.'

'All right, this is all I can divulge at the moment. Please believe me this is a complex profile quite unlike anything I've done before. I've a good record of seeing into the minds of ordinary criminals both rational and in some cases deeply disturbed. In this case I thought I was making progress and Frank Matheson has proved an experienced ally – I'm glad you people brought him into the picture. This is my reading of the situation as I see it now.

'I'm convinced that all four of the murder victims knew their attacker. I am likewise convinced that all four killings are linked to the cycle of cult killings that are occurring throughout the world. As all four victims knew their attacker or attackers, it confirms that the centre of activity in the UK is right here, or at least within here and outer London.'

'I thought all cults were centred on the United States,' Steve was sceptical.

'No, this one is world-wide but Frank has met a South American intelligence operator, and he confirms the cult leader to be resident in this country and, to be more precise, in Southern England. This intelligence man has met her but that's all that Frank could extract from the man and he only got that far because this intelligence officer owed Frank a favour.'

'You say her,' said Steve.

'Yes, the driving force is female and her followers call her the All Powerful One. And that's the most that Frank could extract, and it fits my own profile. The spook turned really frigid after that, and Frank guesses he was told more than he was supposed to hear.'

Kirsten spoke as she looked out towards the shore. 'The kids are back. I can see them and it won't take five minutes for them to swim back out.'

'All right,' said Greta, 'I'll cut to the chase. You remember Jeremy Preston's information about a family called Larranaga. We thought we might have a breakthrough with that but it seems to be a dead end. You see there is good reason to suspect that at least one of the murderers has engineering skills. This garage still exists and it did once belong to a Spanish refugee, name of Larranaga. This man came here in 1939, and in 1957 he married a South American girl who was living locally during World War Two. They had two sons who worked in the business until Mr Larranaga died. The sons appear to have left the country and the business changed hands. It's run now by a local man named Edward Grogan. Surrey police can discover no fault with this man, although they have no record of where he lived before 1980.'

'Yes, we know this Grogan,' said Steve. 'He services the safety boat engines at Branham. He's surly brute and I've hardly exchanged a word with him in five years.'

There came a shout and a splashing noise and Emily appeared climbing the swimming ladder into the cockpit. 'Mum, Dad, why don't you go for a swim? It's lovely.' She shouted joyfully as she stretched out a hand to pull her brother over the side rail.

'All right, why not,' Steve laughed, relieved to have a distraction. He grinned at Kirsten. 'You too, love, and a swimming costume is a definite!'

'I know that,' she replied. 'We are in England – land of the self-conscious prudes.'

'I think this self-conscious prude will come with you. I need to cool off.'

The water was ice cold and took Steve's breath away for a few seconds. Once acclimatized, he found the salt water soothing to his arthritis, and the swim pleasurable, if leisurely. Kirsten was waiting on the sand for him as he crawled ashore. Together they walked hand-in-hand along the waterline to Snowhill Creek, now a trickle of water at low tide.

CHAPTER 16

Emily had never been to a funeral. This was not only a first time but very personal. Linda Zeigler was her teacher and Emily had been fond of her. Linda had been the one to encourage her running and her ambition to be a serious sports competitor. She found herself wiping away tears. It was hard for Emily to envisage her teacher in that wooden box carried so carefully by the grim-faced men.

The church was filled with people she knew. Her head-teacher, Mr Cotton, led other staff as well as twenty of her fellow pupils, all of whom had been close to Linda. As she looked around she saw others that she was less pleased to see: that pervert press photographer Ikes and that horrible policeman Le Bois. He was sitting not far from her across the aisle and he seemed to have no respect for the service or for Linda. He continually looked around, staring pointedly at every corner of the church and rudely at individuals.

Emily had not often been in a church and much of the service was unfamiliar territory. She felt puzzled as Linda's estranged Norwegian husband read the Bible lesson. The man was so obviously distressed and in genuine mourning. Why should that be? She wished she could understand adult behaviour. Her parents, so different in nationality and temperament, were devoted to each other in spite of a fifteen-year age gap and her mother's occasional tempestuous rages. So different from many of her school friends who were from one-parent families and seemed to think this was normal life. She knew she was lucky.

Much more upsetting was the last act; the walk to the graveside and the lowering of the box into that sinister hole. It was then that the full implications of the ceremony struck home for Emily. She wept without embarrassment, as did the other girls. She knew she was in the presence of death and she didn't understand.

It was a sombre group of children who returned to the school mini-buses and to some semblance of normal lessons. The memories from the funeral made her brood. Emily was both angry and offended when, in class, Ms Flotton had told them she had not attended the funeral because it was false and that there was no such thing as God. Somehow Emily still felt Linda's presence but only combined with an emptiness she had never felt before. She found relief when after lunch she was released for athletics practice. Along with three other girls who had been selected for the county team, they had been bussed to the training ground. Supervising the session was Mr Jones the P.E teacher. Jones was known to be grumpy; a fortnight ago it would have been her own coach, Linda.

She didn't enjoy the training. Mr Jones had very little idea of their regular routines, and in the end she was given permission to do circuits of the running track in her own time. She felt a little better doing this but could have done without the spectators at the far end where the footpath led from the town centre. She had been warned that some middle-aged men were drawn to the sight of young girls in running shorts and skimpy vests. Today it was starting to rain, and she saw no spectators apart from two who seemed different. One was an elderly woman who stood with a large man wearing a hooded jacket. Something about these merited a second glance each time Emily passed them. The old woman was scrawny and horrible, but there was something about the man that was vaguely familiar.

'We're ready to go home, Emily,' Jones called.

'Please, sir, just one more circuit,' she replied.

'All right, but make it quick.'

Emily ran at her regular pace for the first part of the circuit, now she began to concentrate on her sprint for the last section. She noticed that the old lady was now standing on the track. Emily was irritated; surely the old bat must know that this was just not done. She glanced back to see if Jones had noticed but she couldn't see him. As she moved to run round this human obstacle the old woman reached out a hand. Emily felt puzzlement, anger and then alarm as the woman caught hold of her bare right arm. Emily cried out as sharp finger nails bit into her flesh. She was forced to slide to a halt.

Then the old woman smiled at her. It was not a happy smile, not a friendly one, but it had an odd hypnotic quality. 'Hello, you're Emily aren't you?' The voice was soft almost sweet. 'I've been watching you run.'

'Please, please let me go.' Emily tried to break free. She struggled and fought, but now the man had joined them and stood behind her gripping both her arms. Emily panicked. She recalled everything she had been warned about, everything she had read. This happened to other children; surely it couldn't happen to her. Now she struggled and she screamed. The man tried to put a hand over her mouth but she snapped her head forward and sank her teeth into it. He swore and jabbed a fist in her stomach. She collapsed gasping for air, but she had heard his voice before and she knew it.

'Come this way, Emily,' said the old woman. 'I want you to have a word with someone who knows your father.'

The two pushed Emily away from the track towards the fringe of trees alongside the main road. Emily was desperate, she yelled again at the top of her voice, but she knew that little could be heard above the roar of nearby traffic. She struggled to break free, but the woman's grip was like a steel trap and there was something in that soft voice that dulled her resistance. A car was parked under the tree with a man standing by the open rear door. He walked towards her and she could see the hypodermic needle in his right hand. His face was familiar: she saw him every week and she knew his name.

'Steve, we've a problem.' An irritated Kirsten had waited two minutes for Steve to be connected to her from his office. 'My car won't start and I'm late to fetch the children from school.'

'What's wrong with the car?' Steve's voice was clear, but the background noise indicated that he was in the sailmaking workshop.

'I don't know, but I think it's the immobiliser. Nothing happens when I turn the key and now the battery is dead.'

'All right, don't worry. I'm nearly through here and I'll fetch the kids.'

'Oh, thanks, darling; I was getting desperate. I asked Dolly if she could go but she says Gerry drove off in their car and he's not back yet. She's a bit worried because the old guy was only going to his allotment and nobody's seen him there.'

'Much better I go and not Gerry. He's eighty six and still drives as if he's in a fighter plane.'

'Steve, I'm worried about Emily.'

'Why?'

'She was going to athletics practice straight after the funeral, and she always phones on her mobile when they finish. Today, nothing.'

'Probably the phone battery is flat.'

'Oh, I know, but with the car breaking down for no reason. It's just I've a bad feeling about this.'

Emily was not waiting at the school but Steve was told that the mini-bus was overdue in returning from the athletics track. He was puzzled more than alarmed but he turned the car around and drove to the sports ground two miles down the road. The mini-bus was still there. The sports teacher was standing among a group of his students. With him were two policemen and another character whom Steve recognised. It was the newspaper cameraman Ikes.

140

'It's Mr Simpson, isn't it?' The schoolteacher looked relieved. 'Emily's gone missing. Can you tell me – did you arrange for someone to collect her from here? She really should have gone to school first.'

'I've come looking for her,' said Steve. 'I've already been to the school.'

'I saw a girl get into a car over there. There was a woman and two men with her,' Ikes intervened 'But I'm not sure she went willingly. She's the one at your house that we thought was dead...'

'Can you describe these people?' Steve clung to hope. 'My wife did try to find someone in our village to collect Emily. You see her car won't start...' He knew he was starting to gabble.

'Car not starting?' It was the police constable who had now been joined by a colleague.

'Yes, she thought it might be the immobiliser,' Steve replied although what all this had to do with anything. 'Did anyone see this person who collected Emily?'

'I took some pictures,' said Ikes. 'It looked like it could be an abduction – a snatch.'

'Description,' said the policeman.

'Elderly bird, grey-haired, with two blokes. The old woman stopped the girl, and then she went with them, but it looked as if it was force.'

Steve tried to get to grips with this. 'I don't know anyone who fits your description.' He knew he was beginning to combine anger with panic. He glared at Ikes. 'Are you telling us that you stood by gawping while my little girl was abducted, and you are saying that you did nothing?'

The policeman intervened. 'Don't tell me, Mr Ikes, that you haven't a mobile phone on you. Why was it Mr Jones who had to report this and we only hear your version just this minute?'

The cameraman looked both sheepish and defiant. 'How was I to know this wasn't a legitimate pick up? It's not as if I know her. I thought her name was Rachel anyway. I don't know what the hell's going on around this place.'

Steve had had more than enough. 'Please, this is wrong – she would never willingly go with someone she didn't know...'

'Right,' the policeman interrupted, 'this is suspicious – I'm going to radio in a report straight away.' He looked at Ikes. 'Did you identify the car? We'll want the registration if possible and we'll need those pictures of yours. All of them.'

'Sorry,' said Ikes. 'But I didn't see the car properly. It was on the road the other side of those trees.'

'Why are you here?' The policeman glared at Ikes.

'I saw the girl at the teacher's funeral. She's connected in some way with that police suspect, Preston. So I followed her to this place. I've no other assignment at the moment, and anyway,' he looked indignant, 'I'm only doing my job, I'm not breaking the law.'

'All right, sir. Keep your cool, we may be grateful for your evidence.'

Steve could hardly take this in. He felt as if he was in a nightmare from which he must awake but could not. 'We have to do something!' he shouted. 'I must search for her. I must tell her mother. Oh, Emily, where are you?'

'Please, sir,' it was the second policeman speaking. 'We'll do everything we can, and there may be an innocent explanation…'

'But you don't believe that do you?' Steve stared at the man who looked shiftily at the ground. That told Steve enough. He climbed back into his car and began driving.

For an hour he drove down every road around the sports ground and beyond until, exhausted and sick, he returned to where he had started. Another car was already parked there with the owner standing beside it: Chief Superintendent Fox.

'Norman, thank God you're here. Have you any news of Emily?' Steve looked for hope in his friend's face and saw none.

'Steve, I'm so sorry,' Norman shook his head. 'We're treating Emily as a missing person. We're computer enhancing the pictures that the man Ikes took and there's no doubt Emily went with an elderly woman we can't identify. There's two other males in the frame but the shots are long-range and blurred.'

'Does Kirsten know yet?'

'We've a WPC with her now, but maybe you should go home, Steve. Just believe me that we are pulling out all the stops. We're treating this as major incident. All our resources are targeted on finding her. Just remember, Carol and I know Emily, so it's personal.'

Three cars were parked on the gravel by the front door of Firs Farm. One was a police panda car, a second belonged to his daughter Sarah and the other was Frank Matheson's. Steve could hardly remember a mile of the homeward journey. He had driven in a sick daze, only wanting to reach home and be with his wife.

Kirsten clung to him as soon as he entered the house. He could see that she had been crying. 'Sarah's upstairs looking after Johnny,' she said. 'Oh, Steve, darling, what can we do? Everyone likes Emily. Why would anyone want to hurt her?'

'We don't know that she has been hurt. Sweetheart, we must be strong,' Steve spoke gently as he ran his fingers through her dark hair.

'I rang Frank,' she said. 'He came straight here.'

'I know, I saw his car outside. Let's go and talk to him and see what he can do.'

Fox returned to his office. He had done his best to put on a brave face when he encountered Steve Simpson. What could one say in this kind of case? It was true that teenage girls ran away from home all the time, and invariably they turned up a few days later, hungry and very chastened. In this case it was a certainty that Emily had been forcibly abducted in broad daylight. The photographic evidence was indisputable. He felt he was re-living the nightmare those years ago when that small boy had been snatched in similar circumstances. Despite everything they'd done, and every resource they had deployed, the child had been found dead. Would little Emily be found dead? Well, not before he himself died in the attempt to find her. He believed lessons had been learned from last time and he was heartened by the steely resolve that he detected throughout his command.

'Please, Sir.' Fox looked round to find a uniform WPC looking at him nervously.

'Sorry, Constable, I was miles away.'

'Sir, we've had another missing person alert, also from South Marshall. It's a Mr Pembelty.'

'That's a strange coincidence. Have you any details?' Fox tried to concentrate on this news, but his mind was filled with the face of young Emily.

'We're not treating it as suspicious. Mr Pembelty is elderly, sir. He's eighty-six. He drove in his car to an allotment he works a mile from his home, but he never arrived there, and nobody's seen his car.' The girl placed a printed report on the desk in front of him.

'Thanks, Constable. You know that name rings a bell. I'm not sure from where, but it'll come back to me. Keep me posted about this one, but the missing child has got to be the priority.'

'Yes, Sir, we understand that.' Like all of them the girl look strained. 'Oh, Sir, DI Le Bois wants a word.'

If it were not for all his other worries Fox would have sworn. 'All right, where is he?'

'He's waiting outside, Sir.' The girl looked at the floor. For a split second an understanding between the two of them went unspoken. It worried Fox that his officers should be openly laughing at a senior inspector behind his back. He suspected that the poor man was heading for a mental breakdown; he could see no humour in that.

'All right, ask him to come in.'

Fox braced himself. He knew that Le Bois had been given permission to return from leave due to the urgency of the situation. Fox had severe doubts about his subordinate's readiness for duty.

Le Bois bounded into the office brandishing a copy of the local paper. Fox doubted if his leave had done the man many favours. Le Bois looked tired and manic in equal proportions. 'Sir, read this.' He thrust an open page into Fox's hands.

HERO AND CHILD MEET IN ACT OF RECONCILIATION.

Fox read the headline and then glanced at the accompanying photograph. Now he had a shock. The picture showed two old men shaking hands with a child standing watching them, and that child was Emily Simpson. Fox read the rest of the article and now he understood. Emily Simpson had been selected to meet Gerald Pembelty, ex-Hurricane pilot and his Luftwaffe counterpart. This was surely too much of a coincidence. Two missing persons from the same village linked by a widespread piece of press publicity.

'I think that explains this case, Sir. Same people, same village. Old man's a pervert. He snatches the girl. He can't have gone far. Find him and we'll save the girl.'

'Has this Pembelty any form as a sex offender? What do you know about him and what's his marital status?'

'We're checking all that at the moment. But he comes from South Marshall, and there's something wrong with that village. I encountered this Pembelty and he threatened me...'

'Wait a minute, Phil,' Fox interrupted. 'That's why I remember the name Pembelty. I know you put in a report but you were on leave then – you'd no status.'

'Yes, Sir, but before that he impeded our enquiries into the suspect Preston. Refused point blank to let us set up a watching station in his house, and apart from that the Simpson girl's parents are dodgy.'

'May I remind you, Inspector,' Fox was angry now, 'Mr and Mrs Simpson are personal friends of mine from many years ago. Anyway, why should we regard them as dodgy?'

'The woman's a foreigner and what's more,' Le Bois lowered his voice in deep disdain, 'she's a nudist – flaunts herself openly. That's

144

got to be suspicious and she lets her two kids run around with nothing, on and that's disgusting.'

'Scandinavians have a different ethos to us and anyway, she's only in her own garden – nothing illegal in that.'

Le Bois shook his head in open disagreement. 'It all smells of typical paedophile behaviour to me.'

Fox heard a knock on the door followed by the appearance of DC McGregor. 'Sir, the officers are ready for your briefing.'

'Fine, Constable, I'll be right down.'

Emily had a headache. She'd had them once or twice before, but never anything like this one. She remembered vaguely that her half-sister Sarah had something called a migraine. But this must be worse because she couldn't open her eyes and she felt sick. Why could she remember Sarah when she wasn't sure who she was herself or where she was? The last thing she could recall was arriving at school, and that she was selected to go to a funeral. Whose funeral? Mrs Zeigler's funeral and she could remember nothing about it. So where was she now? She wasn't in bed at home, but on a nasty mattress. Could she be in hospital, or still in the school buildings? She must have been in an accident.

'Sam! One-oh-nine – he's behind you – break man – break!' An odd disembodied voice was shouting not far away and it didn't make a word of sense. Emily felt her world begin to dissolve into some sort of crazy fairground ride. Now she was falling; spinning into a black bottomless pit and she heard her voice in a silent scream.

'Frank, thanks for coming, we appreciate it,' Steve shook Frank Matheson's hand while Kirsten gave the man a hug.

They were all in the sitting room, including Sarah who had come downstairs. 'Johnny's in bed, and last time I looked in he was asleep,' she said. 'I've put Christine in the armchair beside him and I'll sleep on the floor. Nobody will touch either of them.' Sarah's eyes glinted – no one could doubt that she would defend her charges with her own life. 'Frank, what shall we do?'

'I've rung Greta von Essens,' he said. 'She's working through the night on this one but we've got to give her information; anything, however trivial, you three can think of. The police are taking this seriously, in particular Sussex and Mid-Southern...' Frank's voice faded and he looked embarrassed. Steve knew the man was recalling the little boy in that past tragedy. 'I know,' Frank's expression told its own tale. 'I remember, but they won't let lightning strike twice and trust Greta, she's good on this kind of case.'

The sitting room door opened, and into the room came a young policewoman carrying a mobile phone. 'I've had a call from my chief,' she said. 'We've a three counties alert and that will be nation-wide by tomorrow morning. He asks if you can give us up-to-date photographs of Emily and we'll distribute them everywhere and use them door to door.' She spoke softly and looked troubled. Despite the hell they were all suffering, Steve felt a crumb of sympathy for this young woman chosen for such a dismal role.

Kirsten responded instantly snatching Emily's framed photograph from the wall by the fireplace. She handed it to the WPC and began to pull open photo albums. 'Have we the pictures from the picnic on Saturday?' she asked.

'I'll fetch the camera,' Steve replied. 'They're still in it.' He rummaged for the tiny digital camera and handed it to the constable. 'There you are, take the whole thing; there's lots of pictures in it and they're recent.'

The telephone in the office was ringing. The sound made everyone in the room freeze. Was this news, good news? Maybe it was bad news – the worst. Kirsten looked at her husband. Steve was horrified at her wild-eyed stare and twisted features. 'Wait, I'll go,' she said.

She returned five minutes later, her walk listless and her face blank. 'That was Dolly Pembelty, old Gerry's gone missing. They've found his car abandoned at Petersfield.' Kirsten sank to the floor and buried her face in her hands. 'Dolly says he was only going to the allotments and…and…' she lifted her head. 'Dolly says the police looked at the car and the engine was tampered with. Oh, God, what's happening to us? All of us?'

The policewoman touched Steve on the arm. 'I think we should call a doctor for your wife; give her something to make her sleep.'

Kirsten, who had overheard, reacted with her old spirit. 'No, I will never take any bloody tranquilliser or fucking sleeping pill! I only want my little girl again.' She rolled onto the carpet and sobbed.

CHAPTER 17

'I have here the full report and assessment of Group Captain Pembelty.' Fox looked at Le Bois who was fidgeting in his chair near the front of the morning briefing. 'Mr Pembelty has had no contact with us apart from one conviction for speeding in 1967. He has absolutely no record of sexual deviancy. He is a married man with three children and seven grandchildren. His youngest son, Richard Pembelty, is a serving Navy officer. As you all know, Group Captain Pembelty is one of "The Few": a veteran of the Battle of Britain, and as such is something of an iconic figure. His disappearance would be the highest priority were it not for the missing child, Emily Simpson.' Fox regarded the faces in front of him. All were listening intently to every word. That would be pleasing for him had not the situation been so serious. He had now come to the defining moment.

'Gentlemen, Ladies, I know and I appreciate that none of you had much sleep last night. I myself have been in continuous contact with senior officers of our neighbouring forces and our own chief constable. I have also spoken with our civilian profiler who has a far deeper understanding of the criminal mind than I or any of us have. I can tell you now that Dr von Essens is of the firm opinion that these two disappearances are linked, and that there is no sexual motive. Following her advice, I have agreed that we should treat both as a single investigation.' Fox sat down.

The room remained hushed; only one person reacted. Fox watched as Le Bois stood up and stalked angrily from the room. The man was almost encouraging a charge of insubordination, but Fox ignored him. 'You've all been given your set tasks and your links. Chief Inspector Storey will co-ordinate uniform officers, and our armed response unit will be on call twenty four seven. Now go to it – God speed and good luck.'

Fox had more to worry about now. He knew for certain that a media furore would be breaking over his head within the hour. Andy Ikes' camera had been impounded for the moment, but that had not stopped the *Daily Banner* from producing a lurid front-page story with an artist's reproduction of the abduction as told by Andy.

Little Emily, winner of top young athletes award, was seen being dragged to a parked car ...

Thirteen year-old Emily, daughter of famous Olympic sailors ...

such a happy child say villagers...locals say sex pervert seen in the area...

That last had all the makings of newspaper scaremongering. Worse was to come as the press, popular and broadsheet, resurrected the memory of the little boy abducted and murdered on Fox's own patch. This hurt almost as much as the thought of Emily. The failure then was something that he could never forget and still hurt him as deeply as the day they had found the tiny body buried in that shallow grave in the woods.

Fox braced himself for the ordeal of the first press conference scheduled for midday. He knew that he must make a show of confidence. However sick he felt he must go home, shower and shave, and then dress in his best uniform.

Emily was cold, and this strange room was dark and it smelt damp and sour. She could make out a little from a tiny beam of light that shone down from a high point in the corner. From the position where she lay she could just touch a hard wall. She pulled her hand away. The brickwork was wet and slimy and smelt like rotting fish. Her head still hurt and now she felt an awful thirst. She craved water; how she longed for a lovely deep glass of clear water. Above all, she felt cold as she realised with a shock that she was still clad only in her running gear: shoes, shorts and vest. Now she heard a noise; something small was scuttling and sniffing as it came towards her. She could see it now; a creature a little bit like one of her gerbils but bigger. With a mixture of fascination and disgust she saw it was a rat. The creature moved towards her warily, then sat up staring with expressive eyes.

Emily found her disgust fading. 'Hello,' she whispered.

'Get away you dirty little bugger,' a voice shouted from some-where as a chip of loose cement arced across the light and spattered on the floor. The rat turned and vanished into the gloom.

Emily couldn't understand – where was she and how could she have come to be in this place? She began to cry. 'Mum, I want you, where are you?'

'Is that Emily?' The same voice sounded close by. Emily knew that voice, she had heard it before somewhere.

'Emily, it's me, Gerald Pembelty.'

'Mr Pembelty,' of course that was his voice. 'Oh, where am I? I want my mum and dad.'

'Emily, I don't know where we are. I don't know why we're here but we must both be brave. Be brave and we'll come through. Whatever's happening trust me, we'll win.'

'How are things with Kirsten and Steve?' Greta asked Frank.

'What d'you think – not good. I'm worried about young Kirsten; she's going to break soon and she won't take any medical help.'

'Have they got support?'

'Yes, Stephen's eldest daughter has taken charge. She's a trained nurse married to a surgeon. I remember her from the Lindgrune affair and I tell you one thing, she was also abducted then, with another girl. They weren't kids though; both were twenty, and they were held by bog-standard gangsters and only for a day or so. This mess is different.'

'Frank, it's more than different – it's become critical. Look here,' Greta held a sheaf of computer printouts. 'The sacrifices have started, first ones in the Philippines. An old veteran of the anti-Japanese resistance and his grandson were killed, both burned to death. In Florida, a survivor of the Battle of Midway died with a small girl aged eleven – both burned to death. Similar killing in Mexico twenty four hours later.'

'And the same people are doing this?'

'Yes. I believe this is the culmination. Sacrifice to the sun – a child and a warrior.'

'Greta, this is bloody horrible. Have you heard from MI6? I wish I knew what Costas was up to – he told me he was meeting one of them.'

'I'm submitting all my findings to the security services as well as the police. If the intelligence services know anything they will have to reveal it – and now.'

Matheson was troubled. He could not remain an objective investigator any more. His friends were facing the worst nightmare any loving family could. He stared coldly at Greta. 'Are you holding out on me? Is there something you're not telling me?'

'It's difficult, Frank. You are one of the finest criminal investigators any police force produced, but you're long retired. And this matter is personal isn't it?'

'Too right it is. That little Emily is a jewel of a kid. I feel as protective as if she's been one of my own. I've got to get her back to her people and in one piece.'

'That's just it, Frank. I cannot afford to have you charging around when the things are as delicate as I think they are.'

For DI Le Bois matters were also personal. The stupidity of senior officers never ceased to astound him. Chief Superintendent Fox had appointed him to this ancillary role. For God's sake: a record-keeping task that should be handed to uniform officers. To sideline a detective of fifteen years experience was as pointless as it was insulting. He had an understanding of this case that seemed lost to everyone in the division. They had released Preston, his prime and clear suspect, to kill again and just as he had warned, the consequences were now all too clear. Snobbery and political correctness had blinded his superiors. That village, South Marshall, looked so clean and innocent, so law abiding; so bloody English and middle class.

He came from a small community himself; the whole Island of Guernsey was a close community but wholly different. Deep down and secretly he detested the Southern English just as he detested these snobbish, curtain twitching gossiping villages like South Marshall. Behind their façade of respectability they harboured every vice and every sexual perversion. He had already toured the village making enquiries, and true to form, the locals had been tight-lipped and surly. They seemed indifferent to that Simpson woman's open indecency and as for allowing her kids to play naked – that was rank perversion, and the Simpson man did nothing to stop it.

Le Bois had failed to control his own wife. Had he tried harder and enforced his discipline she might not have run away taking their only child with her. If the Simpson girl had been abducted then probably she had it coming. And that offensive old goat Pembelty was the likeliest one to have snatched her. An elderly woman and two males, the photographer Ikes had said. Pembelty's wife was old and grey haired and she was Australian. Not that Le Bois was prejudiced, but the woman was clearly a suspect. More than likely Henry Preston had a hand in the business as well. He was known to associate with these people, and he had stayed with the Simpson family while on bail.

He knew he was gambling his career and possibly threatening his pension. But that was too bad – he had a point to prove. He had waited for nightfall and then selected the right magistrate: a stupid fat woman usually the worse for drink of an evening. She had signed his search warrant without a word of objection and then pushed him out into the night. Minutes later he was on the road heading for South Marshall. He was breaking the rules by not taking another officer as a witness but that was just too bad. If he was right he would return with the little girl, and tomorrow Fox would see sense and have her taken into care.

'They used to say lightning doesn't strike twice,' Sarah sat on the carpet hugging her shoulders – just like she did as a little girl, thought Steve.

'You mean the time you and Francine were kidnapped,' he replied.

'Yes, but that was different. The men we were with were thugs pure and simple.'

But that hadn't stopped them from coming within a whisker of raping and killing her. Steve had never felt so helpless as he did now; never suffered this feeling of paralysis, both mental and physical. Emily had not been born in this house, but she had come here as a child and everywhere, indoors and in the garden, was rich with her memory. He remembered each minute of their times together, he had visions of her sailing her dinghy, running in her school sports. He remembered Emily in her wilder moments, very like her mother.
An hour ago he had been drawn to look in her bedroom. Emily could have been there five minutes before. He saw the untidy bed, the floor covered in cast off clothing and shoes, the pop posters on the wall and the disordered little dressing table.

For a moment he had lost hope. 'Oh, Emily, where are you?' he cried aloud.

Kirsten could not stay still. She was distraught and she was angry. She had no idea who had taken her little girl, but she could imagine them. She could imagine the fat pervert and smell his stench. She could see herself scratching out his eyes before tearing him limb from limb. Given the opportunity she knew that she would kill the man and feel happy to do so. In the meantime she could not stand still, could not stay inside this house. She had brushed aside the protests of the woman police officer and then stormed out into the night. Light rain was falling, and the wind was rising. She hadn't bothered to put on a coat, and she didn't care. She had no idea where she was walking, and she didn't care about that either. She only knew she had to walk, had to burn off her misery in action. Doing something, anything, was better than sitting around indoors. Oh yes, she would kill the pervert when he was found, and he would not die speedily.

Kirsten was hardly aware of any direction as she walked through the village main street, but she must have instinctively turned up hill into Field Lane towards the Pembelty's cottage. The surface was slippery and the rain was blowing in her face as she walked, dampening her sweater and jeans. She began to slow her furious pace and for the first time to think where she was going. She began to wonder how poor Dolly was faring. She had heard that Gerry was missing but had hardly taken in the news. She made up her mind she would call on Dolly; anything was better than walking alone through these dreary lanes.

She could see the Pembelty house now, through the rain, with lights glowing in the downstairs windows. A car was parked on the lank grass verge a few yards short of the gateway to the house. Something was wrong; a man was walking around the little outhouse that had once been a farm dairy. She wondered for a moment if this was Gerry safe home again, but she could see enough to know this was not so. This man had the movements of one many years younger. She could see him wiping the glass of each window and trying to peep inside.

Kirsten had no fear of this stranger, who was clearly up to no good. She felt her smouldering anger begin to burn again until it flamed into full fury. Somehow she equated this furtive individual with her imagined pervert. She bent down to pick up the only weapon she could see: a short ash pole, probably a piece of discarded firewood. The man never heard her cross the few feet of grass, but he felt the pain and shock as she thrust the long stick into the small of his back. As he turned around gasping, Kirsten dropped the stick and flung herself at the man, her long fingernails gripping him around the throat. She fought with the fury of a tigress cornering the one who had tried to molest her young. She fought, but the man was stronger. For ten seconds she had the upper hand before he punched her hard in the stomach. She doubled up fighting for breath as the man seized her in an arm lock from which, try as she would, she could not shake free.

A torch was shone in her face. 'I might have guessed,' said a voice. 'The woman Simpson. I am Detective Inspector Le Bois and I am arresting you for assaulting a police officer. You do not have to say anything but it may harm your...'

'You can stop that now you useless waste-of-space bludger.' Dolly had emerged from her house. In any other circumstance Kirsten would have laughed. Dolly's acquired posh English accent had dissolved into pure Aussie vowels. 'Kirsten, sweetheart, what's this man doing here?'

'I caught him trying to break into your barn.'

Le Bois clung on to his struggling captive while he tried to delve into his inside jacket pocket. Eventually he withdrew a crumpled sheet of paper and his ID card. 'I have here a search warrant for these

152

premises and for the property known as Firs Farm,'

'Well, you can wipe your asshole with it, because you ain't coming in here, mate. Little Kirsten's going nowhere except back to her hubby and little boy.'

Kirsten staggered over the step of her own front door and sank into a chair head in hands. An anxious Steve appeared and put his arm around her. Shortly after that the young WPC joined them. Kirsten, now emotionally blank recounted the happenings at the Pembelty house.

'You say DI Le Bois was on his own?' The police girl sounded puzzled. 'He can't execute a search without supporting officers, it's just not done.'

'He wanted to arrest me, but I refused to go with him and Dolly was wonderful. He says he's coming back for me in the morning. Oh Steve, darling we're in so much trouble already – why can't that man leave us alone?' Kirsten began to shake spasmodically.

The WPC pulled out her mobile phone. 'I can't make this out,' she said. 'I think I'd better ring into my division and see if they can make some sense.'

Steve looked up wearily. 'You may not get much of a signal with these hills around – use our phone in the office.'

The WPC left them, and Steve knelt beside his wife stroking her dark wet hair. 'Did Le Bois search Dolly's house?'

'Yes, she let him in the end, because that was the only way she could stop him dragging me into his car. But there's nothing in the house or anywhere around it. Gerry's gone, probably fallen down somewhere, and my little girl has vanished and I want to do something but I can't think of anything…' She clung to him shaking.

The police girl returned with an odd expression. 'Mrs Simpson, do you know where Inspector Le Bois went after he left Mrs Pembelty?'

'I don't know, I didn't see him go, but he said he would come back for me and I didn't do anything…' She knew she was slurring her words but the WPC seemed to understand.

'Mrs Simpson, you're not under arrest and nothing's going to happen in the morning.'

'Constable, please,' Steve spoke. 'Is there any news of Emily?'

She shook her head. 'I'm sorry, but this is early in our search and I promise everything is being done that can be done.'

Kirsten sat up in her chair. 'Please, we can't go on calling you, Constable. From now on we're Kirsten and Steve and you are…'

153

The girl smiled. 'I'm WPC Calder but please call me Penny.'

'Thanks, Penny, we will,' said Steve.

'Just one more thing,' said Penny. 'Please try and rest, I know it's not easy, but I advise you to let me answer all incoming phone calls tomorrow morning.'

'Why?'

'If there's any news I'll bring it to you at once. But I'm afraid we're going to be in the middle of a media frenzy and you can do without that.'

In his state of mental and physical exhaustion Steve did sleep fitfully. It was an uneasy slumber, with periods of vivid dream. He saw the harbour at Chichester and then the lake at Branham as both merged into a shade of brilliant blue. Once again, standing among the sands of East Head, he became a spectator watching himself. It was the exact reprise of that same surreal dream that he had experienced fifteen years ago, the day he and Sarah had recovered the drowned boy. This time the sea was benign, and the sun shone from a cloudless sky. Emily was by the foreshore, splashing happily along the tideline. She ran to him, and taking his hand, led him along the beach to where her mother stood open armed and smiling.

The telephone started ringing at six o'clock. Steve, grabbed the bedside handset. He heard Penny's voice ordering someone to clear the line and that she was waiting for news.

A man's voice answered her. 'There isn't any news, we've checked. I want to interview the girl's parents...'

'No chance,' said Penny as the line went dead.

The whole household had been aroused now, and Steve knew there was no possibility of more rest. The full horror of their predicament came flooding back. No news good or bad. He wondered how long he could stand this waiting. There seemed no comfort anywhere. His devout first wife, Miriam, would have found hope in prayer. That was something beyond him. His Irish mother had schooled him in the dourest Catholicism, and Miriam had maintained the same faith to her dying day. For Steve, religion had always been something to escape from rather than a solace. As they were almost certainly going to get a call from the village vicar, maybe he had better think again. Anything that would restore Emily, his own little girl; now his tears were flowing unrestrained: the tears of a stoical grown man who could maintain self-control no longer.

He wiped his eyes, took a deep breath and walked downstairs. Kirsten and Sarah were both there, fully dressed and talking to Penny.

'Who are all these people on the road?' Kirsten asked.

Steve looked anxiously at his wife. She had remained downstairs all night and clearly had not slept. She seemed controlled, but he could sense her anger boiling just below the surface. Steve wanted his little girl back in his arms, but that would not be enough for Kirsten – she was vengeful.

'They've been here for the last two hours,' Penny replied. 'But I've managed to call for backup. I've two more officers already on their way.'

'They're press people,' said Kirsten. 'I saw that man Everett and that horrible little photographer.'

Emily could see daylight through the little grille high in the cellar wall, and at last she could hear footsteps overhead. She knew that she had passed through a night and she had not slept. Her mind was numb, and she could rouse no interest in anything except the cold, her aching bones and racking thirst. She had heard more rats in the night and had shrunk away from them as two had sniffed around her filthy mattress. In the end she had realised that they couldn't hurt her, and she almost welcomed their company.

Now came a noisy scraping and a square of light appeared in the ceiling. She could see old Gerry sitting on the floor leaning against the far wall and he looked ill. A fresh scraping and now a metal ladder came lowered through the hatch.

'Emily, climb the ladder. I have food for you.' The voice was a woman's and the memory chilled her.

It was the voice of the old bat, the one who had grabbed her beside the athletics circuit. She remembered everything now and she was frightened. But the offer of food was too tempting and, more than anything, she craved a drink of water. Very slowly she climbed the ladder and found herself in a small room. At least it was warmer here and better lit. Facing her was the old woman.

'Where am I? I want my mum and dad.' Emily was shivering, only partly from the cold.

'You would like a drink?' said the woman.

'Yes, I'm so thirsty.'

'In a minute – now let me look at you.' Emily felt she was going to vomit as the old crone caught her by the arm and then forcibly pulled off her tiny running vest and sports bra.

155

'Please, I'm cold,' Emily sobbed. She shuddered and almost convulsed as the woman ran her bony fingers and long scratchy nails all over her body and her small firm breasts.

The old bat mumbled something in a foreign lingo that meant nothing to Emily before she spoke in English. 'So good, you are well into your puberty – exactly what we need.'

She handed Emily her vest again and called out once more in the strange language. Two tall men entered through a door from a further room. They were the same two who had forced her into the car by the sports ground. She remembered the whole scene vividly and, of course, she knew their names already. One of these men she'd always disliked, but recognising the other she felt only a sense of shock and betrayal.

Sid Everett and Andy Ikes had detached themselves from the crowd of reporters and paparazzi and were heading for the lower slopes of Marshall Down. This hill offered Andy a perfect long shot of the rear of Firs Farm and the whole of the garden. The site also provided some sort of signal for Sid's mobile phone.

Sid was happy; he had not felt so happy since he'd bugged the flat with the three gay MPs, or seen the police take Harold Shipman away. But a child's abduction was a story to kill for, a story worth waiting years to report. It didn't matter about the outcome. If the child was alive and returned home, then that was the happy ending his readers wanted. Most likely the kid was dead, and then the police would be searching for the sex fiend. There would be extra mileage from the man's trial and sentence: particularly if that sentence was less than whole life. That would give his editor full scope for a tirade of moral indignation. So, pretty satisfactory all round, particularly if the pervert turned out to be the old war hero. What a story – this had to be his lucky day. His mobile phone was ringing.

'Yes?'

'Hi, Sid, it's Sandra – news desk. We've some information just come in and if it's true it's mega. There's a religious cult claiming to have the girl, Emily, and they'll kill her if the police don't back off.'

Penny was firm. 'I strongly advise that you do not watch the television news. We can keep the media away from you until you are ready to make your own statement, but in the meantime don't get yourselves extra distressed by the rubbish that's being written.'

The Simpson family had made no objection to this advice, and that was a relief for Penny. The two uniform PCs guarding the frontage had left her a stack of daily papers and they made sick reading. Emily's picture filled the whole front page of all the tabloids plus the same text that Fox had seen earlier.

BOAT YARD KID SNATCHED BY SICK SEX FIENDS, read the headline in the Banner. Andy Ikes reported witnessing the abduction plus the artist's recreation of the scene. *The police will give no explanation after impounding my pictures…the people have a right to see them…* The other London tabloids all had similar lurid accounts. The more mature broadsheets were little different.

Emily, daughter of two Olympic sailors, Kirsten Schmitt of Denmark and her husband, Stephen Simpson OBE, was forcibly abducted at her local athletics park. Police are unable to comment on a motive but have dismissed the notion of a ransom demand.

None of them seem to have picked up on the disappearance of the old man Pembelty. If the media made the connection they would indulge in a feeding frenzy. Penny was not a detective and certainly not a psychologist, but she doubted that the doddery old fellow was the paedophile that DI Le Bois believed.

Le Bois had been returned to the division late last night and Superintendent Fox had suspended him pending disciplinary action. Everyone knew that the Inspector was heading for a breakdown. Her boyfriend in CID had spoken openly to her about Le Bois' paranoia. It seemed that a household in Surrey had called treble nine and reported a suspicious person loitering in their garden. The embarrassed local police had discovered the Inspector shouting incoherently that the house occupiers had kidnapped the little girl, and that they had murdered their own children as well as killing four other adults. The Surrey family, the Prestons of course, had allowed the police to look around the house and there had been no trace of either Emily or the old airman.

Penny knew that police service could, and often did, drive officers to alcohol, marital failure and mental breakdown. Superintendent Fox himself had asked her to volunteer for this duty, and she had faced it with dread. She had used all her female instinct to handle the mission hour by hour and now, it seemed, day by day. It was impossible to understand fully the hell the family must be passing through. She felt a fondness for them and an admiration for their courage.

Greta von Essens arrived at Firs Farm mid-morning. For the first time she felt harassed. She was not sure how much she should tell Steve and Kirsten, but her earlier meeting with Norman Fox and his Chief Constable had shaken her.

'This has been posted world wide,' she handed the two officers the website printouts. 'And before you ask, yes it's genuine!'

People of Earth. There is only one Power the SUPREME POWER that you in your ignorance call the sun. You have angered the POWER and it is minded to destroy you. In your stupidity you talk of GLOBAL WARMING and claim that it is caused by your own puny industries and your fume filled greed.

NOT SO. The POWER IS ANGRY. So angry he will scorch your lands and boil your oceans if you do not repent.

WE THE CHILDREN OF THE POWER alone can save you and appease THE MIGHTY ONE.

But some must perish in the sacrifice for the good of all. A child beginning his or her puberty must pay the price with an ageing warrior who has proved himself in mortal combat. To this end we have taken the following who will have the privilege of sacrifice.

Fox read a list of names spread around five continents. All were in pairs confirming the contents of the printout. Most were allocated to one nation or region, although Fox was not surprised to see that seven alone were declared in the United States. It was near the end of the alphabetical list that the blow struck.

In the United Kingdom we hold – Warrior Gerald Pembelty with child Emily Simpson. Sacrifice will be by fire.

'This is madness,' Fox muttered.

'Yes, but these people have an unshakeable belief and they have already carried out their first sacrifices.'

'Doctor, have you any idea where our hostages may be?'

'Yes,' Greta replied. 'My independent colleague, Mr Matheson, has had some contacts with a security service operative. You will find the hostages not far from here. I believe one or both may recognise their captors.'

'We've already surmised that,' said Fox. 'We've an officer showing these to Mr and Mrs Simpson and I've clearance for you to have copies.' He handed Greta an A4 envelope. 'These are digitally enhanced pictures of the gang who snatched Emily. We're giving the Simpson family first view.'

The Chief Constable spoke. 'You say the security services are active in this?'

'MI6 have an operative from Argentina who is privy to the international dimension. This man claims to know one of the cult leaders.'

'Oh, does he. Right,' the Chief was angry. 'If MI5 – MI6 or any of them have information that will help this investigation they must pass it to us. If not, I personally will go to London and metaphorically beat it out of them.' He pressed a buzzer on his desk and a civilian secretary came into the room.

'Clare, I want the Home Secretary on the phone now. I want him and him only. Tell his people it's vital to the Emily Simpson enquiry. If she dies because his department withholds co-operation, we might just tip off Mr Everett and The Daily Banner. How many votes for his party in that?'

Despite the seriousness of the meeting Greta saw Fox smile. 'Sir, that's blackmail.'

'Moral blackmail linked to votes – it's the only thing that politicians understand.'

The internal phone on Fox's desk rang. He picked it up and listened. 'Thank you,' was all he said.

Fox turned a troubled face towards Greta. 'The press have caught up with that web site of yours. They're going to make big trouble for us now. Tell me, do you believe these are really the people who've done this?'

'Yes.'

'Come in, Greta,' Steve ushered her inside while keeping a wary eye at the huddle of pressmen just visible at the drive entrance.

She had fought her way through the mob while they surrounded her car and pushed cameras at the windows. Uniformed police officers had checked her identity and waved her through. She was not comfortable with this meeting. Greta was an academic whose successes were based on knowledge and experience. She could cope with interviewing criminal psychopaths, however grisly, but meeting the parents of an abducted child was another matter. She had done so twice before and both had been soul-destroying experiences. Worse, in both cases the child had died. Now she was faced with people she already regarded as friends. She had shared their life for a few short hours and nearly died with them on their beautiful boat. She had no doubt that she was the primary target of that cunning attempt at mass-murder.

As she expected, Steve appeared tired and ill. His round, sun-tanned face looked hollow, and its colour was tinged with an unhealthy yellow. This man loved his child. She guessed he was only realising now just how much he loved and cherished her. Kirsten was suffering as much as her husband, but she showed none of his abject misery. Kirsten was tense and angry – ready to lash out at anyone or anything that crossed her path.

Greta showed her ID again to WPC Calder. 'I've some pictures here from CID,' she explained. 'Have the family seen them?'

'There are some officers from CID due here any time now, but I'm not sure what they are bringing with them. Please, Doctor von Essens, is there any news or I mean…' she lowered her voice. 'I mean…I mean is there any hope?'

Greta was uncertain how to reply. 'Yes, we have hope. Never lose hope.' It was the defining moment. Greta knew that hope rested with her experience and skills alone.

Gerry Pembelty had eventually made it up the ladder into the strange little building in which Emily and he were held prisoner. Emily had helped to pull him over the edge of the stone surround of the hatch. At least the horrible woman had left them something to eat and drink. It was only a packet of cornflakes and five litres of bottled water, but that at least soothed her terrible thirst. Some of her terror was beginning to subside into a horrid sick fear. She felt only hate and disgust for the old woman: like a living creature made of skin and bone. She was now over the shock of recognising the two men who had appeared. She had never liked either of them, but they were adults and her Dad had insisted she show them respect. But why had they taken her here and why old Gerry? She had expected any moment that the men would try and rape her. That's what these sorts of people did of course, and the thought sickened her and made her shiver with misery and revulsion. But why was Gerry here?

Emily could understand why everyone said Gerry was brave. He had stood up to their captors with contempt. Even the horrid woman had seemed startled by him. Somehow his voice had changed. Gerry had ceased to be the muddled old gentleman digging his allotment. His voice and body language had become that of a much younger man. The three captors had taken him into the adjacent room and shut the door. She could hear voices in there; muttering voices and then she had heard Gerry; he was angry and shouting.

'You think I'm frightened of that? My buddies, my closest friend and so many of my comrades died that way and I would not be less than them!'

She heard more muttering, and then Gerry had been pushed back into the room with her. He was red-faced and breathing hard as he lowered himself to the floor and leant against the walls. Emily ran to him and fell sobbing into the old man's arms.

Sarah entered the room. Greta noticed that the eldest Simpson daughter was also suffering from lack of sleep. This family was unusual. She could detect no tensions between this stepdaughter and her stepmother. In the face of this terrible grief she could not conceive of a more united family.

'Johnny's asking more and more questions,' said Sarah. 'He knows something's wrong with Emily and I've tried to make excuses but I don't think he'll buy that much longer.'

Greta spoke. 'Excuse me asking, but is there any way he could find out the truth without you knowing?'

'No, I'm certain of that, but he doesn't understand why Penny the policewoman is here, or why there's all those people and police at the gate. He doesn't understand why I've taken his little radio away, and most of all he can't understand why he hasn't gone to school today.'

Kirsten spoke. 'Greta, you're the psychologist. Should we tell him the truth?'

'Yes, I think you should,' said Greta. 'You see, I believe he's only too aware already and he's upset at your evasions.'

'How much should I say?'

'Just that Emily has been taken away by some bad people and all the good people of England are looking for her.'

'Do we tell him a bit more about who we think the bad men are?'

'How well does he know the men in the photographs?'

'Hardly at all. If it is them,' Kirsten's voice was slurring and Greta wished the woman would accept medication.

Greta had led a lonely single life without marriage or children. In earlier days she had survived three broken relationships and their aftermath had killed her appetite for sex and the possibility of children. She had settled for the security of academe. Yet she wondered how she would cope with the loss if it had been one of her

161

beloved nephews or niece. Every time she had had to face the parents of a murdered child she had wondered that.

That morning, the arrival of the official copies of the enhanced pictures had been traumatic. By any standards it was shattering for the parents to see the actual moment of abduction. For Steve it had almost been too much. Greta had seen the poor man begin to hyper-ventilate while Kirsten clung to him, tears pouring down her cheeks. The woman sergeant who had brought the pictures waited tactfully.

'Please, could you look at the two men. We think you might know them.'

Now it was evening and Steve, for the tenth time that day, scanned each picture in turn before passing them to Kirsten. 'It's got to be him – that's Peter Terring. It's not a perfect shot but I would still say it was him.'

'I think so too,' said Kirsten. 'The other evil bastard as well – it's that Grogan. I wasn't sure when they first showed us, but I am now'

'Greta,' Steve asked. 'Do the police know the names, I mean are they known perverts – what have they to do with this?'

'No, Steve, they are not paedophiles, they are members of a religious cult. That is all I can tell you. The name Grogan has come up in my investigation but his connection was so tenuous that the police lost interest. But at one time his garage business was definitely connected to the cult I'm talking about.'

'So they've stolen my little girl and they want to brainwash her – is that it?'

'We cannot say for certain but it could be so.' That was all Greta dared to say.

Kirsten was staring at her. 'I never liked either of them. Child stealers – they will be dead men when I catch up with them!'

'What about the woman in the photographs?' asked Steve. 'The police must circulate these pictures now, today. What the hell are they waiting for?'

Greta was firm. 'That could be the worst thing we could do. We must not frighten these people into doing anything stupid...'

Greta did not finish the sentence. Behind her, the door was pushed open and there stood a white-faced John-Kaj. The little boy walked into the circle of adults and stood staring. He was crying and his lower lip drooped but there was something resolute about him. 'I've been listening,' he said.

Kirsten rounded on him. 'You must learn not to. It's deceitful. I

162

mean it's just wrong and it could get you into trouble one day.'

John-Kaj seemed not to hear. He spoke slowly and huskily. 'You say Emily has been stolen by some bad men. If one of them is Mr Grogan then I think I know where he's taken her.'

The next morning both press and television reporting had spiralled into a crescendo of hysterical verbiage, enhanced by their own caption writers.

MAD CULT ADMIT THEY HOLD LITTLE EMILY

MPs DEMAND EMILY MUST NOT DIE

SUN CULT SAY EMILY WILL BURN

HUMAN SACRIFICES FOUND IN MEXICO

Worse from Fox's point of view, they had printed the website address of the Children of the Power for all to see. Now questions were being asked in Parliament, drawing cagey responses from the Home Secretary and others which satisfied no one. Fox was committed to bringing Emily's parents to the next press conference. He would give anything to be able to cancel that event, but he knew he could not.

CHAPTER 18

'I think they've gone,' said Gerry.

Emily watched him as he stood still near the barred window.

'Emily, I'm old and a bit deaf – come and listen and tell me what you hear.'

She obeyed and stood by him. 'I can't hear a thing,' she agreed. 'What is this place?'

'If you can hear nothing then it is likely those people are not here. It looks as if this is an old cottage in the middle of a haystack.' Slowly he reached through the bars and pulled in handful of straw. 'Not a haystack. It's more likely a pile of round straw bales. A very clever disguise but not, I think, been here for long.'

'I hate this place,' Emily was starting to panic. She had tried all day to be brave like Gerry, but she couldn't, she was frightened and once more the tears came. 'Can't we get out of here?'

'Now, now, little girl – no crying. Let's treat this as a problem to be solved.'

'Mr Pembelty, what do these horrid people want?'

'Well, I'm not sure why they want me, but your Mummy and Daddy are not short of a bob or two as we say. So, don't despair. They love you and they will pay up.' He grinned at her and Emily felt better. But there was something in the old man's manner that made her wonder if he was telling her the truth.

The door into the other room was locked and bolted. 'We'd need dynamite for that,' said Gerry. Emily followed him as they explored further but the cottage had no doorway to the outside world and the only two windows were tiny, barred and filled with solid straw. At least it was better up here than down in that damp cellar. The cottage contained only a ground floor and a tiny loft reached by stone steps. The roof beams were solid, and the roof itself was insulated with a layer of felt behind stout wire mesh. The loft smelt sour, and cobwebs with spiders dangled from the beams. Emily could just tolerate the rats, but spiders made her cringe. She was glad to retreat down the steps into the lower room.

'I shall have to leave you for a moment and go down there,' Gerry pointed at the cellar hatch. 'I badly need a call of nature – it's old age you know. Perhaps you could help me back up when I've completed the task.'

164

Gerry climbed painfully onto the ladder and his head vanished slowly into the depths. Emily had heard something. A rustling, scrabbling noise came from the window on the left. More rats? At the thought, Emily shrank back; again half disgusted, half interested. She watched from a safe distance as the scrabbling grew louder. Then she saw it, a living creature and it was not a rat.

'Terring vanished at the time of the attempt to blow up the Simpson yacht. Grogan was in his garage up to three days ago. Before that Surrey say the man wasn't hiding. He's been working on an agricultural contract of some sort, and he's been visible around the area.' Fox looked up from his notes.

'But we accept that Grogan is the other man in the photographs?' asked Greta.

'Yes, the pictures have been shown to a dozen reliable witnesses and everyone agrees the man is Grogan, and some of them recognised Terring. The manageress of the Lakeview Hotel says the two of them were in her pub when Nadine was there. She is certain they recognised Nadine, but then all the blokes in the place did.'

'I can give you some more facts about these two,' said Greta. 'The founder of the garage business was the Basque refugee Larranaga. His mother's family name was Terra. Larranaga married a South American woman, Carlotta Mfanywy Terra y Gryffydd who turns out to be a second cousin of Larranaga's mother. Have the security services come up with anything?'

'Up to a point,' Fox replied. 'They deny the existence of Frank Matheson's friend Costas, but they're lying through their teeth – he exists all right. But we think the old woman in the pictures is Mrs Larranaga.

'There's one of that name in a council flat in Basingstoke. It seems she seldom left it; total recluse, but a social worker has identified her from the picture. Hampshire police have visited the flat and she's not there. But residents on the same landing have identified both men from our pictures. So, Doctor, who are these men in the real world?'

'They're her twin sons, not identical twins but same birth date. Records say that the Larranaga boys left the country for South America a few months after their father's death. That was in 1973. The garage business continued under a new owner who has no connection with this crime. He sold it again in 1989 to our man who seems to have shed the name Eduardo Larranaga and reappeared as Edward Grogan. Frank has been asking questions around the area and he has witnesses who say Peter Terring worked as his chief mechanic at that time. His real name is Pedro Larranaga but his grandmother's family name was Terra; so anglicised into Terring, it follows.'

Fox shook his head. 'It's a weird business. Fancy those two both knowing little Emily. That's either an unbelievable coincidence or a nasty dose of fate.'

'That's probably why they chose her. They were looking for a child and she's the sort of extrovert kid who stands out from the crowd. They both knew her so they chose her.'

'Is she alive, your honest opinion please, Doctor?'

'Yes, she's alive because The Children of The Power always acknowledge responsibility after a sacrifice. Secondly, they fire their sacrifices with burning glasses from direct sunlight, and so long as it keeps overcast and raining we've a chance.'

'Is it true the Simpson boy claims to know something?'

'Yes,' said Greta, 'At first I thought he was just trying to be helpful and had dredged something out of his imagination. He's only eight, you know. His mother turned on him and shouted. But Kirsten's on the edge, poor woman – and Steve's even worse. They'll both crack in a day or so if we don't resolve this.'

'What's your opinion of the boy?' Fox was interested and he valued Greta's views. 'Should I have a chat with him?'

'Actually, I was impressed. He stood up for himself even when his mother said he was talking rubbish; but as for you talking to him. No offence Superintendent, but I think any official policeman might frighten him. Let Frank chat to him. I doubt it's anything serious, but you never know.'

Sarah met Frank and showed him into the sitting room. 'I'll fetch Johnny in a minute,' she said. 'Frank do you think the kid really knows something? We don't see how he can.'

'Tell me, is he an imaginative boy? Is he the sort who dreams up wild tales and frightens himself with them in the night?'

'No,' Sarah was emphatic. 'He's a studious little chap but he's not imaginative in that way. He's a whiz at maths, and Dad says he's got a scientific mind even at eight.'

'All right, bring him in. I'll take the interview with tact and care, poor little mite.'

Sarah pushed John-Kaj into the room and closed the door. 'Johnny, this is Uncle Frank. You remember him? He came to your birthday with Lily his granddaughter.'

John-Kaj blinked shyly but he showed recognition. 'Lily said you were a copper, then she put jelly down my shirt.'

Matheson smiled at the boy. 'That sounds like Lily, but John, I'm not a copper. I was one once, but that was a hundred years ago.'

'Can't have been that long ago. Even you're not that old.' John-Kaj was looking interested.

'I'm not sure if that's a compliment. Now, John, I'm here to help find Emily. I understand you've got something to tell me.' He looked at the boy and carefully raised an eyebrow.

'Mum won't believe me. They sent me to bed and I cried.'

'All right, young man, see if I believe you.'

Greta picked up the telephone even as it started to ring. 'Yes.'

'Greta, it's Frank. I've spoken to the boy. He's not telling tales – I think he's got something.'

'Go ahead.'

'When he and Emily were walking by the Little Lake at Branham they saw Grogan come out of the forestry plantation with a bloody great tractor and trailer. My God, Greta, that little boy is as sharp as his sister but in a different way. I've rarely interviewed a better witness. Clear as a bell and wouldn't budge.'

Greta had been feeling depressed. Now she felt a surge of emotion. Was it hope? Could she dare to hope? 'Frank, it all fits. Surrey police have just passed me a report. Grogan has spent the last fortnight shifting a massive stack of straw bales. Apparently he paid cash for them: over two thousand pounds and he's been taking them away with a tractor and trailer to no one knows where. Now he's vanished from his home and they can't trace him.' She paused to draw breath. 'Some of the sacrifices that we know of in the last few days have been straw fires.'

'Yes, and young Johnny is bright enough to notice that the track into the trees was cut to bits by heavy traffic. I think we should tell Surrey police right away. I'll ring their operations room now.'

It was dark and another night without news. The police had finally decided to brief Emily's family concerning the Children of the Power and their claims. Steve had seemed numbed and Kirsten had finally collapsed. Sarah had given her a sleeping pill. She had accepted it without resistance, but it seemed to have little effect. Steve had never felt so empty and numb. 'Penny,' he said, 'I can't take much more of this. If Emily dies I die.'

'Please,' she said. 'Don't even think that way. You've your wife and little John to think of.'

'But you believe she's dead – don't you?' Steve saw her flinch and shy away. Her eyes and expression showed her hurt. She could never fully share their grief, but he knew she was suffering too and he regretted his outburst.

'I think I saw lights and a car stopping,' she said. 'I wonder who that is at this time of night?'

Steve felt his heart beat faster and his stomach tighten. The knock on the door in the night was always the harbinger of bad news. Now Penny's police radio was calling her.

Penny answered it as she walked away to the far side of the room. She returned almost at once. 'That was our officer on your gate. There's a Mr and Mrs Preston asking if they can have a word. It's rather late – shall I tell them to go away?'

'No, tell them to come on in.'

Harry and Liz had already been on the phone. They told of the huge explosion of support that was growing around Branham. Little heart-warming gestures like the mass of flowers by Emily's Cadet dinghy and the yellow ribbons tied around the mast. They told Steve and Kirsten of the nation-wide surge of sympathy: the questions in Parliament, the candle lit vigil in Chichester Cathedral and the multi-millionaires who had offered rewards for Emily's safe return.

Kirsten had come down into the hall looking unsteady and bleary eyed. Liz and Harry had hugged them each in turn and then shaken hands with Penny. She in turn had been tactful and had not openly recognised the Prestons as recent police suspects.

'We had to come,' said Liz. 'Please tell us if we're intruding and we'll go away.'

For the first time in seventy-two hours Kirsten smiled. 'You are not intruding and you will not go away. You are staying the night with us.'

It was past midnight when Greta's phone rang. Her reaction was much the same as Steve's. The likeliest reason was bad news. She braced herself for it.

'Norman Fox here – there's developments. Surrey have passed me your report and we're moving on it. Problem is: that Forestry Commission plantation is vast, nearly nine hundred acres of it. It's the biggest in Southern England. It would take an army to search every inch.'

Greta interrupted. 'An army is the last thing we need. The kidnappers would react and kill their captives as soon as they heard them.'

'All right, Doctor, we're not that thick. No, my chief rang the Home Secretary and he's come up trumps for once. He's contacted the MOD and there's an RAF reconnaissance unit in East Anglia ready to go first thing. There's already a detailed air survey of the forest. They'll complete another one first light and then they'll analyse what's changed.'

'If there's a helicopter buzzing around, won't the cult guess what's going on?'

'No, these RAF boys are flying Tornados at thirty thousand feet; nobody will notice a thing.'

'That's great news and it must be something of a precedent isn't it?'

'Maybe, but young Emily's touched the heartstrings of our nation, plus the sacrificial threat has spread her story worldwide. The RAF boys suspected they might be needed. The whole unit had already volunteered; they're right up for it. The MOD were wary about the cost but they've agreed to make it a routine exercise.'

'Thanks to that website,' Greta replied, 'plus the press and television, the Air Force will know that old Pembelty is a captive as well and to them he's special'

'They will know about him now. We were all for keeping the lid on that one at the beginning. You said yourself we don't want the tabloids accusing the old fellow of being a paedophile. It's the warrior and the child for sacrifice now, that'll be tomorrow's headline. The papers are reporting a dozen sightings of Emily from Glasgow to Vancouver. This thing's going out of control.'

'No it is not – never,' Greta spoke the words with the emphasis on "never". 'To hell with press speculation – we use all our experience and skills. Norman, I am seeing this one through!'

Gerry Pembelty had been taking stock. He had mentally rolled back the years until he had once again acquired the ice-cold logic that made one survive in air combat. He accepted that his days were numbered. Although he still enjoyed amazing health for his age, he was eighty-six years old and he hadn't long to go. These crazy people were going to kill him inside this constructed funeral pyre. He remembered old comrades who had died in the fireballs of their aircraft – maybe it would be the fitting end for him. He had only one compelling aim.

True, he was going to die, but while he had breath in his body little Emily would not die. She must not die, not in this brutal, sadistic fire.

The child had spirit. She showed fear, with tearful fits, sickness and shivering. He knew that her health was deteriorating with bad food and the cold and damp. But she had shown no sign of hysteria. This child was strong, and he was glad that their abductors had not revealed their full madness to her. He could see her cradling the little cat that had crawled in through the bars. That had been a happy distraction for her and a surprise.

'Mr Pembelty, I've seen him before. It was when we went for a picnic at the Little Lake and we saw Grogan on a tractor. I think we're near Branham.'

'As that man knows the locality I suspect you are right.' Gerry sat down slowly and painfully beside the child. 'Emily, I have a plan of a sort so listen. When I was young and fighting as a pilot I used to have a sixth sense. You see, at the height of the battle none of us knew if we were going to be alive at the end of the day. I told you how I half-lost my own fear didn't I?'

Emily looked at him with tired eyes. 'You said you remembered the kids you played with when you were young. They were Jewish and the Germans wanted to kill them.'

'That's right, well done. Anyway, during the battle I got to sense the guys around me. You could tell by little things the people who were breaking up inside. I was always right, because they were the ones who didn't live long. I want you to do something for me.'

Emily looked at him; she was interested now.

Gerry continued. 'The man you named as Peter Terring does not like us, and I'm afraid he especially dislikes you, but the man Grogan is unhappy. For you he has a soft spot. Not, I think, in a nasty perverted way, but he could be wavering about your abduction. You must be a brave girl. You are already a very brave girl, and you must encourage Mr Grogan to like you – understand?'

There was a gleam in the child's eye now. Solemnly she nodded and for the first time he saw her smile.

'Good, that's settled. Now for my second plan,' he groped in his jacket pocket and found what he was looking for. 'Do you know what these are?' He held out the paper folder.

She shook her head.

'These are cigarette papers, they're for rolling your own, and they were called Rizlas in my young day – still are. Don't ever tell your Aunt Dolly that you saw me with them. Now, if you will hand me

Mister Pusscat, we'll see if he can give us a helping hand.'

'Five days gone, she'll be dead, they always are,' Sid Everett pulled his waterproof tighter. Rainwater had been leaking through his collar. 'I dunno what the constabulary think they're playing at. They've suspended Le Bois pending a disciplinary hearing and he was the one copper who'd really got his teeth into the water murders.'

'That's right and I'll tell you some more.' Andy Ikes had been securing a cover over his camera and equipment. 'Le Bois' main suspect Preston is in that house now.'

'Bloody hell, Andy, why didn't you tell me?'

'I wasn't sure until I got my scope on that open window and there he was no doubt about it.'

Sid was pleased, so pleased he slapped Andy on the back. 'I wonder if there's a secret agenda to this business?'

'How so?'

'Supposing this sun cult is a set up – what if this lot are hiding the kid?'

'Why should they do that – what's in it for them? You've just said she's dead.' Andy looked sceptical.

'Have you thought that maybe Simpson's kids are not his at all? I remember Steve Simpson and his Danish bit from near twenty years back. He was knocking on a bit then; looked overweight – bit past his shagging days.'

'I wouldn't say that – my Dad made me when he was near fifty-five.'

Sid laughed. 'I always wondered why you were a pint size. Look, supposing, just supposing that Emily is really Rachel Preston. The Simpsons may have taken over the Preston kids, which is why no one can find them. The sun cult is a fantastic story but maybe it doesn't exist.'

'Much better for us if it does. Come on, Sid, who would give their kids away?'

'Phil Le Bois reckons Preston is a psycho. Maybe Preston didn't trust himself to bring up kids – so his friends did it for him. But we know they spend time at Preston's house – maybe that's the deal.'

Sid watched Andy's expression. His photographer sidekick was not the sharpest tool in the box. His level of intelligence was on a par with their paper's readers.

'Tell you something else,' Sid continued. 'The old pilot who's vanished; they say the cult have got both – right? Le Bois has

171

convinced himself that Pembelty's a paedo and that he's the one who snatched the girl. But the man's got a wife and family and his record's clean. He's a bit of a World War Two hero as well. What if he's the one hiding the kid for them?'

Andy looked unconvinced. 'Oh come on, Sid, you don't really believe any of this, it's fantasy – right off the wall.'

'No, of course I don't buy it. I'm dreaming, but what a great story it would make. Le Bois might swallow it though. They say he's three parts slipped his trolley. Let's wind him up with it and see how he reacts.'

'Le Bois is in the pub just up the street. I tried to speak to him but I thought he would rip my head off so I left it.'

'All right,' Sid grinned. 'Leave him to me. Let's go find him.'

'It's rained most of the night,' said Fox, 'but the skies were clear enough for the RAF to do their photo shoot first light. We've got to wait until their analysts come up with something.'

'Whether they do or not we're looking in the right place, I'm sure of it,' said Greta.

'I've been on the line to Surrey. They say that forest is so big it would be needle in a haystack so to speak. They wouldn't be sure where to start.'

'It must be somewhere near where the little boy saw Grogan and his tractor.'

Fox grimaced. 'Yes, Doctor, I know that, and so do Surrey but little Johnny is a bit vague about where that is. He may have a scientific brain but it doesn't stretch to understanding maps.'

'Then I suggest Frank Matheson and I go to the place with him.'

Fox could think of several objections, but Greta was too quick for him.

'Yes,' she said. 'We would have a police presence provided they kept in the background and didn't make themselves too obvious. Then, locate the objective and go in.'

'I think police tactics are bit outside your remit, Doctor,' Fox was irritated at this academic woman's presumption.

'No, I'm not concerned with how you do it. Softly-softly or crash in with the firearms squad, as long as you free our two and catch these crazy people.'

'We've got to keep the media at bay,' said Fox. 'We're holding a press conference tomorrow and we've invited Mrs and Mrs Simpson to be there and make a statement. They've agreed but it'll be one hell of an ordeal for them.'

'I can't imagine anything worse.'

'Nor can I,' said Fox. 'I would ask you to be there to take some of the flak, but on reflection, I think it would be better you went to Branham with Frank and the boy while we've got the media trapped indoors.'

The long nights seemed to last for ever and it was then that Emily knew fear that slowly merged into frozen terror. She wished she could believe Gerry's theory about kidnap for ransom, but if that were true her parents would have paid up by now. She felt cold all the time, and she guessed her body must stink of filth and urine. At least the two men weren't perverts. Peter Terring had treated her with open dislike. She guessed he'd always hated children – perhaps he'd never been one himself. The ghastly old bat was their mother. The sight of her made Emily feel sick. The woman smelt of fabric restorer and old soap. Several times she'd repeated her awful body inspection, each time sniffing and muttering.

The single door into the room was made of some heavy wood, oak, she assumed. Each time the men came she could hear them unfasten padlocks before they pulled back the bolts on the far side.

'If only I was sixty years younger,' Gerry had remarked. 'I could rush them first moment that door opens. I used to be a bit of a boxer when I was a young man – won the Group middleweight in '38, or was it '39, can't remember – memories going. Sorry, couldn't do it now.'

Emily had worked her charm on Edward Grogan for all she was worth. She even surprised herself with her acting skills.

'Please, Mr Grogan, is my boat all right? I think there may be a leak in the cover and you say it's been raining.' That had been a crafty start. Then, with a supreme effort, she'd managed to switch on her sweetest smile. 'I remember when we took that safety boat without permission. Bob Beale was angry but you were nice about it.'

Grogan had said nothing but Emily detected a small spasm of pain on the man's face, and for the first time she felt almost elated.

Terring had reacted differently. 'Shut your face, you nasty little slut!' He glowered at her, but again Emily saw the same expression on Grogan's face.

'Sorry,' she replied meekly. 'Mr Grogan looks after our rescue boats, and my Dad says he's a brilliant engineer.'

'Look, you filthy little brat, I don't want to hear your voice, and I don't like your father and I don't like what I've seen of your mother,' Terring leaned over her. Emily shrank back, the man was menacing and he stank of sweat and diesel fuel. He swung round and delivered a torrent of words in some foreign language. Grogan shrugged and walked from the room. As he did so he turned and glanced at her. With a huge effort of willpower Emily smiled back. Terring pushed him through the doorway, and they heard the bolts slide shut.

Gerry spoke quietly. 'That was wonderful. I'm not sure you shouldn't be in films.'

'Did I do any good?' she whispered.

'By my reckoning that was brilliant. I think you have weakened the man's resolve somewhat.'

Gerry had stumbled painfully across the room until he was near the window where the cat had entered. 'I wonder how much oxygen is in this place,' he mused. 'There must be some coming in or we wouldn't breathe.'

CHAPTER 19

'We'll take you in one of our cars,' said Fox. 'Then we'll whisk you away afterwards.'

Steve spoke. 'We just want to get it over.'

'Right, we're sending in two extra WPCs to help Sarah with young Johnny and we're increasing officers on the gate. We're sending WPC Calder home for the day but she'll be back with you this evening.' Then Fox told them.

'We need to take young John-Kaj to a place near Branham. He will be under a full police escort and your daughter Sarah will go with them.'

'Why? For God's sake, Norman, we can't risk him out of our sight.'

'No, Steve, he will be out of your sight this morning anyway. Please, we think he may have seen something at Branham, but he can't place where. He's got to show us on the ground. It could be the thing that gives us our breakthrough.'

Steve was appalled but in the end it was Kirsten who, awaking from her morose state, agreed. Steve then conceded – he was past arguing.

It was eight-thirty in the morning and the police press conference was scheduled for midday. Steve had spent another night of exhaustion with fitful sleep and surreal dreams. Kirsten had changed to the point where he hardly knew his own wife. She had sunk inside herself in a surly apathy and surrounded herself with a mental shield that he was unable to break through.

The press conference was not his idea, but Fox had insisted that they face it. He suggested a short appeal in their own words, and then he and his fellow investigators would field the media's questions. Steve had accepted the fait accompli. Personally, he no longer cared about the police. He could sense too well that many, if not all the police around them, believed Emily to be dead. Steve did not believe this; he felt deep in his subconscious that he would know the moment she died. He could not feel this yet, and so there must be hope.

The press conference was in the headquarters of the regional police force. The car they travelled in had darkened windows. The passengers could see out but casual spectators could not see in. Looking from the car, Steve received a shock. Emily's picture stared down from walls, lampposts and private houses. Clumps of yellow ribbon were everywhere.

'Of course they know you in this town,' said Fox, 'but it's not just here – this is everywhere. If it's any comfort you've the whole nation is rooting for you and Emily. The sailing community and the yachting media have started an Emily website and they've had thousands of hits from all over the world.'

The press conference venue was crowded. The room hushed for a few seconds when Steve and Kirsten entered and followed Fox to the table with its microphones. Already seated were two chief constables and a woman inspector, who was introduced as the press liaison officer.

Steve and Kirsten were invited in turn to address the gathering. Steve felt bewildered by the crowded room with its sweaty journalists and the flashing and clicking of cameras. He mumbled the appeal that had been largely scripted for him, his voice finally breaking. 'Emily is special...everyone loves her...whoever you are, please let her come home.'

Kirsten spoke next. 'I know you all want Emily safe home. We thank you for everything you've done to help find her. Now please leave us alone.'

Thankfully, they were allowed to leave before the assembly degenerated into a shouting match.

'Are we going to find Em?' John-Kaj asked.

'No, it won't be as easy as that,' said Sarah. 'But you are going to help. Today you're important, and you're going to ride in a police car.'

Frank Matheson arrived with Greta; shortly afterwards they were joined by Liz and Harry.

Harry spoke to them. 'You two had better ride with us. We know exactly where Branham Little Lake is.'

'Thanks – we'll do that. Steve insists that Sarah and Johnny are to go in the police cars.'

The sergeant gathered them for a briefing. 'We shall travel to Branham Little Lake where we will be met by officers from the Surrey force. They and we shall remain discreetly in the background while you people walk the area and see what you can discover.'

It was spitting with light rain when the cavalcade arrived at the Little Lake car park. The poor weather had left the spot deserted. Frank agreed that it was better to have no casual spectators, and it was even more satisfactory that the news corps were corralled in a probably useless press conference.

The police, now reinforced with Surrey officers plus a forestry official, deployed at a distance.

'If anyone asks, we're searching for some stolen jewellery,' said the sergeant.

John-Kaj looked apprehensive as he led the way with Sarah, Frank and Greta. To a casual watcher they would look like a family party. It took ten minutes to reach the dividing of the ways.

'We walked down there and we saw Mr Grogan on his tractor,' said John-Kaj.

Sarah shielded the ordnance sheet from the drizzle while Greta peered over her shoulder.

'This track leads straight into the middle of the plantations. It's a bit more than a track. I think it's really intended as a firebreak,' said Greta. 'But this forest is so vast anybody could hide away in there forever.'

'There's been a lot of traffic,' said Frank. 'Look at the way the track has been cut up.' He tapped Greta on the shoulder and beckoned her out of earshot of the others. 'There's nothing on the map that looks like a building.'

'There is that little group of dots up a secondary path,' said Greta.

'Lets all go back and talk to the Prestons and that bloke from the Forestry,' he looked around. 'What on earth has Johnny got?'

John-Kaj was ambling back to them carrying an odd shaped bundle. They could see now that it was a dishevelled cat.

'He's my friend,' he said. 'He was here when I was with Em, and we saw the tractor. Em said I couldn't keep him because he might have a home, but I don't think he can have one any more.'

Sarah bent over and examined the furry bundle. 'He's certainly friendly and he doesn't look that well fed or loved.'

'Can I take him home?'

Sarah looked at Frank and Greta. 'I think he could. The cat would be a distraction, and since the gerbils died the kids haven't got a pet.'

Frank smiled. 'Temporarily anyway – you'll have to check with the RSPCA in these parts, see if there's a name chip, but you might be doing it and young Johnny a favour.'

Frank spoke quietly to Greta. 'So long as it keeps raining these sun nutters will have a job lighting their straw fire.'

'If it's some comfort my sources say they need to start the fire by the sun's rays.'

'You mean with a burning glass. Well, the forecast says forty-eight hours of clouds and solid rain.'

Greta agreed. 'Let's hope it's right.'

They all walked slowly back to the car park. None of them noticed the figure that had shadowed and watched them, every step of the way, since their arrival at the lake.

Philip Le Bois' moods varied between depression, hatred and elation. The elation had been followed by a terrible interlude when he had broken down and wept like a child. Yet here he was, a top policeman and a grown man, and neither would ever normally weep like a child. This was what they had brought him to and he would have his retribution. Whatever happened, they would pay for his humiliation. He had no doubt that he was a victim of corruption in high places. He could see through the conspiracy of Superintendent Fox's favouritism and bias that had sabotaged his investigation from the first. The man Preston was a murderer. No one could deny that Preston was present when Arnold Evans had been clubbed to death with a yacht tiller. Who else could have killed the man? And Preston had a motive.

Social services had been unable to locate the missing Preston children. Le Bois did not much care for Sid Everett but the man had made the connection between Simpson's alleged children and the missing Preston girl. Could the missing girl have all the time been Rachel Preston – was that the truth? Was this a plot by Preston to dispose of an inconvenient child? Le Bois couldn't say, but his mood was beginning to lighten while he felt this crazy surge of energy and joy. He didn't deserve this treatment, but suspension or not, he was a free agent now. He was more than an investigator, he was an avenging angel who would rescue the child and destroy his enemies.

He stood under the fringe of trees opposite the entrance to Firs Farm. His watch read eleven am. Fox was holding a press conference with the Simpson couple. He had left with them half an hour before. Four years ago, Le Bois had been present at a similar conference where the alleged grieving victim had turned out to be the guilty party.

He heard vehicles travelling towards him from the direction of Chichester and this time they were the cars he had been expecting. He ducked behind the convenient beech tree. Covert surveillance had always been his speciality, and he was good, no not good – he was the best. The first two were police cars. He knew both the occupants of the third car that had turned into the gateway. That meddlesome Von

Essens woman and that disgraced superintendent Matheson: both cronies of Fox. The police cars parked on the driveway were manned by officers he didn't recognise: Portsmouth division most likely. Twenty minutes more and he saw real movement. The two police cars left, followed by another civilian motor and Alleluia! The driver was Preston with his wife and Von Essens plus Matheson. He ran to his own car and prepared to follow. His mind was racing, his ears were singing; he felt almost as if his head would burst. He was on the trail now, and his enemies would lead him to the missing child.

The evil woman was back and she was horrible. Emily was tired, hungry and she couldn't control her shivering. What did these nasty people want in keeping her here? This night had been colder than ever, and water was dripping through the roof and on to the floor. For the second night Gerry had insisted that she wore his tweed jacket. It smelt faintly of old man's odour and tobacco. It was also very itchy. All inhibitions gone, she had curled up in his arms and exhausted now she slept, although it was a sleep filled with weird dreams.

'Stand up, young one, let me look at you,' said the woman.

In no way did Emily want to obey her, but as before the old bat had that strange hypnotic power that left her no choice. Gerry had remarked how tame and obedient were her two sons whenever she was present.

'You have lost some weight,' the woman had a lilting singsong voice.

Emily summoned all her spirit. 'What d'you expect? You don't give us any proper food.'

Peter Terring snarled. 'Slut! You don't answer back – understand! You speak to the Powerful One when she tells you!'

Emily shrank away – for a moment she thought the brute was going to beat her. She managed to throw Grogan a pathetic and appealing glance. He shook his head but said nothing.

The woman's face twisted into a grimace of a smile. 'We need you in good shape for the great day. So, very well, you shall have food. What food would that be?'

Emily was so startled that she could think of nothing to say.

Gerry grinned broadly. 'Fish and chips.'

'Don't try to be funny, old man,' Terring sneered.

'Curry then,' Gerry replied. 'I don't know where we are, but it can't be far from one of these takeaway places or whatever they're called.'

179

The old woman spoke a few words in the strange language and walked from the room. Emily was watching Grogan. He had moved away from his brother and she could sense him relax now the woman had gone. Terring stood, face deadpan, apparently lost in thought.

Grogan spoke. 'Emily, the Powerful One orders feed you. I will see what we can do.'

Emily summoned up her sweetest smile and looked him in the face. 'Thank you,' she replied.

Philip Le Bois had lost none of his surveillance and tracking skills. These had been trained and honed years before in the MET, as a junior detective constable. He felt exhilaration once more as he discreetly followed his quarry. Preston must be totally unaware of Le Bois on his tail, for the man drove at a steady sixty-five miles an hour up the A3 as if he had not a care in the world. Le Bois would have expected to see some manic tendency and some aggression in the man's driving, or at least some signs of carelessness: signals of the man's innate violence. But Preston's car handling became even more cautious as he turned onto the busy two-way A325. Le Bois dropped back a couple of places, never for a moment losing concentration on his quarry. By now the police cars that had started the journey were way ahead and out of sight. After a tricky passage through a maze of back lanes, the journey came to an abrupt end. Preston turned right into a car park, deserted apart from the two police cars that had started from South Marshall.

Le Bois did not follow them but checked his map against the car's GPS system. He was at a remote spot called Branham Little Lake. A mile away was Branham Great Lake where Preston had deposited the body of Arnold Evans, and close by the site where Nadine Rotherton had died, killed by Preston's wife. He had already noted that the signpost into the lane read Tilford and Tilford was where Preston lived. Le Bois felt a surge of pure joy. He would follow them on foot and they would lead him to the missing girl.

Greta had reached police headquarters at nine o'clock. She was shown straight into Fox's office and there, to her surprise, was Frank Matheson.

'That's right,' said Fox. 'My lord and master has agreed to take Frank as a consultant, but on this case only.' He waved Greta to an armchair. 'That little boy Johnny came good I gather.'

'Yes,' said Greta. 'We were all impressed.'

'Surrey have plainclothes officers concealed and watching the track into the plantation. They had a pretty damp night of it I'm told.'

'Any news on those aerial pictures?'

'They're due here by courier within the hour. MOD emailed us earlier. They say, quote, "...there are a number of inconsistencies...compared with the original survey..." Let's hope to God that means what they're hinting at.'

'What's this report of people loitering?' asked Frank.

'Oh, yes,' Fox picked up another printout. 'The Surrey watchers identified two civilian males hanging around Branham Little Lake and the plantations.' He handed both of them copies.

Male, aged mid 50s, short dark hair, height 5ft 8 approx. Clothing: dark anorak, dark trousers, town shoes. PC Dent thinks he's familiar. May be police but not local. Man appeared agitated.

Male, aged late 50s, tall, shoulder length dark hair, with touch of grey. Well-built, dark skinned, but not Black or Asian. Clothing: long rain coat, short Wellingtons.

'The second one is Costas,' said Frank. 'Can't say who that other one is. Did the two talk to each other?'

'No, the officers were definite about that. The first man concealed himself when the second appeared.'

'I take it the officers didn't speak to either?'

'No,' said Fox. 'They only had orders to look out for Grogan and detain him for questioning.'

Kirsten and Steve were returned home from their press conference rather faster than they had driven on the outward journey. The police car had sped down the A27, leaving the reporters trailing in their wake. Apparently the pressmen had been warned that any of them exceeding the national speed limit would be pulled over and ticketed. In the long term it made little difference. By two o'clock the media scrum was once more in position outside Firs Farm.

Steve and Kirsten knew nothing of the mayhem that they had left behind in the press conference. By now the journalists had discovered that Gerry Pembelty was on the same list of sacrificial victims as the girl: a warrior and a child. Forty-eight hours earlier the tabloid hacks would have implied that the man was connected with Emily's disappearance, but stopping just short of libellous accusations of paedophilia. Now they were gorging themselves on this much hotter story.

A story enlivened by real reports of sun sacrifices in America. An amazing number of sightings of Emily and Pembelty seemed to be winging their way back across the Atlantic. The police press officers had done their best to keep to the facts, but with the media pack in full cry it was futile.

The reporters had then demanded that the police release Andy Ikes' photographs and insisted that they be distributed nationwide. Finally, a television journalist had raised something about "... reluctance by the security services to co-operate with the police". He then implied that MI5 and MI6 had their own fish to fry and weren't too bothered if the victims in this case died.

The presiding officer had glared at the man. Clearly this tiresome journalist was echoing some of the official investigation's own suspicions.

'All sorts of strange people and organisations are always claiming responsibility at times like this. We must all keep a sense of proportion.'

By now, some of the press were diverting their attention elsewhere. It seemed the rumours about a lacklustre MI5 had reached Westminster. Once again the luckless Home Secretary had been on the receiving end of a backbench grilling. When asked whether the Government accepted the existence of the Children of the Power the man had replied: 'Yes.'

Did the Government believe that the cult would fulfil their sacrificial threat?

'Everything is being done to forestall such a horror, but if not, we must prepare ourselves for much sorrow.' It was a reply that reduced the House unusually to a stunned silence.

The Home Secretary concluded by saying that the police had agreed to release the family pictures taken on Mr Simpson's digital camera.

Little Emily Simpson was once again destined to fill the morning papers.

Steve was worried about Kirsten. Her condition drew him away from his own anxiety and misery. She had spent the last five days in a smouldering rage, dreaming of her retribution. Now she had sunk into apathy, hardly speaking or showing any reaction to anything. At least John-Kaj and Sarah were both safe home. They had little to say about their trip to Branham. Sarah had confirmed that Johnny had pointed out the place that he remembered. Johnny had appeared carrying a scruffy cat. Steve could tell that Kirsten was not pleased but her apathy inhibited her from saying much. Steve really didn't care and Sarah said it would be a good distraction for the boy.

'Come on, Dad. Johnny's safe home now. Let's show him how to feed the little cat and groom it.'

Steve looked at the cat cuddled in his son's arms. It was black and muddy but definitely not wild. He could hear it purring contentedly. How he wished his Emily was here – she would love this funny little creature as if it was a baby. Steve wasn't sure why, but Kirsten's depression and apathy had increased his own resolution. He felt cocooned within his subconscious and there he found hope. He couldn't quantify it, but he felt an increasing sensation of hope. He knew that the police officers around them all believed in their own hearts that Emily was dead. Steve would not believe it. Never would he accept it. Until the awful moment when he saw and touched his little girl's dead form he would believe that she still lived.

'Dad, I don't think you've heard a word I've said,' Sarah looked up from the bathroom chair where the cat lay on a towel in an undignified posture. 'I'll have to take him to the vet – he's got fleas.' She pulled back the fur to reveal a tattered flea collar. 'This is useless; it's worn out and somebody's stuffed paper in it.' Sarah had removed the collar and was holding a slip of thin paper up to the light. 'There's writing – who would do that? I wonder if it's his name and address?'

She set the collar down on the washstand. 'The ink's run a bit but…Oh! Oh, Dad, I can't believe this, I can read it now and if it's true…!'

Steve looked over her shoulder, but the writing was too small for him without his reading glasses. 'What is it?'

'Oh, Dad….it says: *Emily OK in ruin near Brham little lk. G Pmblty.*'

'Mrs Pembelty confirms the handwriting is her husband's. He takes that old-fashioned stylus pen with him everywhere.' Fox paused to let Greta absorb this information, 'Secondly, we have the aerial pictures and they are very interesting.' He nodded to a technician with a laptop.

The screen in the conference room filled with a remarkably high definition photograph. 'This is the aerial shot taken six years ago, covering four square miles of the forest plantation.' Fox directed the pointer in his hand to a small square object in a plantation clearing. 'This is the cottage that the Forestry officials located for us. It's called Woodman's End.' Fox moved the pointer to a wide strip running roughly east to west. 'That's the fire break where Grogan's tractor was seen.'

Greta had a question. 'If anyone lived there, how did they reach the outside world? That track is a bog. I've seen it.'

'No, when it was inhabited people reached it via a mile of hard track branching off Sandy Lane; that's this turning off the main Hindhead to Farnham road.' He pointed. 'The track's still there, but in a terrible state. You could possibly drive a small car down it, but it's too narrow for Grogan's tractor. It's a clever spot to choose, you have to give the abductors credit for that. Right in the middle of that bloody great forest, it's probably the only really obscure site in these parts. Talk about needle in a haystack. Next frame please.'

The following picture was a contrast. Greta could see a square where trees had been felled, but the cottage seemed to have vanished. Where it had been was merely a distorted smudge. She felt an overwhelming feeling of failure.

'All right, the close-up,' Fox called.

Now Greta could see the difference. There could be no doubt that where once there had been a dwelling there remained a huge pile of straw covered by a rectangular tarpaulin.

'Not much doubt about that,' said Fox. 'Now the clincher. The deeds for Woodman's End Cottage are in the name of Carlotta Larranaga. So, very well done, Greta, but for you we'd never have cracked this one.'

'Thank you, Norman, but what do we do now? We've got to get the hostages out and damned soon. The weather's changing in twenty-four hours time.'

'We spoke about not using an army. Well, the MOD won't deploy a full SAS unit without a certainty that the hostages deaths are imminent.'

'But, they are...' Greta tried to interrupt but Fox held up a hand.

'Hear me out. The MOD have agreed to loan us two fully trained watchers from SAS Hereford. They are already on the site, and they will deploy a full section when needed. The Surrey police armed response unit have also been briefed, and are on first state readiness.'

'Norman, what are we waiting for? If the hostages are there go in and get them.'

Norman Fox sat back in his chair and grimaced. 'I thought you'd ask that. Everyone is asking that on our side too. But the intelligence services say they need to net everyone: hostages and kidnappers. It seems that this Carlotta is a high priestess of the cult worldwide. Her followers call her The Powerful One. Catch her, and there's every chance the killings will stop,'

'I know that, the Powerful One is referred to on their website. I say don't arrest her – kill her! I know that's unethical, unlawful, but in this case I say no legal proceedings – kill her! If I'm right, that will stop the sacrifices, and we may just resolve this happily,' Greta sighed. 'If we do, I think I'll resign as a profiler. This assignment nearly killed me, and I dream of that little girl.'

'I know that, Greta, me too. The whole country is thinking of young Emily and we don't forget the old man as well. Battle of Britain pilot – that's special.'

CHAPTER 20

Emily had been sick in the night. The food they had been given was real food but she couldn't take it. Sometime in the hours of darkness she had crawled away from Gerry and vomited into a far corner. For the first time she had lost interest in living. She would never grow up and go to university. She'd never win races on the track or become an Olympic sailor. Then, in despair, she knew she would never see her mum and dad and her brother: never see her home and untidy room again. Her life was over. She was going to die and soon. She had given up on hope, and now she had lost interest in life itself, but why? It wasn't fair – she couldn't die, not here in this stinking hole. She lay down and pulled the fusty tweed jacket around her and fell into a half-doze into which horrid visions intruded. The old woman had become a slimy sea creature with tentacles, and at the end of each tentacle was one of those thin bony hands. The slimy creature had turned into a vivid blue, and its head had morphed into the face of the woman. It had come to kill her. Emily lay rigid; she was paralysed, incapable of movement; but the twisted face only laughed.

It was light now; they knew when day came from the light that filtered through the gap in the straw bales, especially the gap where the little cat had entered. In fact the light was better than yesterday. Emily sat up trying to make out the rustling noise that had been in the background of her brain for a while. She could see what it was now. Old Gerry was pulling handfuls of the straw through the window. Already he had a sizeable, fluffy looking pile on the floor. She was about to speak when Gerry shook his head and put a finger to his lips. Then he picked up something and held it out to her. It was another of those little squares of cigarette paper, and once again Gerry had written something with that funny pen.

Emily, they are in the other room. Been there all night. BE QUIET.

She nodded and managed a smile although the news, if true, was frightening. Gerry was writing another message, holding a tiny slip of the paper with his thumb against the wooden window frame.

You go listen – come back whisper.

Gerry pointed at the oak door.

Emily nodded again and crept across the room. She could hear a voice; it was the old woman. Emily recognised it and she wanted to be sick again. The voice continued in a funny drone as if the old bat was reading aloud from a very dull book. Then she heard the men, both of them. She couldn't understand a word, but it seemed as if the men were repeating line by line everything the old woman said.

She tiptoed back to Gerry who bent down stiffly to listen. 'They're all in there but they keep talking in that silly language and I don't understand.'

'Good girl,' Gerry whispered. 'Now, look at this.' He passed her a weird looking little metal box. It was heavy for its size and was shiny. She turned it to the light and saw it was engraved with a little winged badge and some words. She handed it back.

Gerry took it, grinned and then with a snap the box opened, and a bright centimetre of flame burned brightly, throwing little shadows against the walls. Instantly the flame died accompanied by another snap. 'My silver lighter, given to me by my mechanics – got our squadron's crest engraved'

Next he bent down and picked up a little rusty tin can. He tapped it with a finger. 'Found it in the cellar – good old fashioned turpentine – just what I need to help matters along.'

Gerry caught her by the shoulders and turned her to face him. 'Emily,' he whispered. 'When the door next opens I will make all three of them come in here. When I shout, Scramble! you will run through that door and into the outside world, and you will sprint like you are trained for. You will not stop running until you find safety. Do you understand?'

Gerry spoke quietly but his voice had a quality she had never heard, even from her own dad. It was a voice of command not to be disputed, but to be obeyed to the letter.

'What about you, Gerry?' she asked.

'What about me?' he grinned again. 'Never mind me. You will do as you are told!'

'Andy we divert from here to ole' Pembelty's house. His wife's hiding in there. I bet the old biddy knows something. We'll smoke her out.'

Sid Everett was sitting in the bus shelter at South Marshall, tapping busily at his laptop. The tiny building was festooned in yellow ribbons: newsworthy, but of no interest to Sid. Andy Ikes had set his equipment down on the bench but stood looking out into the rain soaked-road.

'I'm going to spin a bit of a new trail. How does this sound?' Sid read from his screen.

'Questions are being asked. Why did the police fail to connect little Emily in the first place with the disappearance of her elderly neighbour Gerald Pembelty, 86? Why was the experienced police officer, who attempted to execute a valid search warrant, suspended from duty? These are the questions the villagers of picturesque South Marshall in Sussex are asking. When will these questions be answered?'

'You fucking reporters!' an angry voice intervened.

Sid looked up into the face of a genuine villager of South Marshall. He hadn't realised that this red-faced individual had been within earshot and big Daryl, Sid's security man, was nowhere to be seen.

'You do spout some shit you people. Old Gerry is as honest as the day is long. We like him and we like Emily and her mum and dad. Nobody's asking those questions here – so why make up this shit?' To Sid's relief, and even more to Andy's, the belligerent local turned his back on them and strode away.

It turned out to be an even worse day for those of the local and national media who, abandoning their watch on Firs Farm, shifted the quarter of a mile to the Pembelty cottage. It had started raining again. Sid and Andy found a good pitch on a high grass bank on the edge of the throng. The lane seemed a sea of mud. Some of the press corps parked through the gate of a grass field. Within twenty minutes an irate farmer arrived and padlocked the gate. More police appeared and restored order. At ten o'clock, the Pembelty's son, Richard, walked out dressed in his Navy commander's uniform, accompanied by a little man who announced that he was the family's solicitor.

This pair was greeted by a hubbub of noise. The solicitor read a prepared statement. Group Captain Pembelty had not come home for six days. He was an elderly man, and the family and police had taken positive steps to find him. There was unconfirmed evidence to suggest a connection with the tragic disappearance of Emily Simpson and the illegal actions of this alleged religious cult. Alternatively, Group Captain Pembelty may have met with an accident.

The media were not to be appeased by this, and replied with a barrage of sceptical questions. Then one man went too far.

'Commander Pembelty, is your father a paedophile – did he molest you when you were young?'

'That's done it,' Sid laughed.

Richard Pembelty had clenched his fists. Sid expected and hoped the man would lash out, but his service discipline held fast.

The solicitor's voice rose above the uproar. 'You, Sir, have made a slanderous comment in front of witnesses. You will be hearing from us.' The rest of his words were lost amidst a shrilling of mobile phone alerts, including Sid's.

'Sid here…what? I can't make you out – sounds breaking up. It's these sodding hills…'

It seemed much the same thing was being experienced throughout the crowd. 'Something's happened,' said Sid. 'I don't know what or where. Come on, Andy, let's go find out.'

'I think it's only fair that you and Frank be here for the last act,' said Fox.

Greta sat in the passenger seat of Fox's car, with Frank in the back with the Chief Superintendent. They had passed through three road blocks manned by police firearms officers before Fox's driver turned right into the car park at Branham Little Lake. It was six-thirty; the rain had stopped and the first hints of daylight revealed a clear sky.

Uniformed police were everywhere as well as some sinister army personnel with blackened faces. Two civilians were standing some-what apart from the activity.

'There's Costas,' said Matheson. 'Come on, Greta, we'll have a word with him.'

Greta followed him across a patch of sand and heather. 'Hello, Costas,' Matheson called. 'They told me you didn't exist.'

'Mr Matheson, well met again,' replied the dark-haired man.

So, this was the Argentine security agent with an insight into the sun cult.

'Who is this man?' asked Costas' companion none too politely.

'He's a consultant on this case, as I am,' said Greta.

'And you are?'

Greta was not going to be intimidated by this spook. The man was tall weedy, nondescript and rude.

'I am the official police profiler,' she replied. 'So who are you and by what authority are you here?'

'I am a civil servant.'

'Leave it, Greta,' said Matheson. 'Costas, how will these sun nutters react when we move in?'

'They will destroy themselves and their sacrificial captives. So, you will have to tread most softly. Your soldiers must not charge in waving and shouting. This is not the Malvinas.'

Fox was beckoning to her. Greta left Frank with Costas and the alleged civil servant and walked back to where the Superintendent was talking to an army man. The soldier was one of the two that she had seen on arrival beside a drab camouflaged Land Rover. Something about this man was different. Greta couldn't quite analyse it. The soldier was not a tall man, never a guardsman. He was short, squat and exuded fitness and menace. His combat fatigues were drab, and his face and hands were streaked with camouflage cream.

The man nodded dourly when Fox introduced her. 'There's a party hanging around near the target. My observer can't identify the man.'

'Description?' asked Fox.

'White, short hair, dark clothing, civilian. Been wandering around the target area all night. If he doesn't shift he'll get himself shot.' The soldier walked away.

'We've had several reported sightings of this person,' Fox said. 'I've a nasty feeling I know him. Could be Le Bois. We know he's gone missing.'

'Would the army shoot him for real?'

'Those guys would. They're the real McCoy – eight of them from Hereford.'

'Special Forces.'

'That's right. That means instructions from the very top. The Government are terrified of this sun cult, and Emily Simpson has come to represent every family's little girl. It's that serious. It means we must succeed – no foul ups. Le Bois has no business here so he'll have to take his chance.'

The soldier reappeared. 'Our unit's in position. Intruder's around somewhere, but they've lost him.'

'We think the man may be a suspended police officer with a mental problem,' Fox replied.

'Understood: our priority is the kid. If that man gets in the way – too bad.'

'What will happen to the abductors?' Greta had to ask.

The soldier looked at her. 'They want a sacrifice – they'll have one.' His hand mimed a throat cutting.

190

Gerry had been working continuously, and with Emily's help they had collected a large pile of dry straw under the window. Gerry had finally given up with exhaustion, leaving Emily to plait a loose tail of straw through the bars.

'If they run to form they'll be in here within seconds,' said Gerry. 'You know your orders. On the command Scramble, you run.'

Gerry looked at her and winked. He undid the cap of the little tin and poured the liquid within over the straw and through into the stack outside. He snapped his cigarette lighter and plied the flame into the base of the straw pile. Then he stumbled to the doorway and began to kick it. The fire was well alight now, and Emily found her eyes smarting. Within seconds she was choking. Fear took hold of her – it wasn't going to work. This was the end.

The door swung open. The two men ran inside followed by the old woman shuffling behind. 'What are you doing?' she screamed. 'It's too early – it's got to be the rays of the Power. You stupid old man you'll ruin everything...'

'Emily: scramble – scramble!' Gerry roared the command before subsiding in a fit of coughing.

Emily obeyed, but as she ran through the doorway Peter Terring made a grab at her. Then the unexpected happened. With an eerie cry, Grogan pushed his brother against the wall. Then he in turn grabbed Emily and for a second she felt despair. Grogan lifted her off the ground and projected her through the doorway. Emily staggered into the tiny room beyond their prison and saw the entrance. The door was open wide, and through it shone the early daylight of the outside world. With a rush of adrenalin she sped out, running as she'd never run before. Running now, not for competition and prizes, but running for her life.

In front of her was an open expanse of sand and short heather with a wall of trees at the far side. She would run for those trees. She must reach the trees – she would feel safe if she could lose herself in those trees. But she was no longer alone; a man stood in her way, and she had seen him before but she couldn't remember where or when. She must dodge him. She could see that he was old and fat. She knew she could outrun him.

As she passed him the man made an attempt to catch hold of her. 'Rachel,' his voice croaked. 'I know you – you're Rachel – where's your brother?'

Emily evaded his grasp with ease and as she ran on she felt elation, a wonderful high. She was running in fresh air and it smelt good – she was free.

Crack – Crack – Crack – Crack! That noise was gunshots, with a horrid nearby whining sound! Bullets – someone was shooting bullets – oh why?

'Stop it!' She heard her voice whimper. 'Oh, stop!'

She couldn't look back; she dared not turn round. She was too frightened to wonder what was happening. She must run; must gather herself for that sprint-finish that she was so proud of. The shooting had ceased. With one last effort, her lungs gasping and her legs and arms pumping, she stumbled into the first of the trees, and for a few seconds, she slowed. The forest was dark and the trees so thick. Behind her came a long rumbling explosion, followed seconds later by a blast of intense heat. Now she ran again, faster than ever, sobbing and wailing as she did so, dodging among the tightly spaced trees, hardly noticing the sharp lower branches scratching her arms.

'Emily, slow down, kid. It's all right – you're safe now.' The voice was nearby and it was a good voice, a man's voice, a nice voice, with warmth and a chuckle to it. She felt a sense of relief and trust. He was a soldier of sorts with a sinister black gun. He looked weird: his clothes were filthy, his face was covered in paint and his head was topped in a funny woolly hat. 'Come on Emily, the whole country's been searching for you. We're going to take you home to your mum and dad.' Though distorted by the green paint, Emily saw the man's happy smile and she realised that he, too, was as relieved as she was.

'What's happened to Gerry?' she pleaded.

'Two of my lads went in to fetch him. They got him out before the place blew.'

'The little girl's fine, Sirs, and it's all clear for the ambulances,' the constable addressed Fox and the senior officer from Surrey. Greta could read the relief in all their faces.

'Tell them to go ahead,' replied the local Superintendent. 'My radio's reported in. I'm afraid your man Le Bois has been declared dead at the scene. Special Forces took him out. I'm sorry, but they didn't have any choice. He tried to seize hold of the girl as she was escaping. They had no clear identification, and they couldn't have known he was a police officer.'

'I know,' said Fox. 'The man had lost it some weeks ago. He was seriously mentally disturbed – his career was over.' He lowered his voice. 'There'll be an official enquiry. I'll see he has an honourable record and I guess they'll rule accidental.'

The Surrey man's radio was calling. The sound was distorted but the officer seemed to comprehend. 'Le Bois's body is going to the morgue with two of the others. The second ambulance is taking the old man to hospital in Frimley.'

'How is he?'

'The army guys say he's fine, but he's inhaled a lot of smoke and he's pretty well crashed out with exhaustion.'

'Thank God for that. What was that bloody great explosion?'

'It seems they packed drums of fuel and gas cylinders all round the cottage. They got the old man out before the whole lot went up.'

'And the kidnappers?'

Well, they wanted a sacrifice to the sun god and they've got one – only it's them that's paid it. The fire brigade are on site but there won't be much left for them.'

Greta could see Frank talking to Costas. 'Who is that man?' she asked.

'The foreign spook?' the local officer replied. 'They say he provided the intelligence for all this.'

'No,' said Fox. 'It's true the man identified the cult leader, in fact he met her right here, but he never found the abandoned cottage. It was young Johnny Simpson who pointed us to it. When Costas finds that out he'll feel less pleased with himself. No, the person who told us about the sun worshippers and then probed right into their minds is the person who is standing beside you. She is the queen of all profilers. Greta, I'm going to break discipline and protocol and give you a kiss.'

A small knot of people was approaching. Frank Matheson went over to meet them. Greta could see two WPCs and clinging to them, stumbling as she walked, was a tiny shrunken figure of a child.

It was midday at Firs Farm when one more police car drove in off the road. Steve watched Penny Calder run to the front door. Another policewoman was standing there, and beside her was a small figure dressed in a makeshift array of baggy clothes.

'Daddy, I'm home again and I'd awfully like a hot shower.'

It was not long afterwards that the news began to break worldwide and it could not have been in a more dramatic way. BBC1 was about to show the House of Commons with the Prime Minister's keynote speech on the Health Service. As the premier stood to speak, an aide touched him on the shoulder. The PM read a note and then promptly sat down. Viewers could hear the puzzled muttering around the house. The aide carried the note to the Speaker, who stood up and addressed the members.

'I have some news. I am happy to tell you that the little girl Emily Simpson has been rescued, and she is alive and well...' The words were drowned in a storm of cheering. 'Order – order...this session is suspended for twenty minutes.'

For Steve and Kirsten, with Sarah, Penny, the Prestons and everyone at Firs Farm it was hours of bewilderment. The emotions were muted as they had been advised that Emily was not ready for a noisy reception.

'Just show her all your love,' advised their doctor. 'I can't find anything physically wrong, but she's been to the edge and come back, and that's going to affect her until the end of her life. Be loving and patient and she'll be fine. She will seem a little bit more adult and serious perhaps, but she'll be fine.'

'We'll give her more love than she's ever known,' said Steve. 'It's a miracle but she's alive and with us again.'

'After a while it will be good if she will talk about it with you. I can tell you I've seen Mr Pembelty in the hospital. He says Emily saved the day – he's full of praise.'

It was only now that Steve and Kirsten began to learn of the great furore that Emily's abduction had stirred, both in Britain and overseas. For the first time the police told them the full truth about The Children of The Power and their belief in human sacrifice. Kirsten's friends had phoned and emailed from Denmark. Emily's picture had been on newspaper front pages, and her story had been told on television. Although Kirsten would never admit it, she was secretly pleased that her fellow countrymen and women still remembered her as a sporting personality. In the days that followed it was a Danish TV team who alone were invited to film and talk to the family.

As they had been warned, Emily's recovery was slow. She actively hated the interrogations with the child trauma counsellor, and after two of these sessions refused point blank to co-operate further. For many nights she could not sleep in her room without screaming in terror. In the early hours she would run to her parents' bed and snuggle down beside them. Only then did she sleep peacefully. Her greatest solace came from the little cat, the same that had carried the cryptic message. No one had come forward to claim him and the vet confirmed that the creature had no identity chip and was seriously undernourished. Emily named her little companion Gerry, and carried him around for hours on end until the animal struggled free demanding to be fed.

Although extrovert by nature Emily had found school difficult. Press cameras had been waiting for her that first day. Kirsten had whisked her through the school gates and into the staff car park. Emily's special friends had met her and shown her pictures of the silent vigil and the display of yellow ribbons. Emily had been distressed to hear that Mr Jones, who had been in charge at the athletics track, had been suspended from duty. She had always found the man grumpy, but this was unfair. Carlotta had been waiting for Emily, determined to snatch her. Why couldn't they find out who it was that had told the horrible woman where she would be that afternoon?

The first few days of her return were difficult for Emily. Her friends were supportive, but others seemed to regard her as a curiosity and Ms Flotton hinted that the sun cult was fantasy and that Emily had run away with a man. Ms Flotton didn't like men and said so. Emily's fellow pupils never accepted this cruel slight, but it became a signal for the school bullies. Emily was taunted openly until she threw a punch at a boy twice her size and broke his nose. The boy's parents had complained, but it was their son who was suspended.

Oddly enough, it was the Danish Television interview that briefly restored Emily to something like her old self. Steve had had his doubts about allowing her to appear in person, and the child counsellor had disapproved. Emily would have none of it. She told of her days in the old ruin and gave a laconic account of her escape with lavish praise for Gerry Pembelty. Steve, much heartened, smiled as Kirsten started to babble in Danish. Emily intervened in her own fractured Danglish version of the language, to the great delight of their interviewers. Apparently the Danes were intrigued and amused to find that Christine, Sarah's little girl, and technically Emily's niece, was three months older than her aunt.

Gerry was released from hospital after forty-eight hours. He entered a media storm that shook him profoundly. Gerry had passed overnight from suspected child snatcher to national hero. He was clearly shaken and very weary but he bore up well under the spotlight. His wartime record was unearthed and blasted across inches of newsprint, and a special television feature about the abduction and the Children of The Power. A week later, a happy, but shy Gerry received a hero's reception at the RAF base from where the photographic mission had been flown. After a lavish lunch in the mess he had been given a framed citation at a ceremony culminating in the Red Arrows roaring overhead.

Gerry and Dolly had called at Firs Farm as soon as they returned to South Marshall. Emily had flung her arms around the old man and wept, but all could see that hers were tears of joy. Then Kirsten had hugged and kissed him, followed in turn by Sarah and by Penny Calder, who had been invited to join them.

'Four lovely ladies,' Gerry laughed. 'You'll make my good wife jealous.'

Emily ran into the garden to join her brother. Minutes later they could hear their joyous shouting and laughter.

They sat their guest down and poured him a slug of his favourite whisky. 'How is she?' he asked.

'She's recovering better than anyone expected. We've stopped the psychologist's probing; that woman's obsessed with sex. The questioning was only making Emily more depressed and she's scared to go back to Branham and sail. It was a big part of her life and now she's backed out of her athletics team. We had high hopes of her sailing. She's still in the Cadet national team.'

Gerry seemed lost in thought, and it was a few seconds before he spoke. 'Years ago I had an old pal who was captured by the Japs at Singapore and spent three and a half pretty dire years as a PoW. When he got back to civvy street, it haunted him. His wife told me sometimes he couldn't sleep for whole weeks on end. Then he was persuaded to go back and visit the places where he had suffered and meet some of the people who were there with him. His wife told me that after that he settled down and never had another nightmare.'

'You're saying take Emily back to Branham?' asked Steve.

'No, I'm saying take her back to that bloody cottage, and show her it doesn't exist.'

'We've never been to this place so we'd like you to show it to us,' Kirsten spoke, as Emily clung to her, burying her face in her mother's chest. Steve stood beside them with Gerry and Dolly.

'You're a brave girl,' said Gerry. 'Remember, this is going to be hard for me too. Will you do it?'

Emily released her grip and faced him. 'Yes, all right.'

Steve's Volvo was parked on the overgrown track that led half a mile from the junction with a narrow tarmac lane. They were now within a short walk of the ruined cottage.

'I'm a bit stiff in the joints,' said Gerry. 'But suppose I lead on and you all follow.' He didn't wait for an answer but began walking towards the gap at the far end of the track where the trees thinned.

'Come on, my darling,' said Kirsten. 'We can do this together.'

Emily walked slowly between her parents, holding tightly to their hands. Kirsten had only the faintest idea of where they were going. She had seen the aerial photographs and some very old pictures of the cottage in its heyday that had been found in a local history book. They walked to the edge of the bare clearing and there they saw – nothing.

The forestry authority assisted by army engineers had been busy. No trace of Woodman's End Cottage remained, apart from a few sticks of burned straw protruding from the topsoil. The site was smooth, although the marks of tracked bulldozers could just be made out in the dirt. The cottage and the cellar beneath had been eliminated, and its stone and bricks carted away.

'Was it really here?' Emily asked.

'Yes, this is it,' said Gerry. 'And now it's gone. Let's walk around the outside.'

'I can see it now,' she said. 'I ran over there into those trees. I found that nice soldier and he was kind. But he wouldn't tell me his name. I asked him and he said call him Jack, but I don't think that was really his name. Come on, I'll show you where he was.' She tugged at her mother's hand.

Steve and Kirsten followed Emily across the broken heather and turf. 'It's funny,' said Emily, 'but it's not anything like as far as I remember.' She stopped walking and turned to face them. Once again Emily asked the same question she had repeated over the weeks. 'The old woman's dead isn't she? Please tell me she's dead.'

'Carlotta Larranaga was her name,' Steve replied. 'And she's dead, don't worry – she's most definitely dead.'

'It was here wasn't it?'

'Yes, it all ended here.'

'I know – I didn't see her die but I heard the bullets.'

Grogan and Terring had died, shot down by the army marksmen. Philip Le Bois, indistinguishable from the others, had also died after he tried to seize hold of Emily. Carlotta had perished horribly in the fire. Wounded but alive, she had run back into the cottage and refused to leave. The Special Forces soldiers saw the rescue of Gerry Pembelty as their priority. By the time they returned to the cottage its

197

outer walls of straw and fuel drums had become an inferno. Carlotta had wanted a sacrifice by fire and, thought Kirsten, she had been granted her wish.

'It's funny,' said Emily. 'She was horrible, she scared me but now I can't really remember what she looked like.' She glanced at them with a wan expression. 'Did they really believe that killing me would stop global warming?'

Kirsten was startled. Emily must have overheard them talking with the counsellors and the police. Greta von Essens had also spent an evening with them, telling them of her discovery of the sun cult.

'There are a lot of strange people around in the world, darling, but these were mad. They've gone now – they can't hurt you.'

Emily looked at her solemnly. 'That nasty shrink woman didn't want me to do this. She's wrong though, and those men never touched me in the way she thinks. I'm glad I came here today, but I'll never go to this place again.' She turned round and stared at the site where the cottage had been. 'You know, Ed Grogan didn't want me to die. It's silly but I can't hate him, not any more.' Suddenly she took off and ran back to where the cottage had once stood.

Kirsten faced her husband and spontaneously she flung her arms around his neck and kissed him with the passion of long ago days. 'What a wonderful little girl we have.'

Gerry met them. 'I think our therapy may have worked,' he whispered. 'We never worried about all this counselling and post-traumatic whatnot in my time, but I think we've worked some real magic today for her and for me too.'

'But you saved her, Gerry,' said Kirsten. 'We'll never forget that.'

'Quick, she's coming back this way' Gerry whispered. 'Emily is a remarkable young lady. Without her influence we should both have died. She achieved something amazing that day. She rose to the occasion most bravely. I call it Emily's Hour.'

Emily joined them. The tears had gone and for the first time that day she smiled. 'Daddy, can we go to the sailing club now? I want to see my boat.'

EPILOGUE

THE DAILY BANNER
FUNERAL OF POLICE HERO
Sid Everett Reports.
Philip Le Bois, dead hero of the Surrey sun cult siege was buried today in the little churchyard outside St Peter Port in Guernsey. Police from six forces in Southern England paid their respects to the fallen inspector...

...Many still ask why no notice was taken of the lone inspector's investigations...there is talk of a conspiracy...did he have to die in the way he did attempting a rescue, alone and unrecognised? These are the questions the people of Britain are asking today.

SOUTH COAST GAZETTE.
INQUEST CONFIRMS MURDER BY SUN CULT.

Joint inquests were held today into the deaths of Arnold Evans, Linda Zeigler and Simon Hexham. After two hours of deliberation the coroner's jury brought in unanimous verdicts of murder.

The coroner, Mr George Weldermann, stated that the over-whelming evidence pointed to wilful and pre-planned murder by followers of the cult Children of The Power. He could not comment on the state of mind of such irrational and disturbed people but it seemed each victim had a connection to weather forecasting. Each was a prominent member of their community and well known in the wider world, and it is certain that each recognised their killer. As we reported yesterday, an identical verdict was declared at the inquest in Guildford into the death of former weather girl Nadine Rotherton.

After the verdicts Chief Superintendent Fox stated that the police were not looking for any murder suspect and that he was confident that all those involved in the crime were dead.

SYDNEY MORNING HERALD
KIDNAP KID IS NEW CHAMPION.
Our yachting correspondent reports.

Little Emily Simpson, 14, has been declared Cadet World Champion here in this week's competition on the Harbour. Racing her Cadet dinghy with brother Johnny, 9, young Emily destroyed opposition from twenty-two nations. After winning five races and coming second in two more Emily and Johnny were able to enjoy a day off leaving the rest to scrap for second place.

This Emily, is the same spunky little kiddo who survived that abduction horror in England just nine weeks ago. When interviewed Emily said. "I've put all that behind me now. I just want to go on and do the things I do well." She paid tribute to her mum and dad, Steve and Kirsten Simpson, both former Olympic sailing medallists. "I would love to do what they did before I get too old like them."

THE END

By the same author

THE NEMESIS FILE

Professional yachtsman and Olympic medallist Steve Simpson has problems. His wife has died and his Chichester sail making business is under threat. When Steve and his daughter Sarah find the body of a young Dane in the sea off the Sussex coast they are inextricably sucked into an international blackmail and drugs conspiracy.

The story describes fourteen days in the late summer of 1990 that will change Steve's life. It is a test that leads him to new love and a rebirth of his hopes.

This tense mystery-thriller moves swiftly from Sussex to Copenhagen with interludes in Portsmouth, Italy and Scotland, and ends with a sea chase in a gale

ISBN 978-0-9548880-0-8 (0-9548880-0-6)

Available from Benhams Books
1 Fir Cottage, Greatham, Liss, Hampshire GU33 6BB

Reviews of *The Nemesis File*:

Journalist Pamela Payne: With locations as diverse as the South Coast of England, Naples and Denmark, *The Nemesis File*'s credible sailing scenes will either have you reaching for the seasickness-pills or signing on for a course; the sex scenes, however, are the most romantic I have read for along time. A great adventure story, which will delight both sexes – sailors or landlubbers."

Yachts and Yachting December 2004. "…Jim Morley is a sailor writing for sailors and his first novel is immersed in the South Coast yachting and dinghy scene…if somebody was going to write a novel for *Yachts and Yachting,* readers this would probably be it.

Yachting Monthly: 2006. Dell Quay based yachtsman Jim Morley has turned his hand to writing thrillers based on his sailing experiences of forty years. His first novel, *The Nemesis File,* is a murder mystery linking a Chichester sailmaker with a failing business, the corpse of a Dane found floating off Sussex and Nazi propaganda minister Josef Goebbels.

Reviews of *The Nemesis File* (continued):

Olympic sailor and coach: Cathy Foster, 11th Dec 2004

Rarely have I read such a racy book! It's carries you along at pace, and holds you fast until the very end. Just then, you think that maybe this is getting far-fetched, but the punch-line pulls you up short, and makes you re-assess the characters and their relationship to events. Suddenly the plot hangs together again in a very satisfactory way, just as good detective stories should.

Instead of long descriptions to 'paint a picture' of all the venues and situations, the writing is succinct and carefully crafted to give the maximum impression for the minimum words. This gives the book its fast tempo, yet nothing is lost because the accurate detailing of locations and action bonds the reader into plot. As a past Olympic sailor myself, I know the sailing venues described in both Chichester Harbour and Copenhagen well, and I can reassure any future reader that the author has definitely done his research. In addition, he's right – you do build life-long bonds with other British athletes and other countries' sailors when you are part of the Olympic team representing your country. It is a pleasure and highly unusual to read a book which describes the joys of sailing and racing so well. Yet it's not a book about sailing, full of technicalities of the sport. Sailing provides the background framework for a story of murder and blackmail where the investigation chases over four countries and three generations of lives. A thoroughly enjoyable read.

Cathy Foster went to the Olympics in 1984 (finished 7th and made history as the first woman helm since the 2nd World War) and competed in two other Olympic campaigns, the last being 2002/3. She's a freelance Coach who specialises in top level racing, including Olympic and Paralympic sailors

By the same author

ROCASTLE'S VENGEANCE

When out of work sea captain Peter Wilson takes a job as harbour master in the Dorset yacht harbour of Old Duddlestone, he is surprised to learn that his own father, James Wilson, was the harbour's wartime commander.

There are unsolved crimes involving this secretive community dating back fifty years. The deaths of the entire personnel of a research laboratory, then a rape and murder followed by a lynching.

Peter, aged ten, witnessed his father's suicide. Now he hears disquieting rumours about his father's dubious activities in Duddlestone. He forms a relationship with single-mother, Carol Stoneman. When Carol's ten-year-old son is abducted, Peter is forced into a situation that nearly bring his own destruction.

This mystery thriller is set on the Dorset coast in the summer of 1997, with a sailing background.

ISBN 978-0-9548880-1-5 (0-9548880-1-4)

Available from Benhams Books
1 Fir Cottage, Greatham, Liss, Hampshire GU33 6BB

Reviews of *Rocastle's Vengeance*:

Unsolicited comment on Amazon. *****
Wow! What a read. You know it is a good book when after a few pages you don't want to put it down, nor answer the phone, door or anything...

Bournemouth Echo, July 2006.
Novelist brings mystery to the coast.
Rocastle's Vengeance, James Morley's second novel, is brimming with references to Purbeck Poole and Bournemouth. The book recounts the tale of a harbour master who uncovers murky secrets when he takes a job in the imaginary village of Old Duddlestone...

Tim O'Kelly. Whitbread Prize judge southern region.
Jim Morley writes with skill and intelligence: a genuine storyteller in the finest tradition.

By the same author

MAGDALENA'S REDEMPTION

If an eight-year-old boy commits murder is he irredeemably evil? Can he ever be rehabilitated or will he kill again to preserve his secret?

Hampshire farmer, Tom O'Malley, finds the dead body of a young journalist. Not satisfied that she is a suicide he makes his own investigation.

Fed rumours about his friend and employer, Hollywood film director Gustav Fjortoft, he angrily rejects them. Yet all his inquiries into his friend's past seem to substantiate the rumours.

Following suspicious deaths in his own community, Tom's quest leads him the American West Coast, where he escapes abduction and near death.

Returning to England he finds the answers he seeks in a dramatic finale in his home village.

ISBN 978-0-9548880-2-2

Available from Benhams Books
1 Fir Cottage, Greatham, Liss, Hampshire GU33 6BB